Devil's Feathers

Also by David Chacko

Price
Gage
Brick Alley
The Black Chamber
White Gamma
Red Bishop One
The Shadow Master
A Long Way from Eden
Like a Man
Less Than a Shadow
The Peacock Angel
Graveyard Eyes
Martyr's Creek
The Severan Prophecies
Echo Five

Devil's Feathers

David Chacko

Foremost Press
Cedarburg, Wisconsin

David can be reached at his website at
http://www.davidchacko.com
or by email at david@davidchacko.com

Published by Foremost Press

ISBN-10: 0-9818418-6-4
ISBN-13: 978-0-9818418-6-1

This is a work of fiction. Any similarity of characters or events to real persons or actual events is coincidental.

For Cem

You are only as sick
as your secrets.

— Turkish Proverb

Part One:

Big Cat

CHAPTER 1

The man dove from the dock into deep blue Aegean water and stayed down so long that Levent thought he might be in trouble. It was a relief when the pale form began to move beneath the surface, springing toward the middle of the bay in a series of strong rhythmic kicks. He was twenty-five meters from the pier when his bodyguard dove into the water after him.

The bodyguard would catch the older man, though they were both good athletes. Military, of course. Intelligence, Levent knew. The old man—his name was Tolga and he was in his sixties—was one of the few operatives who was given lifetime protection. For the things he had done, the Kurds would kill him on sight. Some Arabs, too. Only the Israelis and Americans approved of the mayhem that was synonymous with his career in the service. They may have put up the money for the bodyguard. This government certainly would not.

"What did you say you do?"

Levent looked at the bearded man across the table. An Italian named Federico, he had spoken in English. "I'm an off-line consultant," said Levent. "In Istanbul."

Federico nodded as if he understood. Levent did not usually tell civilians he was a police inspector in one of the world's largest cities. That often made them ill at ease. It sometimes made them disappear.

"So far," said Federico, using his eyebrows forcefully, "I haven't met one person in Bodrum who's from Bodrum. Everyone's from Istanbul."

"In summer, yes," said the third man at the table, a Turk named Turan. "It's a colony, and it was founded by people from the mother city to draw more people from the mother city. Istanbul is such a big busy place. If you want to see your friends, you have to come to Bodrum in high season."

"So they're not here for the water," said Federico. "Seems a shame. Offshore or down deep it's some of the best I've seen."

"Certainly they come for the water," said Turan. "There always has to be an excuse for social occasions."

Was that true? Did it matter? They were making conversation, and Turan was a gifted talker with a fine raconteur's voice who wore his head of gray-black hair like a crown. He had an enormous house outside the city that rode the mountain like a crown, and that was only one of his places of resort.

Levent was out of his social order when on vacation and into the web of connections his wife kept like a dowry. He had let her choose their place, a comfortable, close-to-the-sea rental, but they always agreed on Bodrum. The place had kept him and Emine coming back almost every year since they were married. It was the finest summer resort in the world, they liked to think—a mountain desert surrounded by water. And the water at Bitez was the best of the best.

"The whole thing started when Jevat Shakir was exiled here during the forties," said Turan, who had gotten into the rhythm of his story. "He was the son of a well-known family from Istanbul—a family of artists—who was sent down to Bodrum for shooting his father."

"Dead?" asked Federico.

"Of course," said Turan. "It doesn't seem useful to do less if you've made up your mind."

"Actually," said Levent, "the father had taken Jevat's wife as his mistress. She was an Italian, by the way."

"Understandable," said Federico. "A bit extreme."

Turan looked at Levent either with disapproval or as an oracle. "I hadn't heard that part of the story."

"Well, it provides what's lacking," said Levent. "Motivation."

"It doesn't really matter," said Turan, smoothing his way into the newest version of the tale like a salesman. "He was a great man. A writer. He made Bodrum what it is today. All those eucalyptus trees we see on the road to Marmaris—the ones that sucked up the swamps and made the place what it is—Jevat had them planted. He invented the Blue Cruises that all the tourists enjoy so much. It wouldn't be an exaggeration to say that practically everything we love about Bodrum is his legacy."

"But it doesn't seem like a great punishment," said Federico. "Being exiled to the finest part of the country for patricide."

"It wasn't like that then," said Turan. "Bodrum was such a damned dead place in those days. A fishing village. If you wanted to be rid of someone, this was as good an exile as there was. What you see now is pure sophistication. The Turkish Riviera."

"An overbuilt Riviera," said Levent.

Turan looked at Levent as if he did not like being contradicted, even in casual conversation. His eyes turned from dark brown to the lack of light. He got to his feet abruptly, turning to the back of his chair and the mask and fins he had left to dry.

"I'm going in the water and toward the point," he said. "Anyone join me?"

Levent shook his head definitely no.

"I'm coming," said Federico. "Never go alone, they say, and if possible, with an expert."

Levent watched them gather their equipment and walk up the plank-set waterside to the other end of the dock closest to the point. Each carried a spear gun. Hunters for the tribe. The Good Life tribe. It would nice if they managed a catch as fine as the first—an octopus of generous size gotten not a hundred meters off the dock. They had hired a boy to beat the creature forty times against the stones at the bottom of the beach to prevent the meat from toughening. It had not. Levent thought it was the best lunch he had in some time after the octopus was prepared by the chef at the cafe. That fellow was from Istanbul, too.

The Inspector of Police, Istanbul Homicide, moved from the table where he sat to the rows of chaise lounges crowding the head of the dock. On one of the first in the line, his wife lay. Hers was a highly ritualized encounter with nature, following Helios in its movements through the cloudless sky with the speed of a sundial.

"We might have some fish for dinner if those two get lucky."

Emine accepted the comment as if they had been talking for hours. She sat up, looking over the breasts that were so young, though she was not quite. Her black hair was done up in a bandanna of dark green and gold, shading her eyes as she searched the shore until she found Federico and Turan. Her eyes held as the two men tumbled from the edge of the pier into the water.

"I'm not sure luck is the word," said Emine. "I've heard tell that Turan was once the best diver in these parts."

"In Bodrum?"

"The Aegean," she said. "The Mediterranean, too, if you believe the gossip."

"Seems like an odd skill for an industrialist to have."

"He wasn't always so urbane," said Emine in her story voice. "In the old days when Bodrum had one paved road, Turan was the captain of a working vessel. After he taught the locals all they needed to know about fishing and diving, he went on to greater things."

"The word of his friends."

"And local legend."

"Put those two together and it might settle somewhere north of the truth."

"You're skeptical," she said. "I might be, too, if he wasn't so rich."

"Stories always gather around that much money," said Levent. "The dirtiest ones are often the truest."

"I defer to your expertise," she said. "In the meantime, see to your cell phone. It rang a few minutes ago."

Levent did not like that. He was on vacation and the only calls to his number should be social. Emine always came by those first, so there should be nothing on his machine's mind.

"You're sure it rang?" he asked.

"Why don't you look?" she said. "There can't be two phones on this coast that ring out Benny and the Jets."

Not likely. Levent dug his phone from the white beach bag. Yes, a call came up on the screen of his Samsung.

An unknown number. That was the best or the worst. And there was seldom a best in his business.

* * *

It was the worst—the call had come from the Chief. Levent would have recognized his number anywhere, even in a dark dreamless sleep, but the call had not come from the office phone of the most devious man he had ever known. Nor was it from the cell phone of the most powerful man in the Istanbul police department. The Chief had a new one, it seemed. The old one had disappeared. Or been stolen.

"Left it on the damned table at Mister Chips, just like any citizen does," he said, referring to a well-known bar and gambling den. "Got up to go to the toilet and when I returned it was gone."

"Unbelievable, sir."

"It's an unbelievable nuisance," he said. "And it took a lot of ass. Everyone at that table knew who I was. Everyone in the whole damned place. This is as bad as stealing the imam's master CD for the Call to Prayer. It's worse, because when I find that bastard, his balls are the only thing he'll have left. He might not want them back in that condition, though."

"I'm surprised you didn't arrest everyone there, sir."

"The thought occurred to me," he said. "But I decided that I shouldn't commit the Minister of the Interior, the Deputy Mayor of the city, and my brother-in-law to the same jail cell."

"Perhaps only the last, sir."

"That would have been the least safe," he said. "You don't know my wife well."

"Hardly at all."

The Chief cleared his throat, creating space for the unpleasantness he was sure to announce. "Enough of my problems," he said without meaning it. "I understand you're at Bodrum."

"Yes, sir. And enjoying my time away from the job."

"But I know you, Onur. Two days in the sun is the limit before boredom sets in. So I've arranged to pass something of interest your way."

"That isn't necessary, sir."

"I'll be the judge of what's necessary," he said. "That's my job. Yours is to listen. An hour ago I took a call from the commandant of Jandarma down your way. I'd have been on the phone sooner if I hadn't had to look up your number through my secretary. He's a good man, the commandant, met him at a conference in Ankara last year, but real crime is something he isn't comfortable with. This one has an odor. Apparently, a man was attacked in daylight yesterday in the parking lot of a convenience store. He was set on fire and burnt to toast inside his car."

"I hadn't heard anything like that, sir."

"You wouldn't," said the Chief. "It's a serious crime in a prime tourist area. I don't have to say more. Before they send all the English packing for Manchester, they'll deny that anything took place. A bad carburator or something. So the investigation has to be kept under tight control. Nothing goes to the press and nothing for the hotel staff to gossip about. This kebab never happened."

"I understand, sir."

"I know you do, Inspector. You'll get to the bottom of this and do it without attracting attention. I've guaranteed the commandant that. The man is at a loss, never having dealt with anything more serious than honor killings."

"His name, sir?"

"How do you expect me to know that?" said the Chief. "He has one. I gave him yours so he'll be able to nod politely when you present yourself. You'll be sure to do that right away, Inspector."

Levent let a long moment pass before he answered. "Yes, sir."

"This is a favor to me, Onur. You know I honor my debts."

Levent knew nothing of the kind. He might have known the opposite if pressed. But there was no refusing the Chief, or the Minister of Tourism, who was probably on the other line. The only problem was how Levent would present this to Emine.

"I'll let you know how things come around, sir."

"You'll let me know when you've done the job," he said. "This case is out of our jurisdiction, and out of my mind as of this moment."

CHAPTER 2

The crime was also outside the jurisdiction of the Bodrum city police. That was the reason the Jandarma had gotten the case. They were the state police who took care of all the districts, rural and suburban, that were too small to maintain a force of their own. A sensational murder was outside their normal run of mayhem. A kebab was unusual anywhere outside Iraq.

Due to the population boom on the peninsula, the Jandarma probably should have been replaced by a regular police force, but Bodrum was a series of peninsulas within the larger one, scattering in crooked fingers with small towns sitting on them. This Jandarma headquarters stood like a white fortress at the top of the hill twenty kilometers from the city, the driveway ending at the iron gates of the compound.

The guard on duty was a private, but he had the combat boots and green beret that all the Jandarma wore, as if they were special forces. That was true in the east, where the Jandarma were the first line of defense against civilian crime, and the guerrilla forces that Kurdish terrorists, the PKK, kept in the field. Since Levent's only experience with a man being burnt in a car had involved a terrorist bombing, his mind went in that direction. He knew he should curb the feeling. The facts came first.

"The car was released to the Bodrum City Police to see if their forensics can find anything," said the commandant of the station. "They're aware of the priority and should be back to us today with preliminary findings."

Levent, who had taken a plastic chair that looked like a slice of melon, did his best to come to the facts slowly. The commandant's name—the one the Chief had never spoken—was Metin, which meant solid, strong, and contradicted nothing about him. He was a thick block of a man, not tall or fat but filling every angle of his uniform. His calm brown eyes were the last thing anyone would notice, which was their mistake. Well-spoken and a university graduate, he was glad to have assistance from outside his command while surrendering none of his authority inside his headquarters.

"The crime was committed yesterday, I understand," said Levent. "At about what time?"

"Five in the afternoon," said the commandant. "The car was parked in the side lot of the store and only the cars of some of the staff were there. No one saw a thing, though some people had to pass through the store around that time."

"Have you questioned everyone with a view of the parking lot?"

"The surrounding area, yes," he said. "The road has steady traffic, but it's not like a city street. Between five and five-fifteen any number of cars passed on the road. Fifty or a hundred vehicles probably."

"Nothing from them?"

"Nothing except the man who stopped to say that a car was afire in the parking lot," said the commandant. "The clerk at the register had no idea. Looking back, he thought he might have smelled smoke and heard a small explosion. But he was inside all that time, seeing to some customers and stacking a delivery that had come in half an hour before."

It was not likely that the man who lit the torch would bother to report his crime, or that the clerk was involved. The man should have noticed something, however.

"Did the clerk recognize the victim?"

"The identification wasn't easy," said the commandant with distaste that rode his hairless upper lip. "The body was badly burnt. Even the face was completely charred. But the clerk was sure because of the shoes he'd seen in the store. They were new and white. Deck shoes. They turned several different colors with the fire, but he recognized them. They were a good brand, so he probably fancied them. Most people here wear sandals in summer."

Levent waited as one of the commandant's subordinates came with the tea service. The private with the slick sleeve was well trained, waiting patiently at the door until the commandant noticed his presence. One nod brought him into the room with grave haste. Discipline and hierarchy were the hallmark of the Jandarma as courtesy and a welcome of tea was the hallmark of this land.

"Metin, with those deck shoes, do you think the victim could have been a sailor?"

The commandant agreed with a nod. "I have some of my men checking the marinas downtown and in this area. But there are a lot of boats in the summer. Not only the ones that hook up at marinas, but others that put in to any of the coves. We have a lot of those on the peninsula."

Not an infinite number, but plenty. Three major marinas, several minor ones, and fifteen or twenty coves by Levent's count, which could have been light. One of the first things he would do was find a good map. The tourist never knew an area like geodesic survey did.

"Had the clerk seen the victim in his store before yesterday?"

"He said no. I couldn't find a reason to doubt him. He was cooperative and embarrassed by all that happened. He seemed to think he should have noticed a serious blaze in his parking lot."

"Did you run a check on him?"

The commandant's reaction told better than words. His deep chest seemed to take a physical blow. "No, Inspector."

"Do," said Levent. "I like to think I'd notice a car afire on my watch. I might even have heard a scream from a man who was being burnt alive."

"Yes," said the commandant, scrawling a note to the subordinate who stood outside the door on duty. The man entered the room, took the note from his superior and walked away down the hall. Almost before he disappeared, another subordinate replaced him at the door.

"It did seem odd, Inspector. I asked forensics to have a look at the body to see if the victim was dead before the fire started."

"That should tell us something one way or the other," said Levent. "It would be good if they find out how the fire started."

"We may know something about that already," said the commandant. "We found the gas cap on the ground ten meters from the car. It had been attached to the car by a fastener and probably was blown off when the fire reached the tank. There was a boom. Not Hollywood grade, but a definite noise."

That was odd. If the killer had finished his victim, and afterward taken the time to wick a fire from the gas tank, he was a confident operator. He did not seem concerned that he might be interrupted at his work, or perhaps he counted on luck. In that case, he was an amateur. A bold one.

"What kind of car?"

"A Mercedes," said the commandant. "It wasn't new before the fire took it the rest of the way. Six years. Silver gray. We couldn't even read the plates. Forensics should have that soon."

"So we have some time," said Levent. "Do you think the same clerk will be on duty at the store today?"

"I don't know," he said. "But we have his number."

"Tell him we'll meet him at the store if he's not there already."

"Of course."

* * *

They drove down to the main road, Levent following in his car as several men piled into the large van that the Jandarma used for everything but social functions. They were all heavily armed with pistols and automatic rifles, including a young sergeant with a specialist's patch. What he specialized in should become clear in time.

The store was part of a Turkish chain that ran nationwide. It sat close to the road with several parking spaces in front for quick ins and outs. Why the victim had parked around the side was unclear, but it might have been to get his car out of the sun. The side lot took some shade from the overhang of the building.

The blackened and weirdly scorched area stood three parking places in from the front of the store. It had been a hell of a blaze that left holographic images on the concrete wall five meters away. The local fire department had responded with an array of vehicles, but were hampered as always by the lack of hydrants. He was not sure any existed in the whole country, but the firemen had put down enough chemicals to drench the area in a very bad smell.

The flames had been so intense that several lumps of congealed plastic fused to the asphalt pavement. Levent tapped the biggest one with the toe of his shoe. Nothing budged, but a glint of metal within the blob caught his eye. He bent down to look closely and slowly pried the lump loose.

A curious fragment, a piece of metal with notches or slots. It had a slight concave curve, and somehow seemed familiar.

"What do you suppose this belonged to?"

Metin bent down to look. He stayed down as if he had something to add. "It could be a piece of windshield wiper," he said. "A headlight wiper. The car had one if I recall, hanging from the left front headlight. I don't think they make them any longer, but some of the older models came loaded from the factory like that."

For an expensive car, Mercedeses were common in Turkey, so anything that made it less common was a gift. A small one. Levent placed the fragment in one of the plastic bags he always carried. Why he should have carried it on his vacation made a case for prescience or stupidity.

"Let's go now and talk to the clerk."

* * *

He was a man on the near side of middle-age with blue trousers that hung down to mid-calf, as if he was a seagoing sort, too. Levent did not think that likely. The clerk was short and bent at the shoulders, but it was less a matter of height than the sad crouch of a domestic. He had grown a brush mustache of the kind that had carried the Turkish nation from the wastelands of Central Asia without one frozen lip in the tribe. Otherwise, he seemed modern, even to the Chicago Bulls T-shirt. They had not done well in the playoffs. Levent's team, the Celtics, had taken the crown.

"Are you certain you'd never seen this man in the store before?"

"Not that I remember," said the clerk in a wary voice. "But I'm not the only man at this register. Or woman, either. We have four clerks for the shifts."

"Was there anything about him that you'd call memorable?"

"The look in his eye," said the clerk. "You see it when you go any place you're not wanted. They stand at the door. They only let the pretty girls or the money in."

"He looked like a bouncer?"

"He looked like one who got old in the saddle. I don't know if they all do. He was about fifty or a little more."

"Do you remember why he stopped in?" asked Levent. "What did he buy?"

"Cigarettes," he said. "He took a pocket lighter, too, one of the plastics on the counter there. I'd hate to think I sold him the murder weapon."

"Probably not," said Levent, turning to the commandant. "You didn't find a sales receipt in the car, did you?"

"Paper," said Metin. "Not a chance."

"What about the sales receipt from your register?" said Levent, turning back to the clerk. "You should have it in your back tapes."

"God knows," he said. "That was yesterday. I'd have to dig it out of the bin."

"We can wait," said Levent. "Check now, please."

The clerk went unwillingly but with determination after he looked at Levent's face. He opened a small cardboard box from behind the counter. It was lucky that the tape had not already been sent to headquarters in Istanbul, where all the garbage landed. Levent saw that Metin was not quite sure of the reason for the request.

"It's useful to establish time of death as close as possible. The tape should tell us exactly when he left the store."

The commandant smiled. "That's very good, Inspector. I'm making a list of the things I should have done."

"They're the things time on the job makes automatic," said Levent. "I wish I'd made a list when I started at homicide."

"I'm going to say I believe you for now."

Make that forever, thought Levent, and call it a start. The principle was the same no matter what vector the case took. If a time of death was needed, the investigator had better look around for things that told time. Machines did that best.

"I've got it," said the clerk, coming up from his crouch. He held the roll of tape out by both hands and moved it onto the counter. "Cigarettes and a lighter."

Levent bent down for a close look. Cigarettes, a lighter—and something called a Magnum. That sounded promising.

"What's the last item mean?"

"Magnum's a chockolat bar," said the clerk. "Frozen. I'm guessing, but I don't think they do well in that kind of fire."

No, but there was one surprise on the receipt. The commandant said that the fire started around five, but the machine reported that the victim had still been inside the store at 5:11. Add another minute to get out the door to his car and an indeterminate length of time before the fire was spotted. So time of death could not have been much before 5:15. Possibly later.

That meant nothing yet, but certainly could. Levent passed out the front door of the store, following the path the victim should have taken yesterday if he had gone in the logical way that he should have.

The heat that replaced the air-conditioning was staggering. It seemed to draw Levent into it with the false promise that it could not grow worse. The highway that passed by planed like a boat in the heat, rising slightly higher than the front of the store. The buildings on the other side of the road were higher still. Yes, this had been a hill before man leveled it to his liking.

To the left stood a marble factory store with slabs of product—bright white and probably local stone—displayed in the front yard. The store should have been open at five yesterday.

"I suppose you spoke to the people at the marble shop?"

"Yes, but the owner saw nothing," said the commandant. "He was out back storing his best travertine in the shed. The rest of the marble isn't worth the trouble of moving every night, so he leaves it outside."

Levent was sure the man knew his market. He was not so sure of the next business in the dusty line on the other side of the road. It was a large gasoline station that stood opposite the convenience store at a vaguely convex angle. The gas pumps and service area were so far to the right that it would have been impossible to see anything in the side parking lot of the store.

But directly across the street, three large tanker trucks were parked. They must be used for local deliveries of the oil products that were becoming more precious by the day. One hundred dollars a barrel. One-thirty. Almost certain to make one-fifty. The tankers should be valuable even if they were not fully loaded. Levent bet they were protected.

"You spoke to the people at the filling station?"

"Yes," said the commandant. "They were aware of the fire, but late noticing it. One of the men from the pumps ran over to help, but thought better of sticking his head into the flames."

"They weren't in the best position to observe," said Levent. "Or help once the fire began. But it might be different where the tankers are parked. How many were sitting out yesterday?"

"The same number," said the commandant. "Three. I'm sure."

"So several tankers are a constant," said Levent. "I'd like to know how far management goes to protect its investment."

"What are you thinking?"

Levent shrugged. "A surveillance camera?"

Metin tried to hide his embarrassment again. "I didn't ask. They didn't volunteer. The only men around late yesterday were the ones at the pumps. And they may not know they're being watched."

"Given the price of oil, we should find out how well the station is equipped. It seems like a new installation."

"It is."

Metin motioned for the Jandarma with the specialist's patch to join them, and they walked across the hot dusty road. Levent followed, stopping every few paces to look back at the parking lot at the side of the building where the victim died. He could see the area clearly all the way to the other side of the road.

As they came near the tankers, Levent noticed for the first time the little building standing behind a row of freshly planted evergreens. Midway between the tankers and the service area, it was almost secreted there.

"The manager's office," said Metin as he stepped up and knocked at the door.

The man who opened the door was obviously in charge of the station, though he wore no uniform and clearly would have been uncomfortable in one. Just above six feet tall and fifty years old, the strong foundation of his face welcomed the advance of age from deep eye sockets and brown eyes that seemed sunk in the bed of the earth. Their look changed from cross at having been interrupted to accommodating as he considered the commandant and his entourage.

"Yes, sir," he said. "May I help you?"

"Commandant Comert, Jandarma," he said. "I'm afraid we didn't have a chance to meet yesterday."

"Fazil Gazi," said the man, putting his hand forward for a brisk shake. "I'm the manager of this station. Please, come in."

The commandant made the introductions as the three visitors filed into a wide one-room building. Twin desks stood east and west, as if maintenance of the station required those numbers. Certificates of competence lined the walls, along with photographs enumerating the important career points of management and the details of their lives. That included the declining beauty of their wives and a gaudy circumcision portrait of someone's son. Also a portrait of Ataturk in evening dress. A good sign. It meant the man was secular in his leanings. That sometimes helped.

"Tea?" he asked.

"Of course," said Levent.

The manager rang up his service with pleasure as his guests took seats before his desk. Levent's eyes searched the photos and gewgaws before settling on a large console on the wall between the two desks. Like all the furnishings, it was well made. Levent was sure something important was housed inside.

"I'm sure you know about the incident that took place yesterday across the street," said the commandant. "The fire."

"Of course I was told," said the manager, running his fingers across the hairline that formed a fine widow's peak. "Terrible business. And terrible for business. I don't know what this country is coming to when things like this happen in a public place in broad daylight. I've been living in Bodrum for thirty years and don't ever recall anything like it."

Levent found the man's emphasis correct. He seemed to lament the state of affairs under the current Islamic government. The breakdown of order had advanced at a record pace, fueled by the empowerment of their supporters—the poor. Unfortunately, what the poor often felt empowered to do was criminal.

"Have you had much trouble at this station?" asked Levent. "Say, with theft or vandalism?"

"I suppose we're lucky our customers don't have much choice," said the manager. "When they look at their gas gauge, they know it's time to get off the road. Most of the trouble we've had has been pilfering from the fast food racks. This station stays open until ten o'clock every evening, and we keep three men on duty. It helps."

"What about the evenings?" asked Levent. "Has the station been broken into?"

"Once," he said. "But we caught the thieves on our camera."

"Your surveillance camera?"

"Yes, indeed," he said as if proud to be current. "We have a full array, as all the new stations do. We called the Jandarma at once—not your station, commandant, but the other up the road—and they ran those shameful bastards down in good order. The same day, in fact. That kind of news travels fast among criminals. We haven't had any trouble since, except for some midnight raids on our tankers."

"You're talking about the tankers down at this end of the lot," said Levent. "Are they usually filled with oil?"

"Always some," he said. "The thieves can't steal the trucks because they're immobilized, but they were siphoning off oil late in the evenings. It was a clumsy business that made for some difficult repairs until we installed a camera to cover that part of the lot. We haven't had any trouble since."

"The camera," said Levent. "It should have a partial view of the convenience store across the street, shouldn't it?"

"At long range," he said, drawing his hands apart. "I'm not sure you could find anything to use from the tapes."

The tapes. Of course they should keep them, at least for a while. A day might be all that Levent needed. Even a camera at long range could provide a record. It should be something like a sales receipt in that it kept time.

So they went to the console as the tea service came through the door. The large wooden leaves of the cabinet opened to reveal a surprising number of monitors. Three rows. Nine in all. Levent found out how the sergeant got his specialist's patch in the Jandarma when the young man took the equipment in hand. With no help from the manager, he dialed through the tapes until he arrived in digital numerals near the correct time on the preceding day.

Eight of the monitors were focused too narrowly on the busy front of the station, but one returned something like the view that Levent wanted. The camera, mounted high on the fence, rotated through a semi-circle of nearly one hundred and eighty degrees, taking in the right side of the gasoline station. Basically, that was the tanker view, but as the camera swung to zero and back again to the tankers, the road beyond the station could be seen. The front parking lot of the convenience store and the apron of the side lot came into view between the slow rotations.

Levent could see at once that no significant detail would be gotten from the crime scene three parking spaces deep in the side lot. The range was too great and several obstructions at the front of the station intervened. A small tree at the side of the store that he had not noticed seemed to spread its dusty leaves for the sole purpose of obscuring the camera eye.

But the road was visible periodically, and the sergeant stopped moving through the tape when the read-out on the screen said: 5:06.

"I'll run it five minutes preceding the event and five after," he said, as he worked the backward and forward arrows. "We can't count on accurate clock-time from these read-outs."

The sergeant moved forward with real speed but not in real time. Nothing passed on the road for the first two minutes except two cars. Neither stopped. Neither slowed.

At three minutes, a silver Mercedes pulled from the road into the front parking lot. The driver seemed to hesitate, driving slowly past two empty spots in front before cruising to the side of the store. He was visible as he entered the side lot, and then, damn it, he disappeared. That meant what happened to him later, after he left the store, would not be part of the record either.

Levent's luck worsened when the camera swung from the road to a tighter focus on the tankers. If another car followed the Mercedes into the lot, he would miss it.

He almost did. Nearly ten seconds passed as the camera swung away, and he did not see the man exit the Mercedes or walk to the store. But he saw the rear of a second car enter the side lot. It passed out of sight as the Mercedes had. Levent had no means of identification except to note that the car was dark green.

"Back it up," he said to the sergeant. "Run the sequence again."

The sergeant-technician rewound the tape until he reached the beginning of the sequence where the Mercedes appeared.

Unfortunately, the repeat of the tape was no help. The Mercedes passed. The camera rotated. When it came back to the scene, the rear of the green car moved out of sight into the lot around the side. If anyone got out of the car, he did not show himself for the camera.

"If it matters," said the commandant, "both cars came from the direction of Yalikavak."

Yalikavak was the only town close to the scene of the crime. It was almost too much to think they could narrow the investigation to that area.

"Run the rest now."

It was nervous work watching the tape, especially during the periods when the camera swung away to the tankers. The periods seemed to lengthen even as the machine that performed the functions measured out the same interval. At no time when the camera returned to a frontal view did Levent see a sign of another human being in the side lot. The only thing that he thought he saw—then became sure of—was a startled flight of small birds—starlings probably—that rose in a small cloud from the back of the lot and quickly vanished into the continuation of the hill behind the store. Had they reacted to a movement? A sudden noise?

Then he saw the man. The dead man.

It was no more than a glimpse that lasted a second, but he was the only thing moving toward the side lot. He wore new white shoes.

Levent waited. He saw nothing more for the longest time. He did not know if they were seconds or minutes.

All he had to do to find the time that had elapsed was look at the numbers on the screen. He found he could not. Although Levent was an experienced investigator whose soul had been confiscated by his work years ago, he felt the emotion in his body. A man would die in that lot. A man would die soon. There was no way to shout a warning into the past, but everything in Levent wanted to.

The man was probably dead already. He had walked into the lot at 5:12 bearing on 5:13, not in a great hurry but not dawdling. Though it was hard to judge size from the angle of the monitor and the distance, the victim was not a small man. Broad-shouldered with a tight mound of belly, he was at least six feet from the ground and possibly more. Bouncer material. It would not have been easy to bring him down in a head-to-head confrontation. But an ambush, yes.

Any man, yes.

At exactly 5:18, like a breath of an angel, Levent saw a plume of pale light jet from within the parking lot. He would not have known it was fire without this window from the future. Coming within the heat of the day, the greater heat seemed to glow like a faint gas.

Suddenly, a green car crashed from the lot, digging into the asphalt as it mounted to the level of the road. The killer was no longer cool. Smoke followed his car, first black and then white, as if more than one thing were changing states.

Peugeot," said the commandant. "It's a dark green Peugeot."

CHAPTER 3

Finding a green Peugeot on the peninsula did not seem diffi-cult unless someone was intent on hiding. If that were true, the advantages changed to disadvantages.

The job would have been much easier if the license plate had been visible, but the distance and camera angle were bad. The angle would have been best after the Peugeot turned onto the road, but the camera had swung away to the tankers just then. Nothing could be seen of the driver or any passengers.

So they went with what they had. The sergeant specialist took the tape and left the station. He would send it to Ankara to see if the images could be enhanced to a point where they were good enough for identification. The commandant sent word to his men in the field, and to all other posts in the area, to be on the alert for a dark green Peugeot. It was a two-year-old model. The commandant was sure because his cousin in Adana had one like it.

They might get lucky. The man who did his killing in the vicinity of a filling station with surveillance cameras was not the definition of a professional. Everything the killer had done to this point indicated he was a man on a mission that was less business than personal.

Levent made a right turn from the service station to the marble shop that lay next along the road. He spent some time talking to the owner, who had been on duty the day before, but he added nothing substantial to the take. Serpil Pepe, a man with one brown eye lost to his work in stone, had become aware of the fire belat-edly. Of a Peugeot in any color, he knew nothing.

"If it was me killing a man," he said with an eastern accent, "I'd have stolen a car. You could have done it right there in that lot for all the trouble they've had."

"Trouble?" said Levent. "What kind?"

"Break-ins—more than you can count," he said as if he had counted all of them. "Didn't you see the sign posted in the lot?

'Don't leave anything in your car if you want to see it again. We can't be held responsible'."

Levent had seen what might have been a sign that was badly scorched by the fire. But it did seem the Jandarma should have known about criminal events that were common.

"You mean Commandant Comert keeps busy at that store?"

"I think most of the complaints went to the other Jandarma station," he said. "We've got two around here, but there might be none for all the good they do. There's any number of people, you know, they come out of the store with their little bags of things they just had to have before they shit themselves, and they see the broken glass where their back window used to be, and they just throw up their hands. They don't report it, especially if nothing much was taken."

"What's usually taken?"

"I'd say whatever is in their beach bags. These bandits aren't much for soggy bathing suits. They're usually looking for cameras or cell phones. You can find a market for those on any street corner."

If he stayed in this dusty marble yard for long, Levent might find out where the stolen goods were fenced. The trail might lead to one of Pepe's relatives or his enemies, if that was what Levent wanted. But he would rather have a watcher on this road— the main route from Yalikavak to the city of Bodrum. There was no telling how bold, or careless, the killer might be.

"You're outside the shop a lot," said Levent. "I'd like you to keep your eyes open for a dark green Peugeot on this road. It'll be two years old and probably have a man at the wheel. You'll do that for me, won't you?"

"This is the killer we're talking about?"

"He's a suspect right now. I'd like to move him to a more permanent position on the board with your help."

"A position on the board," said Serpil. "You make it sound like a game."

"It's not like that for him, I'm sure," said Levent. "Let's just say that I sometimes enjoy the chase."

Serpil looked closely at the card Levent handed him, moving his lips. "Istanbul," he said. "It comes here every summer, but never quite like this."

"The second number is my cellular," said Levent. "That works everywhere."

* * *

Not long after Levent left the marble shop—when he was about to turn onto the dirt and wishful concrete road that led to the Jandarma station at the top of the hill—his cell phone rang in his pocket. He might have hoped for a quick report from the marble shop, but Levent was not disappointed to hear the commandant's voice.

"We had word from forensics on the license plates," he said after a brief nod at pleasantry. "I can give you the complete plate, but the relevant numbers are the first two. Forty-eight. That's Mugla district and Bodrum. The car is registered to a Nadir Panter. We have his current address as Konak 3, Number 420."

"Where's that?"

"It's on the mountainside behind downtown Bodrum. I can pick you up and guide you in if you like."

"I'll find it," said Levent. "But we should have a locksmith ready to get us into the place. Panter doesn't have to be married or living with anyone. I don't like breaking down doors in an empty home."

"I'll have a locksmith meet us there," said the commandant. "There are a couple on twenty-four hour call."

Levent turned around and headed down the road that led into the city of Bodrum. It would have been wrong to call the place a city at most times, but to the Greeks or Romans or Byzantines, Bodrum had been known as Halicarnassus, an important place. After the Turkish conquest, it reverted to its original purpose as a fishing village for several hundred years. Now it was a question of where the city limits of Bodrum came to an end, or if they ended at all.

The entry into the town was one long glide down the mountains through country that was arid but not unattractive, with glimpses of the bluest sea on earth opening up at every point of elevation. Levent barely noticed anything but the traffic, which also had not existed before mass tourism struck with soft hammer blows. From six kilometers outside the city, the sides of the roads were crowded with shops selling prefabricated mosaics, slabs of marble and granite, outdoor furniture, pottery, and every quick-stop notion for summer people. Even this long way from the center, roadside inns, restaurants and nightclubs had proliferated.

Levent would soon know Panter's part in this sprawl. He did not think the man had come by his silver Mercedes as a bouncer, though his name might be meaningful. Panter meant big cat. A panther. Though names often meant nothing, his grandfather had chosen it as his symbol when the Republic demanded he should have a last name for the tax rolls. Why that one? Because he had admired the fierceness of the beast? Because that was the name of the village where he had been born? Because that was the way he behaved? All those things?

Levent passed the turn-off to Bitez, where his wife waited for his return. She was used to waiting for her police husband, but not on the vacation she prized so much. The look she had given Levent said he had better return for dinner. It was almost six o'clock. That gave him three hours until the late meal they always had in the south. He was damned if he did not make it on time.

He turned off at the fourth light and climbed the hill into the development that had spawned from dry hills where there had recently been no vegetation or water. The units were painted white to conform with the architecture that had characterized old Bodrum. Near the middle of the hill stood the third *site*. That word, which came from the French, would have been *citee* before Turkish claimed it. Number 420 was one of the last units on the left along a vehicle-crammed street.

Levent was lucky to have arrived at the place before the others. That brought him the last parking space. 420 was on the second floor—the top floor—that was draped in red bougainville. Everyone had a piece of the sun in Bodrum as, eventually, the sun took a piece of them.

Levent had no answer to his knock at the door of 420. The sound seemed to echo, as if to say that no one had been here for a while. For a day at least.

Then he heard the others climbing the stairs. First, he had heard the squeal of the Jandarma van as it braked to a stop in the street below. Now the boots climbed the steps and the commandant's voice sounded strong.

"You must have broken the speed limit coming here, Inspector."

"Just a bit."

"No one home?"

"No one who answers the door."

"We met the locksmith coming up the hill," said the commandant, passing his hand to an anonymous man who followed two Jandarma onto the stoop, crowding it completely. "He'll have us in quickly."

Levent stepped back, bumping one of the privates onto the stairs, as the locksmith, a tiny man with a week's growth of gray beard, moved to the door. He took out his tools and knelt to the lock with the total attention of a man who knew that he was earning credit with the police.

"I received another call from forensics as we drove in," said the commandant in a tone that titled at the end. "They have results on the fire, some quite strange."

"How so?"

"They're good these days at determining the causes of fires," he said. "They can recognize almost any accelerant used to start a fire. There's never more than one apparently."

"Are you saying they found multiple accelerants?"

"Multiple meaning two." The commandant took his notebook from his pocket, flipping through his hurried scrawl. "There are several common chemicals that can cause a fire to jump into a blaze, and that was true in this case. Petroleum derivatives were used. The gasoline family. The car seemed to be doused in gasoline, and the gas tank was wicked with a long length of gauze-like material. The killer didn't want to take a chance on Mister Panter's survival."

That's clear," said Levent. "But he chose a flamboyant way of disposing of the victim. A bullet in the head would have done the job with much less trouble."

"We know what caused the blaze, and we can assume the killer brought the goods along with him," said the commandant. "At least he doesn't appear to have stopped at the station across the street on a whim. He knew what he wanted to do and how to do it."

"It isn't something most people couldn't manage."

The commandant put his notebook away, as if what he was about to say had settled to depth in his mind. "Yes, but before the victim went up in the blaze, he'd been doused in ethyl alcohol, too. You know, the drinking kind."

"He was soaked in liquor *first?*"

"That's the way it looks."

If so, the killing was overkill. Why set a man on fire twice? Why did the killer expose himself to danger by repeating an unnecessary act that consumed time in a public place where he might be seen by anyone? It seemed as if he was sending a message. To whom? To say what?

"What kind of liquor was it?"

"They don't know yet," said the commandant. "But they think they can pin it down soon. It wasn't beer or wine or any mild spirit. It had to be a concentrated amount of a strong alcohol. Since they're Turks, they're betting on raki."

That was fifty percent alcohol and easy to get. Nothing was easier to get than raki. "So he doused the victim in alcohol, then lit him up. He did this before setting the car afire. Is that the way they have it?"

"I'm sure they have it more complicated, but yes. That's it."

"And the man sat passively while the killer did this," said Levent. "A big man who would not be easy to put down."

"He was hit on the head with a blunt instrument first," said the commandant. "It might even have been a raki bottle."

* * *

Levent wanted to think the victim was unconscious when he was set afire—and not simply immobilized. Watching. As personalized murder went, this was an example of calculated fury. Panter must have done something extraordinarily foul to have come upon an end like that. What kind of man had he been?

Levent hoped to find out when the locksmith pushed the door open and stepped aside to let the police pass. The commandant entered first, coming into the foyer briskly, in a business-like crouch, so Levent was surprised when that calm professional stopped and said, "Would you look at this world of shit?"

People sometimes said shit when they meant chaos. The apartment had been ransacked by someone who enjoyed his work and worked fast. Even the kitchen on the left by the door had been searched, the pots and pans, the dishes and dry goods, and the frozen food from the freezer. The last was truly messy. Puddles of melted fluids had run down the counters and the fronts of the white cabinets—red for beef, green for pistachio ice cream, and dark brown for the chocolate bars that were called Magnum.

The rest of the rooms were as chaotic but less liquid. The apartment was laid out on slightly descending levels, three steps to the living and sleeping rooms, and another short step to the balcony. The last was a generous space with hanging plants that could have held twenty people. The view over Bodrum with dusk coming was hallucinatory. The tight squat spaces of the city center, the palms of the seaside boulevard, the tall masts and spars in the harbor, and the great castle that reached into the bay, rose like the misty presence of the past.

Levent waited as the commandant's men sorted paper, books and clothing into coherent piles. In doing so, they cleared space in the study where filing cabinets, a drawer filled with file folders, and a computer were placed.

It was the work area of a man who took some of his work home. While Levent fired up the computer, he took a look at one file folder that said DenizKum Insaat.

Sea Sand Construction.

Sand Sea Construction, reverse order, was more Turkish. The name still didn't make sense, though it was reasonably nautical. Several other folders were marked with the same company name, enough to indicate that Nadir Panter had been an employee.

Correction: he was more. On a letter below his signature near the bottom of the page was his title. General Manager. Although Levent was aware that titles were given out like baskets of fruit in many firms, Panter could not be an underling at this one. A general manager was considerably more than a bouncer.

But construction was an area where a man of no special skill could fit in. Physical strength might have put him in the company at a menial position until seniority made him more. That route was common in Turkey.

Levent read the letter dated three weeks ago. Even before he reached the end of the page, it was clear that DenizKum was responding to pressure from another firm called Kanatli Beton. Winged Concrete. That name did not make sense either, but the bill that was presented to DenizKum by Kanatli had not been paid. General Manager Panter had countered their demands with controlled aggression. He noted several instances where Kanatli Beton had supplied less concrete than they had promised at higher prices than they had quoted. Payment, therefore, would not be rendered until all outstanding issues were resolved.

Feuds like this were common in business and often led to lawsuits when nothing was resolved. What seemed uncommon was the number of unpaid bills presented to DenizKum. Levent scanned four letters and found that half repeated similar arguments to various firms in the area.

Pressure was not simply being applied to the firm. It seemed to have come from every direction—a kitchen appliance firm, window installers, and the plumbers, too. All had bills that were not being paid. All the firms were being put off with complaints about the quality of their work.

Panter's business was in trouble. Levent was aware that he had found motivation for murder. He looked through the folder until the end and found three more bills being put off. The list of suspects who might turn violent was probably longer than that. If any had Mafia connections, the likelihood increased. In Istanbul, the usual Mafia response was a bullet in each leg. A tardy general manager of construction could find that the reminders were directed at his knees. Incineration, well, that was a twist, and not a smart one. How could a kebab pay back his debt?

Levent sat down at the computer. It had the new system, Vista, which meant that nothing could be seen. The password box was busily taking Levent's guesses and kicking them back without remorse when Metin came into the room and sat in the chair beside the desk.

"Any luck?"

"Mine's better than Mister Panter's," said Levent. "His company, DenizKum, appears to be under financial strain."

"Could be."

One thing Levent understood in his short acquaintance with the commandant. He was not a man for possibilities. He knew something about DenizKum and not from their press releases.

"Metin, are you trying to tell me something about this company?"

The commandant sat back in the chair and tapped his nose with the index fingers of both hands, as if summoning up his information through a bad smell. "What I know is that DenizKum has been building a large *site* over by Gumushluk. It's one of those newer kinds where you can look at the deep blue sea from deep inside the swimming pool. The common swimming pool, that is. They built a lot of units quite a way back from the shore, as if distance from real water was what their clients wanted. All the units are for sale, but even with the real estate boom they've had trouble moving them. At least that's what I heard."

"What kind of problems do they have?"

The commandant shrugged, but not like an accountant. "I imagine they're the same problems most of these companies have. They sell their units to people without a deed. In other words, they hand the customer a paper that says he has the right to occupy one-fiftieth or one-hundredth part of the *site*. The paper doesn't bother to say which part of the fraction is theirs and which is someone else's. They don't find out that they haven't been assigned a specific unit until later—about the time they decide to put their place on the market to sell."

"It's the same in Istanbul," said Levent. "But if all the construction firms here do it, why is this one having so many problems?"

"That I can't tell you," he said. "If you get into the computer, maybe you can look at their books. Tomorrow, we'll run down to their office and make noises with the staff. The office is on the main street through town."

"That could be an interesting visit."

"Let's try to make it one."

The commandant left to see one of his men, who called with a question about the bathroom. Levent returned to the password screen without having any luck. Only by accident did he realize that Panter's computer used an English keyboard. A lot of people in Bodrum spoke English if they worked in tourism or related industries.

They usually did not speak or write English well, but Levent decided to try variations in that language for the password. He had punched in four or five alternatives when he thought that he might go with a simple translation of the firm's name.

Sandsea as it might be spoken from Turkish came to nothing. But seasand as it was spoken in English brought results. The password box vanished to be replaced by a wallpaper picture of a woman. Young. Much younger than Panter. And attractive.

It would be useful to know who she was, but Levent found no reference to her anywhere on the hard drive. The correspondence directory told him no more than he had learned from the file folders. Some of the letters were identical, printed by the HP on the sideboard.

The spreadsheets were different. They contained a host of numbers that might be interpreted if he had the time to decipher them. And the expertise to know which were real and which were kept for the government.

Levent had better luck with the email, which opened with the password reversed. Turkish grammatical order. Sandsea. One message led to the Web site of a Turkish bank that was also bookmarked. The screen name and password had stupidly been committed to the machine's memory. When Levent hit Return, the account opened instantly.

Like most Turks, Panter had little use for a checking account in a country where checks were refused by everyone. He did, however, have a savings account that was a find. This man, whose firm was being dunned by half the businesses in the district, had a lot of money put away. The total was upwards of two million lira.

About two million dollars, a portion of which was denominated in dollars. Had Panter done so well in his life he managed to put aside that much money from his pay? Even if he was a partner in the business, that much?

There was another way for him to grow rich. He could have been skimming from the company and salting the theft away over a period of time. In that case, the people he cheated would have been motivated to see to his end.

Those people might have been his friends, or business associates, or both. The killing, after all, seemed like a personal matter.

CHAPTER 4

Levent made it back for dinner without much time to spare, though he had been wise enough to keep in touch with Emine during the day. He had even made one request—for an invitation—that should turn the evening more interesting. That was more than he usually contributed to their social life.

The evening was not likely to be less interesting than the rest of the afternoon at Konak *Site*. Levent had gone through the rest of computer without finding much except for a hint of the identity of the wallpaper woman. She was almost certainly the Skype contact known as Istanbullu24. Her place of origin was obvious, and the number might have been her age.

Canvassing the neighborhood to try to track the man who ransacked the apartment did not turn up much. No one had seen a stranger anywhere near Unit 420. The woman who shared the parking in Panter's cluster unit said that yesterday in the evening she had seen a car parked in Panter's space. She did not remember the make or color and would not have noticed the car at all except that she had gotten so accustomed to seeing the silver Mercedes in front of the jacaranda tree.

The car could have belonged to the killer, who had certainly been here less than a day ago. The commandant left one of his sergeants at Panter's apartment to make sure the man did not return to see what he had missed. The sergeant could also accept calls from anyone not aware of Panter's death. The most likely prospect had him taking heat from people demanding money of DenizKum. If a contractor existed anywhere in the area who did not have a complaint, Levent would be surprised.

"So your business caught up with you down here?"

Levent smiled across the dinner table at Zekeriya Tek, a man with thick white hair so closely cropped to his skull that it was like the down of a bird. A seagull, perhaps. He was a friend of two decades, first known in Istanbul where he ran a business restoring homes. Twelve years ago, he had moved to Bodrum to recreate a similar business in a sunnier place. As was often the case, timing was the thing that mattered. Tek's company thrived, riding the building boom in the area. Other men might know more about that business here, but not many.

"I'm consulting and trying not to break a sweat," said Levent. "The Jandarma has a problem with a man who died before his time. In fact, he went to hell before his time. He was in the building trades, by the way. You might know him. Nadir Panter was the general manager of a construction company."

"The name doesn't sound familiar," said Tek, sipping his raki from a tall thin glass. He was one of the few men Levent had known who drank raki straight. More remarkable, he never let the fifty percent go to his head.

"If you could ask around, the name might become more familiar," said Levent. "Anything concerning Panter or DenizKum Insaat would be a help."

Tek nodded as if he would say more. Though he was a good friend, and they always met for dinner when they were in the south, Tek had arrived tonight on short notice. Emine never seemed to have problems with refusals even when they were last minute requests by her husband. Tek's wife Eser was one of her best friends here.

"DenizKum's a different story," said Tek, shrugging the eyebrows that were also white and cropped. "I went out to their *site* twice. South Beach, they call it, as if you have to be careful not to take a wrong turn at Disneyland. There's no way I could forget that place. The first time out they wanted an estimate on what I could bring their kitchens in for. I gave them three prices for three grades of cabinet work and appliances, starting with what they should do and getting down to what they might do if they were cheating their customers blind. That's the way estimates are given here, if you want to know. But they showed no interest, even with the last estimate. It was clear I was out of touch with their reality. I went away thinking they didn't have a grip of any kind of reality that I knew of."

"So they were cutting corners," said Levent. "I gathered that from what I've learned about the company. I hope it's not typical of construction in Bodrum."

"Actually, I think those goons are from Istanbul," said Tek. "Came down in a pickup truck with the company's name stenciled on the doors. The first time it rained, everything washed off, including the logo."

"I didn't think it rained here in the summer," said Emine lightly. "You're exaggerating again, Zekeriya."

"They brought the rain with them," said Tek, favoring Emine as he liked very much to do. "It was winter, if I recall, and the rain kept on for forty days and nights. I swear I never believed in karma until then. When I do business with people, I don't pass judgment. There's no profit in it. But every once in a while you come across something that makes you think that hidden laws exist. No, God doesn't care if we make ten million or fifteen. He lets us buy the pickup truck on easy credit and get together all the things to start up in business even if we have no idea of what we're doing. He gives us the rope to hang ourselves, so to speak. All this is prelude and brings me to my second visit to South Beach."

"I recall there was a second," said Emine, who knew how much her husband wanted to hear Tek's story. "I admire your courage."

"It almost took more than I have," said Tek, who had begun to enjoy himself enormously. "They wanted me to look at their bathrooms that time with redesigning them in mind. There were about sixty units in all, and I remember when I looked at the things they'd put up and called bathrooms, I kept thinking— times sixty. Lord. It would take the rest of my life to do the job. I don't know who they hired for the original design, but he must have been a peasant with a vengeful turn of mind. I mean, they had the space to make good bathrooms. Plenty. But on the left side, they put up cabinets and a long counter that exhausted two-thirds of the room. That left the shower cabinet with no space at all—or let's say enough for a coffin. You couldn't turn around in it. You couldn't hang a soap dish without the risk of impaling people on it."

"I was told they were having trouble selling the units," said Levent. "It's understandable from what I'm hearing."

"Only another peasant would buy one of those places," said Tek with the disgust of a man who was used to dealing with the best materials and designs. "Every damned thing there is plastic. It looks fine from a distance, at least as long as it's new, but when you move up close you become aware that the enamel on your teeth is reacting in a very bad way with the glossy surfaces. It's as if a natural surface can't coexist with something so unnatural. The tile is something for the books if you're writing horror stories. If you struck a tuning fork, the cabinets would shatter to the core. There'd be nothing left but a heap of petroleum distillates on the floor."

Levent regretted that image presented to him at the dinner table. He could still see the small headlight wiper that he had pulled from a heap of petroleum distillates. A Mercedes should have melted down in a better way.

"I think it's a good thing you didn't take on that job," said Levent. "From what I can see, a lot of contractors who worked for DenizKum are having a hell of time getting paid."

"Those people aren't the only ones in Bodrum backing out on their contractors," said Tek. "But they might be the worst."

"Well, there's always the law," said Levent. "The contractors will be bringing suits shortly if they follow through on their threats. We could see bankruptcy all around for DenizKum. It should make quite a pile of paper. And quite a stench."

"Stench," said Tek gleefully. "That's what I remember. I don't know how I could have forgotten. There was a stench in those bathrooms that I'd never come near to in my life before. The smell wasn't shit, you understand. That would have been too natural. It came up from the drain in the floor like a protest from deep in the earth. If they opened Adolph Hitler's tomb, a smell like that would find its way out."

"Hitler doesn't have a tomb," said Eser. Tek's wife was a good cook, good company, and the sometime editor of her husband's errors. "There's no monument, no marker, nothing."

"Damned shame for my story," said Tek. "But you get the idea. Only bad people can create an ungodly smell like that."

"I believe you," said Levent. "Something tells me the stench from this company will be with us for a while."

"They're born from nature like all of us, but this kind, they go stinking back to the source even before they're dead." Tek took a long drink that finished the last of his raki. "They fuck up the business for everyone else, too."

Part Two:

Deep State

CHAPTER 5

Levent awoke early when the bay was utterly calm, like a darkly silvered mirror. He took his two slices of toast and coffee to the balcony. What came to him was a view of sublime Aegean waters hemmed by hills that had changed forever. Fifteen years ago the surrounding hills were as beautiful as the sea. Tangerine groves flowed down the slopes into the valleys and almost to the shore in shades of deep green spiced with bright color. Bitez had once been called Agachli—Full of Trees.

Idly, he counted another concrete *site* that had been built since last year. Nearly every year Levent made the same count, wondering not when the march of progress would stop but when it would be called by a better name. He did not know the name— greed, degradation, the rites of pollution—but he could not deny that everyone was entitled to a slice of heaven. Not all people were like the Inspector of Homicide, a man who liked to rent; who liked to leave no trace of his passage; who liked not to own even when owning was wise.

When his cell phone rang, Levent grabbed it quickly off the table. Benny and the Jets was not for everyone, especially Emine in the morning. She liked to sleep late on her vacation, maintaining with some reason that Levent preferred to brood by himself until the caffeine took over.

Levent recognized the familiar name that appeared on his screen. "Erol, good morning."

Detective Erol Akbay, Istanbul Homicide, coughed on his first cigarette of the day. "Boss, I ran this man you asked me about last night. Ready with a pencil?"

Levent liked Erol for several reasons, not the least his lack of sentimentality. He did not want to know about the weather in Bodrum, which was constant and good; nor did he ask after his superior's well-being, which he assumed was constant if not good; and he never wasted time on anything that he had been assigned.

"I have a pen in my hand," said Levent. "Go ahead."

"This man Panter," said Erol with what was almost a laugh. "You told me he was dead. Well, I can confirm that he doesn't exist. He never existed from what I can see. He has no record with us or anyone else in the country and owns no real estate anywhere that shows. He was put on this earth with a set of keys to a Mercedes and nothing else. In other words, he's a Turk."

"I don't need notes for that, Erol."

"I'm done saving you ink, Boss. What comes next will move you out of your lounge chair fast. You seem to have stepped into something ugly here. Nadir Panter isn't a man so much as an alias. There's no record of his real name or even if he has one. He only appears twice in the records, but when he does it's as spooky as things get in this country. What I mean is, he wears his dick outside his pants. He's *Derin Devlet* for sure."

Derin Devlet. The Deep State. It was the name the media had given to what they called the shadow government that operated behind Turkey's public government. They were never known by their names, but sometimes by their aliases. Something had turned up that put Nadir Panter in the light.

"I'm listening, Erol."

"First you said 'shit,' Boss. I heard you. But don't worry. I went outside to make the call. This is a clean phone."

"No phone is clean enough," said Levent. "So now you can give me the really bad news."

Erol made a strange nonverbal sound that seemed to preface an explanation. "You remember the Turk they caught running drugs in England a few years ago?" he said. "Hard drugs in big quantities. It was more than enough to keep their soccer hooligans quiet until the next match. Well, this man had some fruity English name like Reginald, but his last name was Okbash. The British nailed him through phony buyers, and they were waiting with cuffs when his men made deliveries of the product. No way out for Reginald, it seemed."

"I do remember something like that," said Levent. "Tell me again what happened to him."

"They let him out on bail, thinking he couldn't go far without a passport," said Erol. "I guess the British think in straight lines—A to B. They don't understand our alphabet. It turns out that Reginald somehow got his hands on a passport—very official—and walked out of the country without waving goodbye. They stamped his passport like they do all the tourists. Now the clever detective would know the name on the passport he walked out of the country with."

"Nadir Panter."

"You win, Boss, along with some sharp fellows in the British media. They got wind of the customs walk-through. A couple of days later they came out with screaming headlines and even printed the name in the paper. You have to imagine the noise they made. The Pink Panter was the best thing they said. There was a lot of stuff about heavy breathers, too."

The connections between drug running and the Deep State were constant and not unusual. Criminal enterprises needed a ready supply of cash to enable their operations. Enable. That was a nice way of putting it.

"But you said you came across the alias twice," said Levent. "Was it earlier or later the second time?"

"Later."

"It doesn't seem like a good idea to use an identity that's already been compromised. Especially when the British press know it."

"It might have something to do with arrogance," said Erol with the harshness in his voice that appeared when he looked up and saw only dark space in the bureaucracy above him. "Or carelessness. You know these DDs are connected high up. When they started out under another name, they were protected by the CIA because they were such fine communist killers. Later, they were protected by our military because they were such fine Kurd killers. No matter how many drugs they run, they make sure to spread the money around. They're confident they can find someone with the juice to bail them out. It doesn't matter how dumb they are. To prove it, I'll tell you that an identity card in the name of Nadir Panter was one of the things us cops found when we made the very first Ergenekon raid."

That was a well-known event. The Istanbul police after a long investigation had broken a conspiracy that specialized in political assassinations. Some of the right-wing extremists who made up the Ergenekon group were interrogated and jailed. The Islamic government was relieved because some of the group's activities pointed toward a coup d'etat.

"I see the thread in this, Erol."

"It's the kind you don't want to pull on hard or the Sunday suit falls apart," he said. "But I did my duty, as requested. I don't know what you're going to do with this. I've been in touch with London and asked them to send scans of Reginald's prints and what he used to have for a face. They said they would."

"I'm going to say thanks with reservations."

"You always keep something in reserve, Boss. This time you might need more than you think. You're going up against legends. They're covered with slime and they stink like hell, but they're bigger than life. Your size."

"Goodbye, Erol. Send the London information to the Jandarma."

"Glad to oblige."

* * *

Levent did not like being depressed when he brooded. A human torch was disturbing, but the Deep State was worse. Any group that had sanction for murder was a homicide inspector's nightmare. Under different names they had been doing exactly that since the early days of the Cold War. They had gone by many names—Gladio, Grey Wolves, Counter-Guerillas—but the names were variations on the same theme. These were Turkish patriots who killed anyone who was not a Turkish patriot.

Of course, they controlled the definition. Foreigners were not Turkish patriots. Minorities like Kurds and Armenians were not. Anyone who criticized a tremendously imperfect state was not a Turkish patriot, which meant that newsmen, as well as the rest of the media and arts, were always under suspicion and liable for assassination. And yes, there was a list.

The worst thing was that they were tolerated. The military used the Deep State to do things that they legally could not. Politicians fed off the drug money that the groups provided. Almost anyone could be corrupted by the elixir of patriotism and black money. The police, who were usually conservative and sympathetic to nationalists, could be co-opted to the cause or to silence.

Adolph Hitler's tomb was not in his own country.

It was here.

* * *

"Mind if I do the questioning?"

Levent asked that of the commandant, who sat in the front seat. Metin had consented to ride in the nimble Honda that Levent had driven from Istanbul. Even he saw the disadvantages of rolling into DenizKum Insaat with outriders in a paramilitary van. If he regarded Levent's request as a process of emasculation, he did not show it.

"I'll pay close attention to your technique, Inspector. This is a chance to learn that doesn't come along often."

Levent said nothing. He had told Metin nothing of the Deep State vector in this investigation. Although it was not much more than a rumor, Levent was sure it would grow to be more. The Jandarma were the most right-wing of all the police forces, and the most sympathetic to sanctioned kills. Feeling the commandant out about these matters would be a gradual process that might never come to a good end.

Levent pulled into the parking lot of a small building on the wide boulevard. It was the main road in what might be called Bodrum New Town, and it ran along the upper part of the hill as the feeder route through the city. The two-story building set slightly back from the road was one of the older units that had been put up perhaps ten years ago. DenizKum Insaat occupied half and the other half was a real estate agency. Had either paid their rent?

The DenizKum office was dominated by a gigantic idealized portrait of South Beach ("For Those Who Have Arrived"). It wrapped the back wall through two corners, superimposing the swimming pool and clubhouse at odd angles. Several desks were spread liberally with advertising brochures and promotions— except one desk near the door that gave space to a middle-aged woman.

The nameplate on her desk said that her name was Pinar Seles. She was overweight, but not terribly so. Her eyes were blue but nothing like the sea, yet they seemed alert and intelligent. Surprised by her visitors, she rose from her chair to greet the commandant in full appreciation of his uniform.

"Welcome, sir," she said in a voice much smaller than her size. "What can I do to help you?"

"We'd like to ask you some questions," said Levent, moving her attention toward him. "They concern the death of Nadir Panter."

Clearly, she had no idea that a key member of her firm had died. She took hold of the chair that stood in front of her desk as if bad weather had suddenly come up. "Mister Panter," she said. "He's . . . dead?"

"Murdered." Levent directed her into the chair that she still held to. "We're conducting an investigation into the circumstances surrounding the murder. When was the last time you saw him?"

She fell into a long count, as if distancing herself from the question. Her eyes took a sheen that could have been grief—or calculation. "Why, I haven't seen him in two days, though I called his house," she said. "He was in the office Wednesday."

"The day he died," said Levent, like an accusation. "Was it a special day? How did he act? Did he say anything to you that indicated he was upset?"

"Upset," she said. "Mister Panter?"

A poor choice of words. If Panter was the thug he seemed to be, he had plenty of experience hiding his emotions. Showing them would have been unnatural.

"Did he seem worried about anything?"

"No," she said. "Not that I could see."

"Perhaps he was distracted," asked Levent. "Or forgetful."

"I don't think so."

"Did you notice him making uncharacteristic mistakes?"

She almost offered a quick no, but held back. "There may have been one thing," she said. "In the afternoon, Mister Panter told me to fetch the client and visitors books for South Beach. The client book is the list of people who bought units at the *site*. The visitors book is a list of people who stopped at the *site* and left us their names. Mister Panter gave me the name to look up, telling me he wanted to find it. I scanned the books, but found nothing about this man. He apparently never came to South Beach even on a virtual tour."

"And that was an unusual mistake for Mister Panter to make?"

"It wasn't a large mistake," said Pinar. "But not many units have been sold at South Beach—not a third of the *site*—even after prices were reduced. Mister Panter should have known most of the names of the buyers by heart. The visitors less so. All I'm saying is he wouldn't normally do something like that."

"What was the name he gave you to look up?"

"Varan," she said. "You know, like the tourist company. I thought the name was Turkish because of that, but Mister Panter said no, it's French."

"Have you sold many units to foreigners?"

"No, sir. Two or three. To my knowledge they were all English. That's what mostly comes to Bodrum, and that's why I thought it odd."

"What did Mister Panter say when you told him the name was not on the list?"

"He didn't seem surprised," she said. "He shrugged and said he wanted to check to see if it was there."

"And that was all he said?"

"Yes."

The lapse, if that's what it was, did not seem like much. Levent made a note of the name, but only because it could be foreign. Out of character for Bodrum and Panter made it in character for homicide.

"One thing in all this surprises me, Pinar. I don't see how Mister Panter, as the general manager of the company, could be as calm as he seemed with all the creditors he had to face."

Pinar looked at Levent as if trying to judge how much he really knew. "I wasn't involved in financial matters here," she said. "That was Mister Panter's area."

"It was an area where he did not do well," said Levent. "I'm surprised he didn't confide in you, Pinar. Did he ever suggest that you would be wise to look for work with another company?"

"No," she said.

"Then he was more dishonest than we thought," said Levent to the commandant. "He was a very dishonest man not worth loyalty from his employees." Levent turned back to Pinar. "When was the last time you were paid a full salary?"

She lowered her head, turning her pale blue eyes out the door to the busy road. "Three months, sir. I've been on half pay."

"I'd like to think you have money saved," said Levent. "Mister Panter certainly did. He was a rich man in fact."

"He's the general manager, sir."

"Would his position here give him the means to put away two million dollars, do you think?"

Her gaze hardened and her spine in the chair seemed to find equilibrium. "No, sir. Not from his pay. He hasn't been with the company from the beginning. The last eight months is all. I don't see how his pay made him millions of dollars."

"But from the operations of the company? How about that?"

"I wouldn't be able to say, sir. The money to finance DenizKum came from the parent company in Istanbul."

"The parent," said Levent, knowing this was important. "Who is that?"

"Bozkurt, sir. Bozkurt Commerce."

The nerve of these people. They hid their identities but never their intentions. They wanted the public to know who they were so the public could be better intimidated. Bozkurt meant Gray Wolf. Ergenekon was the mythical valley where the Turkish tribes lived trapped between mountains with no way out, no way to expand, no way to realize their destiny. A gray wolf showed them the secret exit from the valley. And so we all believed there was a secret way to our destiny.

"Can I have the address and phone number of the company?" asked Levent. "And the man to contact there."

"Yes, sir," she said, turning from the chair to the desk drawer as if to all the good things. "I have the address and number, though I don't often talk to Bozkurt. When I do, it's never to a man."

"A woman then?"

"Yes, sir. Sultan Kara is the general manager there."

Levent was surprised. Though he had known women chief executives, and heard of many more, he had never associated any with the Deep State. They were a masculine club of killers. Until now.

* * *

Levent stayed with Pinar for forty-five minutes that were well spent. She talked in a relaxed fashion once tea came from the service that even bankrupt Turkish firms kept. When Levent suggested she should call Zekeriya Tek to enquire about a position at his firm, and to use the Inspector's name, she responded with thanks.

Although Pinar had a propriety feeling toward the company for which she had worked as a secretary for more than a year, her reserve had been completely penetrated by the truth. There was nothing subtle about the discovery. Financial truth is always the most immediate.

Levent was most interested in finding out the real name of Nadir Panter. He still could not believe that the man would take the name of an international felon for his own, regardless of the power of his backers. Doing that was more than stupid. It was arrogant stupidity that always exacted a price.

When Levent asked Pinar if she had ever heard Panter called by another name, she said no. A moment later she said, not really, but—. It would not be an exaggeration to say that the tea in her hand stimulated her memory.

Early this year she had taken two calls from what seemed like the same man. He had a low purring voice and asked for the general manager. He had used the name Fish (in English) to refer to Panter. The man sounded friendly but commanding. Panter had spoken to him in a more respectful and congenial fashion than usual.

When Levent pursued the lead, Pinar offered no further help. She had never received correspondence for Panter from anyone under a different name, first or last. She had never heard anyone call Panter by the name Fish in the office or on the street. She thought it might have been a nickname. The man who called was possibly an old friend, though someone who mattered. The two had talked of both business and pleasure, and some of their references seemed to come from a shared past.

Had she ever heard the stranger's voice before Panter came here as the general manager? Pinar was not sure. His voice was distinctive, but she had little to compare it with in the early days. Experience in the business had told her which things were usual and which not. There were several things about working in this office that were not.

Panter had been the second general manager of DenizKum Insaat. The first was Ali Berman. He was experienced and spoke excellent English, but after six months had been hired away by a firm in a town near Fethiye. She had never heard from him again, though she found out through a friend that he had gone to work for another construction company in that town on the sea to the east. He was said to be doing well.

Panter had been sent from Istanbul last fall. Pinar was told of his coming by Berman, but had been surprised when the new general manager took control because he seemed to know little about the construction business or how to promote sales. He told her that he could not have done without her. That was true. Luckily, the fall and winter were slow seasons in Bodrum and by spring Panter had mastered most of what he needed to know.

Pinar did not think that blame for the firm's troubles should all be laid to Panter. He had made some innovations that Pinar thought were good. He paved the road from South Beach all the way to the main highway out of town, so access was not a problem. He organized "Inspection Tours" from England to bring foreigners in for long weekends of pressure looks. He replaced the firm's web presence with a state-of-the-art site, hiring a local man to revamp it. The Web site now got ten times the amount of hits.

Many of the problems that Panter faced were a product of the times. Housing stock in Bodrum was overbuilt even before South Beach came onto the market. New *sites* with ample backing and larger staffs were common, as was usual in Turkey when there was money to be made. If Panter could be faulted for anything, it might be for his personnel decisions. He often hired men who had little experience in the construction business, putting them into almost any position.

"Why did he do that?"

"I'm not sure of the reason," said Pinar. "Frankly, I wouldn't have done it. But no one asked my opinion."

"He must have been trying to cut costs."

"Possibly," she said, but as if she reserved her doubts. "But inexperienced men can cost more in mistakes than they save in pay."

"Did these men come from Istanbul?"

"No," she said. "They were local, but usually not from Bodrum. I mean not from the city, that is."

"Where did they come from?"

"It took me a while to discover almost all of them came from the same place," she said. "I suppose I should have realized it earlier, but some of them had addresses in the city. They weren't city people, though. Most came from a village back in the hills. Or they'd come from the village before settling in town."

"The same village?" he said. "All of them?"

"I really can't say that, Inspector. I didn't make a study of their backgrounds, and I picked up information as I went along. A lot of them came from that village. It's sometimes like that, you know. Word gets around that work can be had in the big city—and this is a big city now. The villagers don't want to stay where they are. They want to have cable television and shop in the chain stores. At least they want to have some wages instead of working on their father's farm for the food he puts before them."

Everything she said was true. Having lived in the area all her life, Pinar knew the way the boom in tourism had drawn young men from their villages. But Levent felt that gathering most of the workers for any purpose from a single place was strange.

"What's the name of this place?"

"Yelkenli."

The word meant sailing ship. Levent did not understand how a mountain village came to have that name, but there might be a reason.

"Where is it?"

"I can show you on the map."

* * *

Levent made a note of the location of the village, hoping that if he decided to go, his Honda would have enough for the climb into the mountains. He liked the car, but knew it rode low to the ground. Back roads with potholes and boulders that appeared at random were not the things it liked best.

Pinar did not know if Panter had ever gone to the village, but if he did he had driven that silver Mercedes. He took it everywhere, as if it were as much a talisman as a car. Once, he told her that it had been a present given to him by his ex-wife, when she had been in love with a younger and more athletic man.

Panter assured her this story was true. He told it more than once, as if trying to impress on Pinar what she might do to please him. A Mercedes was beyond her imagination, and an affair was something she never seriously considered. Panter may once have been an attractive man, but that was before his hair thinned, his belly thickened and his mind told him that no further input was necessary. He was a typical Turk of late middle-age in those respects.

She would not have liked being married to him even if the subject had been discussed. Nothing about Panter marked him as a family man. Even when he spoke of his family, it was as if that thing was hopeless. His parents were dead or denied, and his ex-wife pursued her own life. He had a son and a daughter. He spoke of them as if he was proud, but even so, could not keep hints of criticism from his gruff voice.

When Levent described the young woman who performed as computer wallpaper, Pinar said that yes, it sounded like Melisa. Pinar had met her when she came to Bodrum in the spring after she graduated from the university in fashion design. She called occasionally. Pinar learned to recognize her voice and transfer it to her father's phone, even if he was at the *site*, where he sometimes went.

The girl's phone number had certainly been in Panter's cell phone directory, but if so, it was one more thing that had declined into hydrocarbon debris. Pinar promised to ask Sultan Kara at Bozkurt if she had the number.

Levent had no objection to that happening immediately. He told Pinar to call Bozkurt, thinking it was better to overhear the conversation. She seemed not to mind and made no attempt to find privacy in another room. There was one in the back of the office with a hotplate and cabinets and a toilet that Levent had asked to use. He found nothing of interest there. Having been forewarned by Tek, even the smell seemed familiar.

The one-way conversation he listened to was more useful. Though speaking woman to woman, Pinar did not presume upon their relationship. She was considerate in the beginning and on the steady side of somber when she gave the news of Panter's death.

The reaction on the other end of the line was odd. It seemed clear that the general manager of Bozkurt knew about Panter's gruesome death, a fact that Pinar confirmed after she hung up the phone.

How did she know when the authorities had done their best to obscure the event? According to the commandant, no information had been released to the media or other police departments in the area. Levent trusted Erol Akbay to keep his information quiet, especially since he had been told to do so.

But there were ways of siphoning the pipeline if your sources were well placed. Obviously, Panter and Bozkurt had ways of intercepting information. The Chief knew what had happened, but it was remarkable how unguarded people at the top could be. They liked being in the know. They liked it more than anything except power. And knowledge was power.

Sultan Kara also asked Pinar to keep Panter's death to herself. Nothing overhung prospective sales as heavily. The general manager of Bozkurt would be in town shortly to help with the transition to better times. She was in fact about to deplane at the Bodrum airport, and would be in the city, traffic permitting, in an hour or so.

CHAPTER 6

Turkish was a logical language, but there were exceptions. One had to do with names. Sultan should have been a man's name since it was the title of the rulers of the Ottoman Empire, who were never women. A woman could rule through the harem, however. That was a very old Turkish tradition.

Levent waited at the hotel when Sultan Kara appeared in her red BMW rental. She had the bellhops truck her luggage in pods of pale leather to the front desk, sweeping through the lobby like the queen of the night that was so famous in Bodrum. Her black hair, long but bright and glossy, framed a face with a high forehead and higher cheekbones. Her nose was a classic Ottoman scepter and her body swum in and out of her silvery dress in smooth visible strokes. Though nothing like the usual CEO, her manner showed that she was accustomed to being treated with executive privilege. She seemed to note only the things that should serve her.

Levent was not included in the group of underlings who vied for her attention while knowing they would never have it as they wanted it. This was a woman more expensive than their hotel, which was very expensive. The desk clerk had greeted Levent like something wet and gross that had dried on his mouse-gray livery. But he promised to tell the sole occupant of 401, the penthouse suite, that an inspector of police awaited her in the cafe. This public servant was not to be put off, said Levent, if there was justice in the world.

Sultan Kara did not like being redirected from the progress of her arrival. She gave instructions to the bellhops about the luggage, gave them fifty lira to guarantee obedience, then entered the lounge where Levent watched and waited.

"An inspector of police," she said, standing before him as before the conquered. "May I see your credentials?"

Levent showed her his shield, understanding that this was part of the process. She might have known who he was, and his home address, but wanted confirmation for her records.

"Istanbul," she said. "Aren't you out of your jurisdiction?"

"I'm assisting the Jandarma in their investigation of the murder of Nadir Panter of DenizKum Insaat. You should know him, Miss Kara. It is Miss, isn't it?"

"You're not proposing marriage?"

"I'm proposing you have a seat," said Levent. "I have some questions I'd like to put to the parent company of DenizKum."

"I should have them in writing," she said with a late smile. "And you should call me Sultan."

"I'm afraid you'll have to take the questions as I put them," said Levent. "I'm on vacation and wouldn't want to waste my time. Or yours."

She sat. She even tipped her cleavage, so anyone in the room, but especially her closest audience, should have the full view of its bounty.

"Now what can I help you with, Inspector?"

"I'd like to know who your general manager was in real life," said Levent. "Nadir Panter is something of a cipher in our records."

This case could be cracked with an honest answer, but she gave nothing like it. "Mister Panter was the general manager of DenizKum," she said. "I understand he was hired in as someone who knew the business and could carry it on after the first manager resigned."

"You had nothing to do with his appointment?"

"Absolutely nothing," she said. "He was recommended by our first manager, who spoke highly of him. We approved him on that basis."

"I'd like to have the current address of that manager," said Levent. "His name is Berman, I'm told."

"That's correct. He went to work for another firm. I'm sorry I can't recall their name. I can have it for you tomorrow."

"Today would be better."

"I'll see what I can do."

"You should," said Levent. "I don't see any reason why this investigation has to be extended to your firm. It doesn't have to be, as long as I receive cooperation from you, Sultan."

"Perhaps you might want to talk to our attorneys."

"For information? Or the opposite?"

Levent wondered when she would turn on the charm that had brought her to the top, and he was quickly rewarded. Sultan smiled as if honoring his humor, knowing that the honor was all hers. She withdrew a cigarette from her purse—a vacation bag of great size and colors—holding it out for a light.

"I don't smoke," said Levent. "But there's a pack of matches on the next table. This is a first class hotel."

She pretended not to mind as she reached to the table at her left for the matches. Her movements were sinuous, extending from her long arms to her fine shoulders and breasts with after-shocks. Nothing was wasted and much, perhaps, gained. Her skin even in more intimate places was tanned, though not to a deep brown. It glowed from within in golden tones.

"We should have a drink," she said.

"It's early for me, but have what you like."

She called the waiter over by a glance that she flung like a lance from horseback. He responded instantly, wanting to be close to greatness, but stopping before he came completely to the table.

"White wine," she said. "Seleccion. Make sure it's ten degrees."

A good brand. Sultan could not have gone much higher. Levent wanted to know just how high this subterfuge went. He knew it would stop in Bodrum before carrying on to Ankara or Istanbul.

"Bozkurt," he said. "What made you choose that name for your firm?"

"I'm afraid it wasn't my choice," she said, putting dense smoke between them. "I took over as general manager two years ago. It was a going concern at that time, but perhaps not going in *exactly* the right directions."

"But it is now."

"Oh, yes," she said with a smile that showed all her teeth. "We're making money. If there's another measure of success in business, I don't know it."

Levent waited while a waiter—a different one—came with Sultan's white wine. He poured the glass from the bottle reverently, like a holy man on three legs, before he withdrew with small backward steps.

"I'm surprised to hear that your company is doing so well, Sultan. I know what a drain on your resources DenizKum must be."

"You're quite sure of that?"

"The creditors of DenizKum are quite sure," said Levent. "I can put you in touch with them if you're not aware of *exactly* who they are."

"Inspector, you're trying to tell me that operations at DenizKum have not met our expectations. I'll concede that and go further. We're disappointed. But we anticipate much better."

"Global warming," said Levent. "That will save South Beach. The *site* is far enough from the shore. Eventually, it should be waterfront."

"We're prepared to wait if we have to," she said. "Land is finite, Inspector. Land near the seashore in a vacation venue has become rare in the last few years. Perhaps you don't know these things. If not, perhaps you should."

Levent knew real estate as most Turks knew it—as a bank that held its value in land. What the general manager of Bozkurt had outlined might be a plan, but it was not far from the normal calculations of companies in business to wash black money. They did not particularly care about the worth of a project or how it measured up in the market place. They waited. They wrote off expenses. They wrote off subsidiary companies. When the land became rare, they cashed in their bet, knowing they had already found genuine value.

"You must be well capitalized," said Levent. "I suppose I'll have some idea of that when I look at your tax records."

"You might," she said without enthusiasm or apparent interest. Obviously, she knew that the police had resources, but did not really fear what might be found. "I can't stop you there."

"I'd be surprised if you could stop me anywhere," he said, daring her to voice her connections. "Perhaps you should ask people you know in Istanbul how easy it is to steer me wrong."

"I'm sure it's not easy," she said. "Or wise. I plan to spend the next two weeks in Bodrum, working to make sure Mister Panter's death doesn't set out operations back more than it has to."

"A new general manager?"

"That will be necessary," she said. "I have to find someone with a good head who has enough experience to run the business."

"That would be more than Panter had when he took on the job."

She placed her cigarette, smoked to the filter and cool, in the ashtray. "I'm feeling hostility from you, Inspector. I'm one of those people who don't like dealing with friends who're less than they seem. I prefer declared competition."

"You have plenty to declare," said Levent. "You might want to settle DenizKum's debts before dropping the mess on a new general manager."

She smiled this time with meaning that was not hard to read. "I should have you on my board."

A joke. But it was a joke that could become more real if Levent showed interest. "What would be my compensation?"

"We could talk about that."

And she was not offering her body, yet. "I need solid information to settle this case," he said. "When I get it, we'll talk about . . . ramifications."

"I'd prefer that this matter didn't ramify," she said. "You'll have my cooperation in finding the killer of Mister Panter. He was an important member of our organization. I don't expect his killer to enjoy his life as he knows it for long."

"He won't."

"Confidence," she said. "I appreciate that in public servants. It's considerably harder to find than land close to the shore. You can rest assured that when I have all the information you need, I'll pass it on immediately."

"I'll need his real name for the record," said Levent in his computer voice. "His occupation—and not the job you gave him to while away his late middle age. The reason you gave him the job—and not the one you'd like me to think. His background from his early days to the moment when his flesh began to melt from his body in the parking lot of a convenience store. His family and friends, with correct addresses and phone numbers. And most of all, his connections—the ones that brought him to his position in spite of his lack of knowledge of the job. In other words, I'd like everything that you pretend not to know."

Her laugh told Levent he had struck the things that she liked to hide. "This will make your work easier?"

"Quicker," he said. "I'll find these things out in any case. Whether I have them from you will determine how well we prosper."

"I think it will be very well."

"I'm sure."

Sultan looked at her wine, which was mostly gone in the tall glass. Knowing she had the concession she wanted—time—she threw the wine off like an extra wrap that was no longer needed. The delicate glass struck the table like a temple bell.

"You'll be hearing from us, Inspector."

Us. Levent thought so, too. Sultan Kara had all the talent that Panter had lacked. She was deft, stunning, and confident, too. But she was not the one who ran this brazen show. That entity was still unknown.

It was Deep State and Levent had just stepped into the shadows.

CHAPTER 7

Levent met the commandant at the forensics garage, where he had his look at the Mercedes that had surrounded Panter in the last moments of his life. The car sat sullenly in the clean floor, as if it had developed a personality by being subjected to the ravenous heat. Small slabs of paint had flaked off, marking strange leaf-like patterns around the perimeter. One last piece fell off, nearly silent, as Levent circled the car.

Although the burn had been thorough, the shell of the car was intact except for the trunk, which had buckled badly when the gas tank blew.

The motor might be salvaged for spare parts, and the chassis for scrap metal, but the interior was completely gutted. The driver's side door lay on the floor as if glad to be rid of the rest. The steering wheel was bent like a vine, and the dashboard had collapsed into a nest of wiring that was intermittently bright. Levent would not have known the upholstery had been a pale cream color if he had not been told. The famous headlight wiper hung like a damaged eyelid near the teeth of the grille.

The body had of course been removed. That was a hell of a job, said the man in charge, a serious sort named Mahir. He had a nose like all police technicians should have; big, bony and bent in a way that made him seem low to the ground. His hands, long and bony, were of the same material, and he used them to shape his words.

"Never seen anything like it," he said, drawing his hands wide open to indicate the impossible. "The flesh was fused to the damned leather in some places, as if they were the same material. And I suppose they are in a way. Skin of animals—mammals. Of course, the ethyl alcohol wouldn't make a fire nearly that hot. It burnt out long before he was dead."

"So the blow on the back of the head didn't kill him."

"Definitely not," said Mahir, touching has head high at the back where Panter had been struck. "He was alive until the gas-fed fire reached him. Maybe not conscious, because he was sitting in the position where you'd expect a driver to be. His body fell over to the right, though not a long way. But he didn't open the door. I doubt if he tried."

"What do you think he was hit with?"

"Something hard," said Mahir with his long fist. "It could have been a tire iron or the butt of a pistol. Not a bottle unless it was completely full. We weren't able to settle on the murder weapon, but it probably couldn't be a chunk of wood, at least not the pine you usually see around here. Nothing we found in the debris matched up with a weapon, by the way."

"Do you think he could have been struck before he entered the car?" said Levent. "Were the doors locked?"

"Not the driver's side or the passenger's," he said. "The victim had an electronic door opener. The usual kind. Depressing the button once opens the driver's side door. The second time opens the rest."

"So the victim could have opened the doors from a way off," said Levent. "Or the killer could have been waiting inside the car if it was left open."

"I'd say the first is more likely," said Mahir. "There was a lot of junk in the back seat. We found debris that had to be a CD case, though the CDs melted. A pile of papers on the seat that didn't survive well—A4 size with figures, normal business printouts. Clothing for the beach, or least it seems that way. A plastic bottle—three liters—water before it boiled away. Frankly, I don't know how a man could get comfortable in the back with all the crap that was there."

If the killer had not hidden in the back of the car, he must have taken the victim when he was outside. So he was fairly athletic. Panter was a good-sized man to wrestle into the driver's seat and screw behind the wheel. And there were a lot of ways to kill a man without going through the considerable trouble of burning him alive.

"Any fingerprints?"

"Fingerprints and high heat don't mix," said Mahir. "About all we found that we couldn't match with the victim were partials on the gas cap. It'll be hard swearing they belong to someone even if you find him and roll him real good."

"Did you find anything else?"

"A couple of things," said Mahir as if they mattered more. "We took a pistol out of the glove compartment. A new nine-millimeter HK. German made. It wasn't badly damaged."

That was a surprise if Panter was an innocent victim, but not the criminal he seemed to be. "The ammunition didn't explode?"

"There wasn't any," said Mahir. "A man goes to the trouble of putting a weapon within reach, but doesn't load it. We haven't been able to tell if the gun was ever fired, but we should have the information tomorrow."

That should be good to know. If Panter had bought the gun recently, that might mean he expected trouble. He did not have many choices for gun shops in Bodrum, and he would also need a permit. That could be checked.

"What about the second thing?" asked Levent.

"We found money," said Mahir. "In the trunk in a small box. It was badly burnt up, but there was once a lot of it in a big wad. Some of the bills toward the middle were just about intact. They were American hundred dollar bills. From what I could tell from the ashes, all of them were."

So Panter kept a supply of cash in his car. Not many people did unless they had plans to dole it out on his rounds—or to run. "How much money would you say was there?"

"Hard to tell for sure," said Mahir. "Not a couple of thousand dollars. I'd say more like eight or ten."

A serious payload. Levent did not wonder where it came from after looking into Panter's bank account, but where was the cash going? And why keep it so handy? What business was Panter really in? Or—how many?

* * *

After hearing Zekeriya Tek's description of the qualities of life at South Beach, Levent had put off going there until it was necessary. Now he wanted to trace Panter's movements on the day he died. Pinar said he was in the office until almost three o'clock before leaving for the development.

That was her estimate. Panter had said nothing about his destination other than to request the client list earlier that day, but he often went to South Beach in the afternoon. He seldom told anyone where he was going at any time, as if concerned they might know too much of his movements.

If he went elsewhere before making his last convenience stop, Levent would like to know. The progress of a man's day required no logic, but if Panter knew he was being pursued, his movements could have meaning. Levent liked to think that many innocent things did. Gumushluk, the town nearest South Beach, was called Myndos in ancient times. It was to this westernmost part of the Bodrum Peninsula that Cassius and Brutus had come after assassinating Julius Caesar. They were hiding, too.

The guard at the gate of South Beach—a young man in a wrinkled uniform who carried a sidearm on his hip—waved them in at a glance, standing to attention when he noticed the commandant's beret.

The *site* had been carved out from the base of the small mountain almost to its summit, yet there were several pockets of free land where more units could be built. The construction in the older parts was still underway in small ways. Subcontractors' trucks, with painted names and numbers to call, careened up and down the mud roads. In the newer part, a large backhoe noisily dug into the mountain as a concrete truck roared by to drop its heavy load at the next cluster unit. Levent wondered what the residents who had already moved into the *site* thought about the racket, but knew their complaints would not be heard over the din.

The completed units were like every vacation *site* in Bodrum—poured concrete, painted white. They did not vary until the last rows at the top, when they expanded by a floor and grew wider.

These would be the largest, most expensive units; two bedrooms with bigger balconies to accept the rays of the sun. They were all air-conditioned, solar-paneled, with small gardens in various stages of completion.

The reception office was halfway up the slope with a parking lot that seemed like the only nicely paved surface in the *site*. All would be paved eventually, said the brochure that Levent had taken from the DenizKum central office. They had the most precious thing in a desert, a water supply, and were all "fine contemporary examples of vacation homes."

So much for Tek. Levent expected that man's opinion to be contradicted at every turn, and he was not disappointed by the salesman behind the reception desk. Hakan Rehber, a small limber man with a mole between his left eye and sideburn, wanted to be free with his hands, like most of his kind, but backed off with a quick police handshake. The monolithic demeanor of the commandant had something to do with that. It was a concern to Levent, who liked more relaxed interviews.

Still, Rehber was as friendly as he was paid to be, asking them to be seated at the circular sales table piled with the same brochures. He told the young male secretary to bring tea for their guests from the kitchen in the back room.

"I hope nothing's wrong," he said. "I could swear all the permits were properly filed and the taxes paid."

"We're here to investigate the murder of Nadir Panter," said the commandant. "We understand he came here two days ago shortly before his death."

Rehber put his hands to his belly where it lapped over his belt, as if he was trying to hold something in. Levent did not necessarily assume it was the truth.

"Well, I didn't know that," said Rehber, as if the greatest crime was ignorance. "I mean, about his death. It seems incredible. Impossible."

"Why?" asked Levent.

Rehber shook his head. "Not being alive is hard to imagine with some people, I suppose. Nadir was self-contained."

"Always alert?"

"Yes," said Rehber. "Not to be distracted, if you know what I mean. He could look at a set of figures, talk on the phone, smoke his cigarette, take his tea, and still handle interruptions that came up." Rehber took back the fingers he had used to demonstrate Panter's talent. "Not the man to be taken unaware. Nadir was always on top."

"Did he seem practiced about that?" asked Levent. "Professional?"

"I'm afraid I wouldn't know how to answer," said the salesman. "Can you tell me how it happened?"

"He was hit on the head," said the commandant, who seemed to like answering questions he should avoid. "Then his car was set afire."

"You mean, he was alive when . . ."

"He was," said the commandant. "Though he might not have been conscious."

"That's mercy," said Rehber, holding his hands out in supplication. "God's mercy. We all need that no matter who we are."

"Who was Nadir Panter?" asked Levent abruptly, not wanting the interview to bog down in tears. "You could do us a favor if you tell us that. No one seems to know."

"Know?" Rehber looked at Levent like the last man at the sales counter. "That's a strange question. Nadir was well known here. I've lived in Bodrum all my life, but if I really wanted to know how things were at any place, I asked Nadir. He could tell you the best clubs and barber shops, the best goods and discounts, and he knew the local histories of every place—I mean the details—all the way back to the Cyprus War."

"You mean he was familiar with Bodrum in the past as well as the present?"

"Absolutely."

"Yet it's my understanding he came from Istanbul."

"Like a lot of people," said Rehber, including Levent in the long progress. "It doesn't mean he couldn't drive a car here in less than a day."

"Did he?" asked Levent, who felt something new had entered Panter's biography. "Was he just a visitor in your opinion? Or more?"

"More, I'd say. Of course, I couldn't prove it, but the way he spoke of things as they used to be was like someone who'd lived here for some time. I mean, he knew everything, everyone. He spoke of Zeki Muren as if they came down in the same pink convertible. That hilarious faggot, he said."

Muren, the pop singer, had made Bodrum the favorite playground first for gays and then Turks through his advertising of its hard-drinking, hard-living virtues. That was at least twenty years ago by Levent's count.

"So you felt that Panter was one of the instant pioneers of Bodrum," said Levent. "Coming back as the general manager of DenizKum was a homecoming."

"If I had to say yes, I'd say exactly."

"Do you know any of his friends?"

"We didn't share," said Rehber. "Not friends, and little outside of business. But he did tell me things about the place I'd never heard before. He knew the owner of this land. Mrs. Ogun sold the property to DenizKum several years ago. She was the granddaughter of one of the people up on the mountain. I won't call them important people, but they owned most of the land around here. The sons inherited the best of it, the acreage back from the sea. It was safer that way. In the old days, no one knew who would show up on the shore at night with a boat, a pair of pistols and blood in his eye. The British used this area for target practice during the First World War. So the old folks gave the land near the shore to the daughters. It was just about worthless—until recently."

The primogeniture story might not be true, but Levent drew a tentative conclusion that Panter had a part in the genesis of South Beach. How else would he know the owner of the land before he became general manager of the company's only asset? Who was this man? He was certainly not the one Sultan Kara said she knew.

"What was Panter doing here the day he died?"

"He came to check up on things—the usual—and to look in on the apartment he'd put aside for himself," said Rehber, pointing toward one of the units high up on the hill.

"Panter bought a unit here?"

"At a discount," said Rehber. "There was a stink around here about that, since it was one of the prime units. They're the ones we like to show even if they're not the ones we usually sell."

"More expensive," said Levent. "How much more?"

"About forty percent," said Rehber. "You're finding yourself now in the neighborhood of three hundred thousand dollars."

"Did Panter bring in all the money for it?"

"Half," said Rehber, slicing the total with the blade of his hand. "The rest came due when the last unit was sold at South Beach."

That made another calculation—one hundred and fifty thousand dollars added to the cash in Panter's bank account. Why did he bother to delay the payment until the end with so much money at hand?

"What did Panter do when he went to his unit?"

"I don't know," said Rehber. "He didn't ask me in for a drink. If he had, that would have been the first time."

"You've never been inside the place at all?"

"No," said Rehber carefully. "Except in the beginning. Before Nadir came to the company. When the unit stood empty."

"But not since?"

"No one ever went inside the place," said Rehber with emphasis that created distance. "We might not have been under orders, but we certainly felt as if we were."

"No one went in," said the commandant. "Not even a maid?"

"Not even that."

Levent wondered how Rehber knew, but it might be because he missed a large commission when the unit was sold inside the organization. What Levent did not believe was that Rehber had never since been inside Panter's apartment.

"How long did Panter stay at his place?"

"I don't know," said Rehber. "A while."

"An hour?"

"I'd say more like half an hour before he left."

Levent's eyes met the commandant's long enough to see that they were making the same calculation. The drive to South Beach took forty-five minutes. Another half an hour put the time past four o'clock. Panter might have been able to stop somewhere else once he left the *site*, but not for long. South Beach could have been his last stop.

"I'd like to see the unit now," said Levent.

"I can take you up there," said Rehber, as if the trek was long and difficult. "Hell, I'd like to see what he did to the place myself."

Levent did not ask if Rehber had the key. He had one from the beginning, and if the lock was changed when Panter became the new owner, Rehber probably had that key, too. The only question was how much in business those two had been.

* * *

The upper units, including Panter's, had marvelous views of the Greek islands across the straits. Rugged Kalimnos. Kos, where Hippocrates made his oath. Rhodes at the margins where the Aegean made its invisible turn into the Mediterranean. Two small islands, uninhabited, that had nearly started a war between Greece and Turkey ten years ago when both sides sent marine commandos there to starve.

"Open it," said Levent to Rehber as they stood on the rear deck at the back door. "Don't pretend you can't."

The salesman took a large ring of keys from his coat pocket, twenty or more. Laboriously, he went through several possibilities before finding the key to 754. With a sound of delight meant to surprise, he snapped the lock open and stepped inside Panter's discounted unit.

The contemporary vacation home. A small kitchen, a living room not meant for serious living, two adequate bedrooms, the grossly inadequate bath, and another huge balcony that could house a dinner party. The interior took on a better tone when Levent opened the sliding glass door and relieved the pressure of a place that had clearly not been ventilated for any period of time.

None of the rooms seemed to have been lived in, in the sense that a presence could be felt. Levent cruised the unit, unbuttoning everything he could find. At a quick look, there were hardly any utensils in the kitchen cabinets—glasses, plates or pots. He found only two changes of clothing in the standalone closets in the bedroom, one so old and sorry they must have been work clothes. One pair of underwear in the top drawer of the night table alongside a bed with sheets and nothing more.

All the furnishings were plastic, Tek. All cheaply made and more cheaply bought at volume discounts. The walls, painted the same white as the exterior, gave a surgical appearance to Panter's second home. Nothing seemed to have been improved by the owner, including the bathroom with its coffin-like shower cabinet. Nothing could be said to be interesting in that it told anything of the owner. Levent made two sweeps of the rooms before he came to that conclusion.

Then what had Panter done here on the last day of his life? Was he making sure nothing could be found in his second home? Why come here at all?

"Did he leave with the same clothes he arrived in?"

"I think so," said Rehber, who seemed to calculate everything for the distance it put between him and his manager. "I only caught a glimpse of him as he left in his car."

"Did he drive the car up to his unit?"

"No. He walked."

"Did you happen to see if he carried anything away from the unit?"

"Probably not," said Rehber. "Again, I can't be sure. It depends on how big the object was. Nothing large certainly."

"Did you notice if he put anything in the car?" asked Levent. "Did he open the trunk?"

"No."

If Rehber was right, Panter must have had the money—the eight or ten thousand dollars—in the trunk already. He had apparently done nothing at South Beach but check on the state of his inert apartment. Possibly, he checked on something he had left behind, but dirty clothes did not qualify. The overturned teapot in the drying rack on the kitchen counter said he may have done something about his thirst. The kitchen knives would not have served for self-defense in an attack by a child.

Levent checked each room again, looking more carefully. Only one thing seemed to stand out, and it was not much.

"He put curtains on the windows," said Levent. "Unless he was a seamstress, they must have been installed by someone from outside."

"Yes, they were," said Rehber. "I remember. It was about two months ago."

"You'd be aware if Panter had other work done on the place, wouldn't you?"

"Probably."

"Then tell me what it was."

Rehber took a moment that might not have been for calculation. "I noticed one thing," he said. "A little after the curtains were installed, a van was parked outside the unit part of one day. It was a natural gas van. I'm pretty sure."

Levent crossed from the main bedroom to the kitchen that faced the living room across a natural, or as Tek would have it, unnatural, break of space. It was a vacation kitchen not made for heavy duty cooking or storage. The refrigerator was small, the sink smaller, and the stove not much more than an enhanced hot plate.

The gas tank was under the sink. It should be connected to the stove that stood between the sink and countertop. Most of the gas in the country was bottled, brought to homes by gas companies in vans. Having a van come to Panter's unit was not unusual.

"Do you think Panter did much cooking here?"

"I don't know," said Rehber. "I doubt it. He usually wasn't here at lunchtime and hardly ever stayed until dinner."

"Not overnight either?"

"Rarely," said Rehber. "Close to never. Anyway, he wouldn't do much cooking for breakfast. There's an electric coffee maker and a tea maker in the cabinet. You don't even have to turn on the gas."

Levent had noticed that, too. The appliances were self-contained, plugging into the outlets in the ceramic tile above the counter. He had not seen much in the way of breakfast supplies either. Not the olives or bread or cheese that served most Turks in the morning.

"Do you have a screwdriver?"

Levent knew that Rehber had one on his key chain, a collapsible one that was the most practical thing he owned. When he stripped the screwdriver from the chain, Levent took it and loosened the burner units that held down the stove.

Carefully, Levent pulled back the burners in case he might be wrong and the units were connected to the tank. He had nothing to worry about. The connection to the gas line had never been made. It seemed that the gas tank was unserviceable in spite of the company van.

"Give me a hand with this."

Rehber moved toward the sink until the commandant shouldered him aside. Together, Metin and Levent toppled the tank onto the tile floor. They were careful, again, though there should be no danger from the fuel. The only reason was the primal fear of explosion and fire.

The top came off with minimal force. It should have taken more, Levent thought as he peered into the interior of the tank. What he saw was a dark interior with glints of light toward all the sides and more material lining the bottom.

"What do you think?"

The commandant put his hand into the tank, but not warily. When he pulled it back slowly, he held two plastic packets by the tips of his fingers. Both were filled with a vaguely brownish substance. Levent had seen things like it before.

The commandant opened one of the packets and spilled some of the brown powder in his hand. He took a dab of the powder on the finger of his free hand and sniffed deeply.

"It's heroin," he said. "Or my ass smells like roses."

CHAPTER 8

The discovery of heroin in a natural gas container roused the commandant to action as murder never had. He wanted to question everyone, including the workers scattered about the *site*, to find information about the cache. He told his men to blanket the *site*, making sure that no one left.

A lukewarm trail that had become hot usually had that effect on police. Metin considered Panter's sideline as an invasion of his territory. It seemed as if the heroin must be part of a distribution ring on the peninsula that should be shut down with all the force the Jandarma could bring to bear. He was disturbed to find that Levent did not agree with him.

"He hid the drugs, Metin. We might find a gathering of addicts somewhere in Bodrum who left off their raki for a quicker fix, but it's more likely the heroin was in the process of transshipment."

"All right," he said. "From where are they shipping?"

"That's hard to say." Levent moved to the window overlooking the *site* from the sales office. "Bodrum's a port of call for boats of any size that can put in with minimal intervention from authority. They need very little space to store a package that size. We can't shut down the tourist trade, especially the yachts that come from all the best places in the world."

Metin knew the restraints he worked under, but wanted to push against them now. "There should be a connection between the drugs and Panter's death, damn it. He might have made someone so angry they set him afire when he didn't deliver the product. That's the man we want."

"We're lucky that he stashed the drugs the day he died," said Levent. "Unless he was a stupid man, Panter would never lay off a large payday to anyone else. The most useful thing for us would be to use the heroin as bait. After you finish your questioning— especially of Rehber—back your men off, all but one. Put him on Panter's unit to see if anyone shows."

"Fine," he said quickly, almost angrily. "But what I'd really like to know is who this fucker is."

"I don't know, but he has very good connections," said Levent. "We'll find out who they are soon."

Levent did not want to expose Panter's link to the Deep State. Nor did he know who would go up against the Gray Wolf to steal his drugs, which was the same as taking his blood. They had put the pretty face of Sultan Kara on their operation, but their reach was ugly and international, starting in the poppy fields of the east and extending with minor logistical problems to their clients in Europe and America.

Interrupting their networks was dangerous for anyone. That was not Levent just yet. It would not be the commandant until he received a call from Ankara congratulating him on his good work and telling him he had completed it to the satisfaction of his superiors. Further investigation would be counterproductive.

"Let me know when you have something with Rehber," said Levent, looking at the pamphlets on the tables that told the virtues of South Beach in lies. "He knows more than he's telling."

"It seems like everyone does but us," said Metin. "Do you think he could have been the one who broke into Panter's downtown apartment?"

"That's possible," said Levent. "Take him to Panter's apartment and show him and his car to the woman who recalled seeing something but wasn't sure what. Tell her to act as if she remembers him—very well. That might bring him around if he's the one who did it."

"You sound like you're leaving us, Onur."

"I'm going to the village on the mountain to talk to the women," said Levent, moving toward the door. "Someone has to chase the easy leads, and it should be the man who's on vacation."

* * *

Levent drove along a narrow winding road strewn with gravel and rock as he climbed the side of the steep mountain. He was aware that he was not thinking of the road. Often, when he did stupid things without consciousness of doing them, he marveled when he arrived at his end safely. It could often be said that he arrived better.

He decided to pay more attention to the road. As he neared the top of the mountain it grew better, straightening and widening. The view was the same as from South Beach, but with the greater height the lowlands receded to the picturesque, and the Greek islands became like slabs of dark mountain in a massive pond. These were the favored lands that the sons had received as their inheritance. They looked down on their sisters like sovereign rulers even as they grew poorer by the year.

The village that appeared around the last turn was not a significant settlement. Twenty houses stood on the steep slope as if they might topple down the mountain into the sea. The village had probably been Greek before the diaspora took place after the War of Independence. The Greeks had been resettled on the islands, and the mainland, after they and their foreign allies were defeated by Ataturk in the twenties. Their stone houses were all they had left behind.

Levent parked his car at the side of the road near the entrance to the village, where a sign said there was an upper and lower level to this place that was called Zamir. Skirting what must have been camel shit on the road, Levent walked to the first house that showed signs of occupation. The middle-aged man who answered the door told him that the house of Mrs. Ogun stood on the upper level of the village. That big one on the lip of the mountain, he said.

It seemed she had cashed in her land near the water while staying in the village where her ancestors had done her that great backhanded favor. Her house was more than one mound of stone, though from the road most of it was hidden by the overhang of the mountain. As Levent climbed the path that could hardly be called a driveway, he saw the rest of her estate slowly emerge. The house was at least two houses, all built of large blocks of stone.

But the owner was a surprise. She answered his knock dressed in a halter and shorts that complemented her lean body, though she must have been fifty. Her hair was blonde, bleached from a bottle and the sun, and her skin deeply tanned. Her diction told Levent that she had been out of this village for some schooling.

"A stranger in the village," she said. "Are you lost?"

"Who would come here any other way?" said Levent. "I'm a police inspector looking for information."

She found that amusing as a smile lit at the corners of her mouth. "You could get everything you need to know if you'd bought a tourist manual. We were written up in a couple that describe the hidden delights of Bodrum. We have a bed-and-breakfast in the village now, and an ashram, too."

"An ashram?"

"A place to park wayward energy," she said without smiling. "They chant all night long some times. Most of the customers come from Istanbul. They think this place is the absolute pit of nature. Natural, that is."

Levent accepted the information without having an idea if it was exaggerated. He was sure that the corruption had spread at least that far, though he could not find the word ashram anywhere in his vocabulary.

"I wanted to ask you about a man you must know," he said. "I'm investigating the murder of Nadir Panter."

"Good luck," she said. "I don't know him."

"The name means nothing to you?"

"Not a thing."

Levent was sure Panter had some knowledge of this woman even if she had none of him. She could be lying, but did not seem to be. "Let me describe Mister Panter," he said. "Perhaps that will jog your memory."

"If you must."

Levent did his best, though he had never had a close look at Panter in life. He sensed he had lost his audience before he finished, but kept doggedly on. Yet until he described Panter's car as a Mercedes with headlight wipers, he found no response.

"Now we're getting somewhere," she said with a smile that could only be called vengeful. "That son-of-a-bitch almost ran me over one day as I was walking up the hill. It was about three months ago. You wouldn't believe it, but I remember those wipers on the headlights best of all."

"Did he stop when he almost ran you down?"

"A Mercedes doesn't stop for anything on this earth," she said. "They get a special license when they buy the car. It says the road belongs to them and anyone else is a visitor."

"But he must have come to the village," said Levent. "Unless the road leads farther on?"

"Not a chance," she said. "If you manage the drive up here with the guidebook on your lap, you find yourself at an end. This is a destination. I told you that."

"But you have an idea of where he was going. You must."

"Well, he didn't pull the grand Mercedes into the bed-and-breakfast," she said. "So he must have gone farther. Except for the goatherd's cottage, there's only one thing farther and that's the ashram."

"So he went there."

"I didn't say that, and I think you should be more careful about what you assume. But from what you tell me, he must have been in need of salvation. That's their business. As I hear it, they do well. A hundred and fifty euros a day."

"A hundred and fifty?"

"That includes board," she said. "They're serious about all the foolishness. They don't want you eating anything that hasn't been grown locally. They don't want you to be bit by anything but local scorpions or snakes. When you come up here, you're written in for the complete experience. And you're theirs for as long as it takes."

"How long is that?"

"I wouldn't try to guess," she said as if she could. "I suppose it depends on how much repair your system needs. The state of your karma, so to speak."

"Panter must have been there for a while then."

She shook her head as if chasing an image that was best left behind. "You know him better than me."

* * *

Levent felt he would come to know Panter eventually, though he never thought he might find the answers at a contemporary center for the mystic arts. The ashram, called The Hole in the Ground, sat at the end of the village and the end of the road. Levent saw no hole, but several village houses grouped in a small complex overlooked the valley below from a precipice. A man who wanted to make a hole in the ground could do no better than walk off the edge.

The houses of the ashram rose from the parched brown earth in graduated shades of familiar Bodrum white. Climbing vines covered the sunny sides of the houses, but the entrance had no person or dog guarding it. Levent called "Hello" with no response until he noticed a little bell at the side. It was a strange thing that would not have been out of place in Tibet. When Levent pulled the clapper, it rang with pure luminous tones.

Someone came like an echo. She was a chubby young woman in a flowery shift that reached all the way to the sandals on her feet. Her body seemed to move beneath it like something that had not yet learned its place, but she opened the three-quarter door and spoke pleasantly.

"Hello yourself," she said in English with a Turkish accent. "If you've come for the drumming circle, you're early."

"I'm afraid I haven't," said Levent, answering in her language. "I'd like to speak to the owner of this . . . establishment."

"Reema is busy now," she said. "But I can give you a schedule for the events this week. You might find something you like."

"I'm sure I would," said Levent. "But I'm a police inspector looking for some information. Nothing serious."

She took his words very seriously, her dark brown eyes flattening into a steady gaze. "An inspector of police?" she said.

"I don't want to disturb your day, but if you call your supervisor I'm sure we can have my questions out of the way quickly."

She blinked as if wanting badly to vacate her space. "If you wait here, I'll find Reema. She should be able to help."

Levent entered the door that she opened onto the interior of the ashram. It was a green place with deep splashes of color; the grass, bushes and flowers well-watered in the dry heat of Bodrum. Banks of bougainville and bushes of oleander boomed in the sun, with roses in the midrange and impatiens hugging the ground.

What had seemed like three buildings as he approached were now five on rapidly descending levels. At the highest point stood a village house that had been modernized and expanded. Levent watched the young woman enter it and vanish.

The rest of the buildings were smaller but somewhat wider, ending in a semi-circle of three running nearly to the edge of the cliff. If Levent was to guess, these were the dormitories, or whatever they were called in the New Age tongue.

He saw no movement from the houses and heard no sounds. One hundred and fifty euro a night seemed to buy quiet if not peace, though the difference might be hard to define. Levent found everything hard to define until a sudden movement came from the large house in three directions. First, a middle-aged man in shorts and a T-shirt that said Godhead left by the front door. He walked quickly toward the cluster of buildings on the lower level, moving at a lurch as if he would rather run.

The man was followed at a surveillance distance by the young woman in the long shift, who did not look once in Levent's direction. She, too, continued to the lower level, where she followed the man into the first building on the right.

When the stage was clear, a striking woman who knew a lot about entrances appeared at the door of the large building. She was tall, with large breasts and hair dyed red in a color that was usually seen on emergency vehicles. Her long dress was more striking than the one the young woman had worn, yellow and black with embroidered figures of birds of paradise. Levent found it hard to guess her age, though she was not young. Women like this descended to earth for lengths of time that varied tremendously.

When she opened her arms, palms raised, Levent understood that he was to approach. As he moved closer, he noticed her clarion blue eyes and the lines in her face, great tracks of time that marked out passages of change. Yet she was not ugly. Commanding, say.

"My name is Reema," she said as Levent entered her aura. "I understand you're with the police. I should say welcome, I suppose."

In spite of her name, she had spoken in Turkish—good Turkish—though English was the language of her business as euro was her currency. Her voice was deep, as deep as a man's, but with more power in the register.

"I'm a police inspector based in Istanbul," he said, "but working with the local Jandarma."

She smiled without touching any emotional register. "You're the second policeman I've welcomed to my ashram. The first didn't say what he was. He came to our meeting and sat down in our circle as if he was one of us, but I never saw a man who seemed so confused. He was obviously gathering information for the government to decide if we were a menace to society. I'd like to say we converted him to a different way of life, but he missed the point. He went away as confused as he arrived."

"Did he pay the euro?"

"Yes."

"Then there was no harm."

"I don't know that," she said. "What do you think resulted from his visit?"

"I couldn't say. That's not my department, and I don't know whose it is. I'm with homicide."

"Homicide," she said. "So we can assume someone has been murdered. What connection can it possibly have to this place?"

"The victim came to your ashram about three months ago," said Levent as if that was a fact. "He was a big broad-shouldered man who drove a silver Mercedes with little wipers on the head-lights. His name was Nadir Panter."

Finally, Levent saw a reaction to the man's death that was not canned like bad meat. Reema said nothing, but her silence drew a charge of emotion from the colors in her garden. It seemed purple, like the bougainville climbing the walls. This time it was Levent who blinked. When he did, the color returned to its origins in her garden, but did nothing to change Reema. She was stunned.

"You knew him, Reema."

She stared beyond Levent for seconds, then nodded as if not trusting the voice that was her finest feature.

"You knew him well."

She nodded again. "I thought so for a time."

Levent was happy not to rush the past from the place where she kept it. He knew he could have it. Only if Reema had a great reason to hide her relationship with Panter would she lie.

"Would you like to sit down?"

She did not seem to be aware that Levent had invited her to find comfort in her own home. Reema walked from the portico by the door to the patio that was shaded by grapevines at the side of the house. Her movements were automatic. Things like this at moments like this remain unreported to the waking mind. She slipped into the leaves of a canvas chair with the movements of someone who was afraid to exaggerate them. Barely under control, she did not speak until she was sure of mastery. And mastery could only come from knowledge.

"How did he die?"

"In his car," said Levent. "We're sure he was murdered. Some-one hit him very hard on the back of his head."

"So he died like that?"

"He died when someone set the car on fire," said Levent fac-tually. "We think it's possible he didn't know when the flames reached him. That's our guess."

"Your guess," she said. "I understand."

She understood a lot. Everyone with whom Levent had talked seemed surprised by the way that Panter had died. Reema was not. She seemed to have expected it and only to be surprised by the length of time of its coming. Panter's death was a fact, but it was not news.

"I was told that the Mercedes he died in was bought by you," said Levent. "That's quite a present for any man."

"I don't know where you heard that story," she said quickly. "It isn't true."

"I had it from the secretary in his office," said Levent, trying to leverage her emotions by mentioning another woman. "I don't know why she'd lie."

"Perhaps she wouldn't," said Reema with a shrug that was lost in her garment. "I'm sure he was trying to impress her with the things women did for him. You might see that as an attempt at seduction."

Levent saw it. Though Pinar had guaranteed that no affair occurred in the office, no one would ever know the trade-in value of Panter's courtship. Most men did it, and Panter might have used it before. He might have used it on Reema.

"I'd like to understand how you two came to know each other well," said Levent. "You'll excuse me, but I find that odd."

She accepted the compliment. "It was out of character for me. Very much."

"You're speaking in the past tense," said Levent. "I wish you wouldn't. I know Panter came here three months ago to see you. If I ask around this village—not a big place—I'm sure I'll find that he came other times as well."

"Don't ask," she said like a businesswoman in cabaret clothes. "That would be inconvenient. The people in this village aren't really equipped to understand what we do here. The best they could tell you was that the man you know as Nadir Panter came here three times."

So she knew his other name—the real one—and had no wish to hide it. "What was Panter's real name?"

"I knew him as Yunus Harman when we met in New York," she said. "He kept to that name for some time."

New York and the name Yunus could solve a double mystery. Panter had learned English in America. The man who had called DenizKum's office asking for "Fish" might have been learned his there, too. In Turkish, Yunus meant a fish. A dolphin.

"What were you doing in New York?"

In Reema's smile, pleasure and regret lay tangled. Her blue eyes took up the pleasure but not the other. "I was studying at design school. Yunus worked for something called the Turkish Folklore Trust. That was its name anyway. Charming, I thought. I had visions of peasants in local dress dancing around the village on holidays. I wasn't aware that he probably worked for the Turkish government as well. I thought I'd left those types behind at the airport in Istanbul."

"Probably is a big word," said Levent. "It has legs like a centipede."

"It could have even more," she said with surprising bitterness. "I wasn't joking about the man who came to our circle to spy. He was obvious. He was the only one who took off his shoes at the door without being asked. He was the only one with an accent from south of Denizli. He was the only one who mumbled into his stocking feet instead of chanting."

"What did Panter—Harman I should say—do for the state?"

"I didn't think it was anything sinister when we met in New York," said Reema. "I was sure he came over after the coup in '80 and stayed on gladly. I even thought he might have been hiding from the junta at first."

"When did you come to a different opinion?"

Reema shook her head regretfully. "Let's say I found out some things gradually, even though he never talked about his business. He seemed to work odd hours. He always had money. When I asked him about his job one day, he said that he was working on a database of Americans of Turkish descent. He said it as if he didn't expect me to ask again. When I did ask him again later—pointedly—he said he was raising money from Americans of Turkish descent to send back to various good causes in the homeland. He was using the database he had gathered to trace them.

There are a lot of foreigners who go to America on tourist visas and stay on without telling the authorities. What he was doing seemed to make sense."

"But it was bound to be illegal," said Levent, who saw calculus in the shadows. "Asking for money from people who don't want their presence known is the next thing to blackmail. Frankly, I think it is blackmail."

"That didn't occur to me until much later," she said, shaking her head at her own innocence. "I thought it was a good idea when I first heard it. But I eventually came to realize that every name in his database was a potential victim."

"At what point did you understand that?"

"I might never have," she said with a modesty that was not quite believable. "Not on my own. But one day after we were married, a man came to our apartment door. He was older than Yunus—older and more worn—but it was clear he'd come to plead with a man who could do him harm. I tried to tell him I had nothing to do with Yunus' business, but he wouldn't listen. We were standing in the foyer, and I hadn't even offered him tea. He kept saying I should tell Yunus he would have the money he wanted as soon as his wife came home from the hospital. Then he could work full time again driving his taxi. He made good money when he worked full time, but the operation for his wife cost a lot. They took one of her breasts, he kept saying, and it was a very expensive thing to do."

"So Harman was shaking down illegal immigrants," said Levent. "He must have had access to information. It isn't usual to go up to a man in the street and tell him that he should give you money in this phase of the moon."

Reema agreed like a woman who was used to moving on. "That's when I knew that Yunus' database worked best in reverse. I hadn't thought of him as a thug until then. It wasn't a bad marriage until that day, and I'm sorry to say I let it go on for much longer—almost two years longer—before I found the courage to divorce him."

"Most women never find that courage," said Levent. "The man who earns a good salary is the man who stays married until *he* decides otherwise."

"Of course," she said. "But knowing your husband is doing terrible things for his money isn't the same if he treats his wife well. Yunus never beat me. He lost his temper at times, but was ashamed of it later."

"I'm surprised he agreed to a divorce," said Levent. "In those days, it could put a black mark on a man's career in government service."

"I didn't know if he ever was a government employee. I should have found out a long time ago." She smiled, trying to keep her spirituality to the fore. "Do you think I could claim his pension?"

"I should be able to check on it now that I have his real name for the records." Levent nodded seriously, deciding he would not tell her that her husband had been a rich man. "I'll let you know what I find."

She lowered her uncommon lapis-blue eyes. "Thank you, Inspector. You understand this is a business here. I'm sure you don't know how many people depend on me for their livelihood."

Levent had only met one, and she seemed not to need much maintenance. He was also sure of one thing: more than love kept Reema (false name) and Yunus (real name) together. New York was an exciting place as long as there was money to enjoy the show. It was certainly where Reema served her apprenticeship in mysticism. That must have been expensive.

"How long were you in America?"

"I stayed on after the divorce," she said. "I was there for eight years. Yunus left the year after the divorce."

"Was he called back?"

"Yes," she said without hesitation. "I'm sure of that, but not of the details."

"He went where—to Ankara?"

"I never knew what really happened to him afterward," she said. "He returned to Turkey, and I was aware that he spent some time in Azerbaijan. He also lived in eastern Turkey, around Urfa, for almost two years."

Harman's path made a good fit with the Gray Wolf's arc of interests. They maintained close links with the Turkish-speaking countries of Central Asia, considering them part of the Greater Turkish Nation. It was interesting that when the Kurdish War heated up in southern Turkey, Harman found his way there, too. A loyal soldier.

"Do you know what he was doing after he left New York?"

"No," she said. "I assumed it was nothing I'd want to learn about. I was an American by then. What's done is done. In other words, ours wasn't a Turkish divorce with one of the parties on the phone begging money from the other."

"Why did you return home?" he asked. "Not everyone does."

"I couldn't stay," she said, as if she would have had it otherwise. "We had two children. Yunus wanted them raised in Turkey. I had a green card, but when I applied for citizenship, I was rejected. I asked why, of course, and so did my lawyer. We never had a proper answer."

"So you think that Harman's wishes prevailed behind the scene."

"I'm sure of it, but couldn't prove it," she said, allowing the sorrow lines in her face to deepen. "I didn't learn more about Yunus' place in government, or even in the shadow government, but I came to the conclusion he had one that was more important than I thought. He had gotten to the American authorities. Someone had."

Levent did not think Reema was being honest. She would have reasons for marrying Harman and continuing with him that did not sound best when presented to another person. They might have something to do with love, home, children. They might have a lot to do with money.

"It would seem that Harman had friends in government," said Levent. "Did you ever meet any of them?"

"Not many," she said. "One young man—I can't recall his name—came round to the apartment, drinking until he passed out. Yunus wanted to invite him back, but I said no, drink with him in a bar. It's safer for the furniture."

"Did you ever meet his supervisor?"

"Twice," said Reema, holding up one finger as if that was more than enough. "I have to say I was impressed. The Turkish Folklore Trust may have been a dummy, but this man was not. He was handsome and intelligent. Smooth. As smooth as glass. He knew the right questions to ask, even to the wife of one of his employees. Whatever he was talking about, he made you to feel that he was confiding in you. More, he made you feel as if he was telling you a secret. Something important that no one else knew."

"He sounds like a brilliant con man."

"I thought so," said Reema. "He had devil's feathers, if you know what I mean."

Levent nodded. The phrase did not translate nor did it need translation. It was one of those things everyone understood. They knew what it was it in spite of the fact that they never saw it often. They knew it because they could not forget the man who wore the plumage so well.

Reema laughed for the first time, a good round sound. "You know, when Americans see a man like that, they say he can talk a dog off a meat wagon."

"That's good, too," said Levent. "But I like devil's feathers. Evil isn't quite the same as an animal following his nose. Tell me, did this man have a low voice?"

"Yes. Very pleasing."

"Did you ever hear him call your husband Fish? Fish, in English?"

She shook her head until the side-to-side motion vanished. "I don't recall hearing that, but something seems familiar. I suppose even a Turk can find another name given to him in America. They like nicknames. They use them especially among their friends."

"So if someone called your ex-husband Fish, they would be his friend."

"Definitely."

He was a friend who impressed Pinar at DenizKum with his command presence on the phone. Could a boss be a friend? Not in the usual sense. But it would depend on how much they had shared. Or were complicit in.

"What was this man's name?"

"It's been a long time," she said with her first wary response. "I'm just not sure any longer."

"His last name?"

"I can't recall."

Levent did not believe her, but decided not to press. Reema might talk about her dead ex-husband, but not the men around him who could still be alive and in positions of power. She knew the ground was dangerous.

"Did you ever see this man—the boss—afterward?"

"No," she said quickly. Too quickly?

"Do you know what your ex-husband was doing here in Bodrum?"

"He was in construction," she said. "You didn't know that?"

"I found out," said Levent. "But I wonder what a man like him was doing in a business he knew little about."

"I wondered about that myself," she said. "I asked him and he said he was in the same business as always. The names change, he said."

"His, too."

"Panter," she said. "I thought it wasn't a bad one for him."

"Did you think he was in trouble when he turned up using an alias?"

"That was always possible with Yunus," she said with another turn to regret. "He once told me that the Kurdish terrorists had put him on their list. I'm in the single digits, he said. I assumed he meant an extermination list."

"That's why you weren't surprised to learn he'd met a violent end."

"I suppose not."

Reema spoke as if she did not want to again. Levent expected her to fold back into sorrow when she confronted the figure of her ex-husband in this place, but they were bound to come to that point.

"Why did Harman come here to see you?"

"His visit concerned our son," she said defensively. "He was arrested at school at a demonstration against the headscarf girls. Yunus wanted me to speak to William. He didn't object to what his son had done, just that he'd been caught. Not being caught was what his father did best."

"You said William?"

"I planned to stay in America, as I said. I wanted our boy to have an English name. It would make things easier for him."

"Your ex-husband didn't object?"

"Oh, he did," said Reema. "But we'd compromised with our girl, the firstborn, giving her a name that went to both cultures. Melisa. It was different with William because we were on the way out of our marriage when he was born. I really didn't care what Yunus thought by that time."

"It sounds like he maintained contact with the children."

"To some extent," she said as if she wished it had been less. "I couldn't deny him that, and when I moved back to Turkey I didn't try. Besides, he treated them like his children. He loved them, he said, and he contributed money to their schooling. I was grateful for that."

"You said he came here three times."

"Did I?"

"Yes."

"The second time he wanted to talk about the boy our daughter was dating," said Reema, as if the subject had closed before it began. "We had an argument—nothing serious. For all his faults, Yunus is a Turkish father. I told him the quickest way to get a bad response was to tell Melisa she had no idea of what she was doing. Remember us, I said. We had even less."

"Did he listen to you?"

"I think so," she said. "I heard nothing bad from Melisa, so I suppose he watched his words. She's of age anyway. This isn't a day of arranged marriages except for those who need the arrangement."

"Your daughter works in Istanbul?"

"She's doing well," said Reema with the pride of an independent mother. "She's one of the editors of a fashion magazine."

"Do you mind if I talk to her?"

"Yes, I do," she said. "You look like a Turkish father, too."

"I'm not," he said. "But my job means that I pursue any leads I come across. Can you tell me now about the third time your ex-husband came to see you here?"

"It wasn't the usual visit," she said. "At least, it wasn't about the children in the usual way. Yunus wanted me to know he had provided for them. He said that he had a private account at a bank in Switzerland. He gave me the name of the bank to contact if something happened to him."

So Harman had more than a premonition about his end. How strong? Levent continued to be surprised by the money the man had put away. More than two million lira at a Turkish bank and an account in Switzerland. Drug money, of course.

"Why do you think he told you about the account?" asked Levent, knowing the question was important. "I mean, why tell you now?"

"It was the obvious reason," she said. "He was afraid of something. Of someone. The Kurds of the PKK was my guess."

"Did he say anything specifically?"

She considered her answer carefully, turning her eyes away from Levent to the place where she kept her worst memories. "He said a man never realizes when he does things that they can come back on him. He said some people never forget."

"That was all he said?"

"That was the sum of his life as far as I knew." Reema looked to the dormitories at the edge of the cliff. "After he left, I spent some time thinking about what he said. I journeyed, looking for an answer."

"*Journeyed?*"

"The name of this place is The Hole in the Ground," she said, slipping into the voice that she used to tutor her euro visitors. "We enter the underworld by an opening in the earth. It's an ancient shamanic practice I've adapted to modern ways. An experienced journeyer can see things that will guide him in the future. He can do it quickly."

Levent was always at a loss when facts were replaced by anything else. This was worse. It seemed infinitely worse.

"What did you see when you journeyed?"

"Bodrum," said Reema. "The inner city. The castle. The harbor."

"Nothing else?"

"There should be nothing else, Inspector. If you're looking for the key to Yunus Harman, you'll find what you're looking for there. I wish I could tell you what it is, but I'm sure we'll know in time."

CHAPTER 9

Levent could have spend more time talking profitably with Reema, but she had said all that she wanted. Her drumming circle began on the hour, and she needed time to prepare for the ceremony. Levent could not imagine what journeying took place to the sound of crashing drums, but he excused himself with thanks.

He did not tell Reema about the two million plus. The money might come to her children, though he doubted it would come soon. Funds obtained through criminal enterprises were often confiscated by the government. It might depend on which branch of government lay claim. Harman-Panter seemed to have worked outside normal channels of the state. How informally was the question.

Now that he had a name to research, Levent put in an immediate call to Istanbul. "Yes, Boss."

Erol Akbay's voice was so hard and flat that Levent found it unaccountably soothing. He was all fact, all cynicism, a proper detective who knew that a hole in the ground was good for only one thing.

"I have another name for you to research," said Levent. "The same rules apply. Maximum stealth. Cover your tracks."

"It's that animal again. The Panter."

"This time he's aquatic," said Levent. "His real name is Yunus Harman. Let's hope we're down to the last one."

"That's good enough for me," said Erol. "I like chasing phantoms."

"Look especially hard in the narcotics files," said Levent. "I'll take anything that sounds like a dolphin."

"How about a farmer?"

Erol was punning on the last name. Harman meant threshing floor, or harvest time. It did not mean the port of Bodrum, though that was an idea.

"If you find anything that points to Mugla district, follow it as far as you can," said Levent. "There has to be something in Bodrum that connects Harman and the past. I don't know what it is yet."

"You will, Boss. I've got confidence in you."

"Do you think you have enough to keep you busy, Erol?"

"Right, Boss. Just having some fun. Enjoy the water."

Levent intended to do that as soon as he cleared some time for his holiday. He realized that he could walk away from this case any time. Even the Chief would have no objection once he learned that a drug stash had been discovered. The case could be laid off to a war between gangs staking out territory in Bodrum. No one objected to them killing their own.

It could have happened that way. Another gang, or gang member, who wanted to remove his boss—or rival. Levent had even heard that the Russian Mafia bought a hotel complex near Gundogan.

The terrorist angle could work, too. The PKK were not known to be strong in Mugla district, but Istanbul was the largest Kurdish city in the world, and Izmir had a population, too. Both cities were drivable in a day; Izmir in an afternoon. A flight took less time. A flight from almost any place in the country was an hour.

Levent was less than halfway down the mountain when the phone on his belt made its NBA sound. He did not recognize the voice of the man who spoke, but felt that he should have.

"Yes. Go ahead."

"This is Serpil Pepe, Inspector. The stone man."

"Yes, Serpil. Do you have something?"

"I have a green Peugeot," he said. "I'm not sure of the year, but this one wasn't old, and it headed down the road to the city a couple of minutes ago."

"Did you see the driver?"

"Not well," he said. "He had dark hair and looked young."

That might be good enough.

* * *

Levent had always wanted to engage in a high speed chase, though Istanbul traffic made that next to impossible. The empty mountain road gave him the chance to bet his life on his skill as he roared down the mountain, the front tires of the Honda constantly threatening to break their hold on gravity. He hit a rock that almost put him over the side near the bottom of the hill, but managed to keep his momentum into the wider stretch that opened up onto the main road.

The commandant was moving to close, too. He said he would call ahead to set up a vehicle-specific roadblock before the city limits. Levent hoped that was good enough. The road into the city was fairly straight, but several roads fed off into the smaller towns and random developments along the way. If the Peugeot turned off on any one of them, finding it fast would be impossible.

How many green Peugeots might be on the peninsula was a question Levent did not ask. The commandant had run the records for cars of a similar make and color and found nothing. But the Peugeot could have come from anywhere in the tourist season. Expanding the search nationwide brought up far too many possibilities.

Levent kept hearing Reema's words. She said he would find what he needed in the city center, and it seemed the Peugeot was headed that way. God, but Levent hated to think that a mind on a mystic journey could do what logic and the police could not.

At the twenty minute mark, Levent came down the last straightaway before the road forked right to Ortakent. He hesitated, knowing he could turn to cover that direction, but at the last minute kept going toward the center of town. Reema's direction. He hated doing that, too.

Not far up the road he saw the light roadblock that had been set. The two police cars were at the verge of the road, not stopping everyone but looking for color-correct Peugeots. Levent slowed when he came up to their cars, but when he shouted, asking if they had any luck, one of the three men told him what was obvious.

Levent kept going for the city center, running two red lights. When he came to the first turn for downtown, he caught a green. If only he had some idea of where to concentrate the search. Cruising for a green Peugeot that might have passed before the roadblock was set meant depending on luck.

And he found none. He hardly saw anything green and nothing of Peugeots, but he tried to narrow the scope by assuming that the man was not a tourist. He should have another destination. It was late for lunch and early for a drink, so perhaps Levent could eliminate the restaurants and bars. That meant skipping the Old Town. Minimal attention to the restaurant strip that ran along the harbor. It was possible the man might have gone to a beach, but those near downtown were second-rate and strewn along the left side of the harbor.

Where would he go?

Levent slowly cruised the front street, scanning for green along the harbor, but saw nothing except an old Renault parked at the curb. Why would the man even go to the downtown area? Because Reema saw that on her journey? The harbor? The castle? It did not seem likely the man had walked to the castle unless he was a tourist. Levent was halfway along the harbor street when he pulled over to a valet parking attendant who stood before a restaurant.

"Have you seen any green cars pass by in the last few minutes?"

"Probably," he said. "Hell, it's likely."

"Think on a Peugeot."

The man, who was barely old enough to be called that, jingled the short set of keys of the cars he had parked. He finally shrugged. "I'd say there was one."

Levent did not ask which way a probable green Peugeot had headed. The street was one way and nothing else lay in that direction but the back way—the only way—out of town. And the marina.

Was there a chance he would head for a boat? That was not a good guess either, but if the man entered the marina gate, he would have been seen by the guard.

It was the only option that did not depend on a random sighting. When Levent reached the end of the harbor street, he pulled off into the entrance to the marina. The guard stopped him.

"Have you seen a green Peugeot pass through?"

The young man with a small goatee actually paused to stroke it. "About ten minutes ago, maybe fifteen," he said.

"Which way?"

"Straight ahead toward the cafe."

Levent drove ahead, scanning for green cars, but saw nothing in the parking areas by the cafe. Reaching the end of the lot, he turned back. Nothing again. He had a choice of running down each of the parking lanes or trying for height.

He stopped his car and got out, moving to the outdoor stairs that led to the second floor of the cafe. He did not have to go all the way up to the landing to get the look he wanted. Halfway was good enough.

Nothing in the first two rows, but two green cars stood in the third. The far one looked like a Peugeot. Levent tried to imagine the car in motion, and smaller, to see if it fit the image from the surveillance camera. It seemed close.

Levent returned to his car without doing anything to attract attention. Driving to the second row, he parked several cars back from the Peugeot.

He walked past the car slowly. It was a recent model—two years old, with no visible damage or particular marks, but the license plate would go immediately into the system. The first two numbers were 48—Mugla district. Unfortunately, that did not narrow the search down enough. Years ago all plates could have been traced to the city of origin by an additional number after the 48, but no longer. The bureaucrats had made bad luck for the police again.

Levent moved close enough to see that no one sat inside the Peugeot. Turning to the front of the car, he put his hand on the hood. It was hot. Almost all the cars in the open lot would be superheated in the afternoon sun, but this one seemed to have been recently run.

The doors were locked, and Levent did not force them. Finding the driver was the important thing, and that would not be easy. Hundreds of boats lay up in the marina, big and small, nose to the docks, sails furled. A lot of them could hide a man easily, and Levent had no detailed description.

But the man should return for his car. That meant a wait, but it seemed that yield was almost guaranteed. Unless he decided to run for the open sea, he had to come back. He might do that if he thought he was not being pursued.

Levent called the commandant, who was at the roadblock. He told him to get as many men as he could spare to the marina on the double.

"I have a green Peugeot in the parking lot."

"The right one?"

"We're going to find out."

* * *

Levent thought that the odds of locating the man were good until the commandant arrived. His hulking Jandarma van came speeding across the lot until Levent hurriedly flagged it down. The huge blue vehicle could be seen by many of the boats in the marina if anyone bothered to look. And they always did.

"Turn around and get the van out of this lot," said Levent into the sliding door that rolled open at the side of the van. "Have your men get as much out of uniform as they can."

The commandant had bailed out of the van like a man with nothing on his mind but a quick arrest. He realized his mistake, jumping back into the vehicle and turning it around out the gate. Levent heard him shout at his men as if the noisy arrival had been their fault.

Levent hoped he had put enough distance between the Peugeot and the van not to draw attention to his location. He followed the van to the gate, though not far enough to lose sight of the target.

What would the man do if he had seen the commandant's entrance? He might run. He had no option except the gate unless he was nimble and vaulted the fence. If he had access to a boat, the sea could be his way out.

Nothing seemed to have moved from the marina from the gate or to the sea, but Levent's visibility was not good enough to track all the possible exits. The commandant and his men abandoned the van on the far side of the gate and returned to the lot. They had removed their blue berets, but their uniforms were still visible down to the pant legs stuffed into the tops of their boots.

That might not matter, but plainclothes were the only thing that really worked for surveillance. Levent took the commandant aside and spent time posting his men around the lot, one at a cafe table and another at the boatyard where a sailing vessel was being refitted. The last man, Levent moved inside the gatehouse.

That would give the watchers enough of an angle on the Peugeot if they could keep a low profile, but stealth was not what the Jandarma did best. They were not used to much more than intimidation.

Metin called the harbormaster for help with sea-pursuit, but nothing was available except two Coast Guard boats that cruised the waters offshore, and they were well away. One had gone to Yalikavak and the other to Gocek Bay. The helicopters were already spoken for, on constant fire duty in this very dry place.

"I'll see if I can find the manager of this marina," said Levent to the commandant. "Don't make any move until you're sure a man is headed for the Peugeot. And call me on the cell the moment you see anything."

"I'll run the plate while you're gone," said the commandant, who seemed annoyed at having his narcotics lead interrupted for mere murder. "That should give us an idea of who we're looking for."

It might. Even a rental should. Levent walked toward the end of the docks. He tried to keep an angle on the fence that ran along the boardwalk in front of the marina. Any man could get over it, but he would be seen. If he was quick, he could zip into the mall that paralleled the walk and make his way into the city. Finding him there would be difficult.

The manager was not in his office near the middle of the marina, but the old man on duty—the assistant manager, as he called himself—said he might be able to help. He was in his late fifties and had seen better days and many better nights, with a two-day growth of beard that would have been fashionable on someone else. An old sea hand who had retired to shore probably. When Levent asked if any ships had left the marina in the last hour, he put his hand out toward the castle.

"Three ships," he said. "One sail's still visible toward the point at Bardakchi."

"What's she look like?"

"A small pleasure craft," he said. "He's been here for the last month and likes to run out to Kos for the day. Comes back with duty-free raki for him and his friends."

"You know him then?"

"Name's Peter," said the man. "About my age. English, it seems. He keeps talking about bad weather and how it's never here, so I guess he comes from some place like that where the sun don't shine."

Levent did not have a description of the man he wanted except that he was young with dark hair. And even that was chancy.

"What about the other two ships?"

"The second was a Turkish vessel," he said. "Been here a long time. The owner is Mehmet Ozkan. He likes to be on the water when he isn't back and forth between his business. He runs a tourist agency on the harbor road."

"He went out alone?"

"Him and his girl," he said. "At her age, I'd say his mistress."

"He's young?"

"Not this decade." He ran his hand along the top of his head where nothing much was. "Hair's as white as Russian snow."

"What about the first ship out?"

"A new one," he said as if he had admired it. "Large vessel, eighteen meter, two-master. It put in last night. The owner's a woman—middle-aged but not bad looking. She asked if I knew a good place to eat in town. I sent her next door to the restaurant."

"She sails the ship herself?"

"There was another woman on board last night," he said. "And two men. I'd say she sleeps at least four. The two men were with the ship when she put in. Another man I hadn't seen before went on board just before they put back to sea."

Levent was alert for any late arrival. The Peugeot could have been as much as a half an hour ahead. Not more than that even with the time Levent and the Jandarma had spent setting out surveillance.

"The ship must have been waiting for the last man."

"Maybe so."

"Can you describe the men?"

"The first two were tall for Turks, if that's what they were. One was young, the other not. I didn't get a good look at the last man to board. Not from the front. I'd say he was something like young by the way he moved. Good shoulders."

More interesting. Levent was looking for a reasonably young man, and strong, who could have taken out a large man in the parking lot.

"When did they leave the marina?"

"About half an hour ago," he said. "They left quick, running on a damned big accelerator. I'd say they're long gone out to sea."

"What about the ship?" asked Levent. "Distinguishing characteristics?"

"She had a purple stripe along her side," he said. "I don't recall the name on the stern exactly, but I might be able to dig it out in the records. A fancy script. Something like Jeune Marie."

"French?"

The assistant manager measured Levent as if he knew he was talking to a landsman and should talk down as far as possible. "Well, the woman spoke some Turkish, though not real good. And all ships have to fly the Turkish flag in Turkish waters, you know. If they want, they can fly another that tells the world their country of origin. Or the place they'd most like to be if they wasn't in God's own paradise for sailing vessels. This one flew a French flag from the stern."

Where had Levent come across a Frenchman in Harman's life? When he had talked to Pinar at DenizKum. Harman asked about a man named Varan, who was not Turkish but French.

A Frenchman might own a Peugeot. Levent doubted that many people would drive from France to Turkey or bother to mount Turkish plates. But the killer could have rented a car he was familiar with. The killer? There was a lot of feeling in that and not a lot of fact. Was Levent still stuck on that mountain with a woman who was as rational as she was odd?

"Do you have any idea when the ship will return?"

"I'd be surprised if she did," he said. "I never saw her before yesterday and don't know if I'll see her again any time soon. They spent most of the morning taking on supplies. They even loaded liquor on board from the store on the other side of the street. I saw the delivery truck."

"What about the third man?" said Levent. "Did he take anything on board?"

The assistant manager hesitated. He used his hands to right the man in his memory, as if lifting something. "If I remember, he had a bag."

"Small? Overnight?"

"Not so small," he said with his hands again. "When he came on board, one of the other men helped him in with it. I'd say it was a load."

Not good. A man with a large bag should not be planning to return soon. Why would he leave his car in the lot if he would not return to pick it up? Levent felt his lead slipping away, though he did not feel it was lost yet.

"From which berth did the ship go out?"

"The fifth slip," he said, pointing down the wooden wharf extension. "It's right over there. You can see it."

"Show me."

The assistant manager of the busy marina did not like being asked to leave his plush but thoroughly patched chair. He shook his head and stopped to lock the door to the office before he turned away up the planks. With a stubborn bow to his back, he led Levent to the fifth slip.

It stood empty between two twelve-meter sailing vessels. A hose hung loose from the utilities hookup, and the metal flap that covered the electrical outlet was half closed. Levent saw nothing worth remarking until he walked to the end of the slip where a small tan plastic bag caught his eye. It rested against one of the dock posts.

"Is that the ship's garbage?"

"Should be," he said. "If it's French, it's probably worth its weight in gold."

That might be true.

CHAPTER 10

"The car is a rental," said Metin as they sat at the restaurant table. "It went out of the lot two weeks ago from a firm in Fethiye called Mediterranean Blue. I couldn't locate the man who wrote up the rental. He isn't at work today, and the secretary knew nothing but the name on the credit card. It was signed by a Francois Gaspard."

Levent did not know the name. It was not the one Pinar had given him and did not have to be genuine. A man who came from France to murder another man—a drug trafficker—could have the resources to obtain a bogus card. And other identification. He would unless he was careless.

"We'll want to talk to the person who rented the car," said Levent. "Priority on that. In the meantime, run the name through passport control. We could find out if that's his real one and when he entered the country."

The commandant nodded. "Right," he said. "Though if he came aboard ship, he could find a way to dodge that."

"With luck he's a frequent flier," said Levent. "He didn't have to use his real name on the rental, but he probably came through Dalaman airport if he took the car in Fethiye."

"It's a long drive from Fethiye," said the commandant. "He obviously coordinated with the ship to pick him up here."

"What do we have on the vessel?"

"She's called the Jeune Revanche," said Metin, who looked at his notes to be sure. "Registered to a woman named Suzanne Vardan."

Jeune Revanche. Young Revenge. The theme of ruthless pirates carrying out pitiless revenge was unfortunately common with vessels and the sea.

"Is the owner Turkish?"

"The surname might be," said Metin. "You can't be sure about that. At least, I can't. Turkish, French, German, Turkish French or German. Take your pick."

Vardan meant nothing in Turkish, but it was close to Varan, the name that Harman had Pinar search for in the visitors' records. He had said the name was French, and the vessel flew a French secondary flag. Levent knew the French had a drug trade that had gone worldwide at one time and might still. He did not understand why the man would murder a member of an organization as powerful as his in a way guaranteed to attract attention. But perhaps that was the point.

"The vessel's been in these waters for the last six weeks," said Metin. "I'm checking to see if we have times and places along the coast."

"The assistant manager is sure he'd never seen the boat before yesterday."

"She was on an overnight?"

"Not longer," said Levent. "The owner asked the assistant where to find a good meal in the city. He pointed her here."

To the marina restaurant. They had set up headquarters at one of the tables. It was too early for Turkish dinner, but the place was beginning to fill with tourists. Even they were looking at the remnants of the commandant's uniform as if they had entered the wrong place.

Levent had taken the precaution of calling Emine and suggesting they meet here for their evening meal. He said nothing about surveillance. No one had made a move toward the Peugeot in three hours, and Levent was afraid none would come. The best he hoped for was domestic peace.

"The fire chopper is out looking now," said Metin. "He can't do a thorough sweep, but he's on the alert for a purple-striped two-masted vessel."

At the height of the yachting season in good weather, he would have to look hard. Several vessels had put in and out since the Peugeot was discovered. None were their target. The Jeune Revanche did not have to return to port—any port—especially if the passengers had good reason to be elsewhere. One of them almost certainly did.

"Tell the chopper pilot to concentrate his search toward Fethiye," said Levent. "That ship can't disappear completely, even in a place with endless anchorage."

Endless," said Metin. "That's the word for the day. Except for that turd Rehber, we've got nothing so far."

* * *

The commandant meant that he had gotten some return from questioning Rehber after taking him to Harman's *site* in the city. Faced with a woman who swore she had seen him two days before when he parked his Fiat in Harman's space at Konak *Site*, he admitted he had ransacked the apartment. He also said he had never searched Harman's unit at South Beach, but that was for the gullible to believe.

The truth was that Rehber had found nothing there. If Levent had not noticed that the gas tank was improperly connected, he would have had the same result. Rehber had not known what he was looking for, he said, but he was aware that Harman had financial resources that were considerably more than his pay. Buying the South Beach unit, half in cash, proved it. Refusing to rent out the unit for the summer months proved almost as much. The bars and restaurants that Panter frequented, along with the foreign women he liked to date, were more evidence if it were needed.

"He's lying of course," said the commandant. "He knew what he was looking for. He's in drugs up to his skinny neck. What I don't understand is how he knew about Panter's death so quickly. He went into that house the same night Panter died. I thought at first he could have had a piece of the murder, but I checked with some people at South Beach and they alibied him for time of death. A little while later he left the office, probably to wreck that apartment. He's a professional accomplice, our friend, but not one that puts himself too close to the fire."

"So either Rehber knew the killer, or someone told him of the kill not long after it happened."

"I don't know who that would be," said Metin. "We responded fast, but I didn't put the news out until later. And it was very quiet news."

But there was always another possibility. "Where does Rehber live?"

"Gundogan."

"He would have driven past the convenience store to get home," said Levent. "He could have seen the car."

"And headed out for the break-in?"

"He might have headed for a phone," said Levent. "If he called Panter's superiors, they would have told him what he had to do."

Metin did not ask who Panter's superiors were, which was a good thing. "It's plausible," he said.

"Check his cell phone records," said Levent. "Find out who he called that night, then beat him to death with it."

"Time, again, Onur. Your speciality."

* * *

The wait continued for the next two hours. Levent was happy that the city police released three of their men in plainclothes to help with watching, but the results did not change. No vessel of the proper description put in. No one made a move on the Peugeot. It was easy to leave a rental car behind for a man who planned to run.

Eventually, Levent hoped for some return from the garbage off the ship. There were several beer and wine bottles, along with other items, that should take fingerprints well enough for the lab to pull up. But unless the prints matched in this country, he would not hear from them for a while that might extend to days. If the prints did not match in any system, the while would be never.

This investigation needed luck. Luck in homicide was usually the result of the killer's mistakes. Levent had his share when he tracked the Peugeot to the marina with nothing to follow but a vision of Bodrum harbor. He was content knowing that the supernatural had limits even as he wished for none.

The ship might put in at a Greek island, where she would be safe from interference no matter what bulletins were sent out. She could have put in at one already and did not have to return to Turkey. The man could board a plane at any of the islands except the smallest. He could catch a ferry for the mainland or other destinations. He should have changes of clothing, if not identity, in the bag he brought aboard.

It seemed he would return soon or not at all. Levent thought he was unlikely to unless he had more work to do. He had burnt alive the man who could have delivered the drugs. It was unreasonable to assume that drawing information about a payload was his purpose when he ambushed Harman. Only a lunatic would take the time to threaten a man with fire when another car could have come into the parking lot at any moment.

Levent did not like to think about lunatics, though murderers often were when they crossed the boundaries that had held them all their lives. He was wondering about that when the commandant took a call from the car rental agency in Fethiye.

It seemed they had received a call saying that the Peugeot had been dropped at Bodrum marina.

* * *

That news effectively ended the surveillance. Though Levent was tempted to keep a man on duty in the lot, he recognized the personnel limitations and the fact that the commandant wanted to return to his office. He had one lead to follow up and a mountain of paperwork to do.

The office manager at Med Blue, as he insisted on calling his shop, was irate at having to send a man on a trip of several hours to pick up a car that should have been dropped in his lot. He was even more angry when the commandant told him that he would have to wait to retrieve his property. The car would be tied up for at least two days while the police lab looked it over.

That did nothing to calm the manager, but he understood that a police investigation should not be impeded. He said he had received the information about the Bodrum drop from a woman who told him she was calling for Mister Gaspard. That man had apparently taken sick and could not bring in the car.

That told Levent something. The woman, perhaps the woman who owned the vessel, knew that her passenger was not the usual freight. She knew the name on the credit card he had used to rent the car, false or not. Her passenger was probably as sick as murder could make a man.

The manager did not know where the call had originated except that it had been made from a cell phone. That might mean the ship was still in Turkish waters. Though it was not impossible to call from a Greek island, or from a cell phone with an international number, the connections were often bad, and the manager noted nothing like that. Clear as the weather today, he said.

The weather was also a factor in locating the employee who had rented out the car. He had gone to sea in a boat himself and had not answered his cell phone the entire afternoon. With night coming on, he would return to port, or come in close enough for contact soon.

At this stall point in the investigation, Levent had no choice but to wait.

* * *

He still had not heard from the car rental agent when Emine appeared with three friends, including the Italian Federico. He brought along two good-sized sea bream that he had speared, and wanted them cooked by the restaurant kitchen. Federico had definite instructions for the chef, who did not want to hear of anything but fish cooked on a grille. Making the bream into an onion dolma was more than he wanted to bear.

Levent translated Federico's instructions, adding basil and butter. The cook left muttering, but promised to bring the fish back with limited damage.

"So you went out with Turan again," said Levent. "I'm told he's the best guide to these waters you could have."

"We went out this morning early," said Federico. "But Turan had to leave to meet someone who came in from Istanbul. He took Tolga and the bodyguard with him. So I brought these devils in all by myself. They tell me that wild bream can't be compared to the farmed."

"They're right," said Levent. "The taste of the wild never leaves the fish. It gets into his body and can't be gotten out. You'll see."

"I'm sure," said Federico. "I've been diving for years and never had an idea of what I was doing until I began going out with Turan. That man has instincts. I'm starting to develop them since we met."

"Be careful there," said Eren, another Istanbullu who spent his vacation time in Bodrum. "You can't be so attentive to the fish that you forget where you are. Turan is a different story. He was brought up in these waters. From the time he was very young, his father would take the family out on their boat for diving and a late dinner. When the meal was finished, they'd throw the plates overboard to be washed. No plate ever hit bottom when Turan went over the side after it."

"I wouldn't believe it of anyone else," said Federico. "With Turan, it's easy. He's half fish."

"Fish," said Emine. "Money. It's all the same. Everything runs in schools, following the leader. Turan has so many companies under his hand that he finds it hard to remember their names. But the direction—that he never forgets."

"I didn't know he was raised around here," said Levent.

"His father worked for the maritime department of a shipping line," said Eren, who was in the textile business. "He went for his schooling in Istanbul, but the family—at least the mother—comes from a village back in the hills."

"Which village?" asked Levent. "Was it Zamir over by Gumushluk?"

"Not that I remember," said Eren. "The one with the odd name. It has something to do with the sea, though you can't see it from there or even smell it for the goat shit."

"Could it be Yelkenli?"

"That should be the one," said Eren. "A sailing vessel stuck on a mountaintop. Seems like just the thing for Bodrum. And Turan."

Levent made a note. Most of the men who had been hired by DenizKum to work at South Beach came from that village. Everyone came from somewhere, but it should be interesting to talk to the man who knew the place from the cradle.

"So Turan's a villager who made good."

"Good isn't quite the word for what he's made, and Turan didn't really grow up in the village," said Eren. "I had some business with him several years ago, and he gave me the genealogy over dinner one day. His father had married a local woman, a villager more or less, but divorced her after Turan was born. He married for a second time to a woman from Istanbul who went out with him on the boat one day and fell in love with the captain." Eren shrugged. "It happens. It seems to happen with rich women more than it should."

"Romance and the sea," said Emine wistfully. "I wish I could get my husband interested in something like it."

Levent did not respond to the bait. He had spent his life trying not to run in the same school as most, to say nothing of what passed for high society. Emine had been born to a lower branch of that tree only to leave the nest for a middle-class university graduate who liked to solve problems that had an end in justice. She really did not mind except on her vacation.

"I'd like to talk to Turan some time," said Levent. "Do you think he'd invite me up to his castle?"

"For dinner, not a chance," said Eren. "He knows you're the police, and he knows that can bring no good."

"He doesn't like us?"

"No one really does," said Eren with a broad looping smile. "Businessmen spend their time trying to find ways not to attract the attention of the authorities. Only the ones who can be bribed are invited up to share the view."

This was second time today that Levent had listened to the subject of money changing hands under the table. The first was serious and unfriendly, the second the subject of conversation. Although that might be normal for Turkey, it was decidedly abnormal for Levent on his vacation.

"I'd like to know what Turan has to hide," said Levent. "It must be something buried deep."

"Oh, something's there," said Eren. "The whiff of the past is strong around Turan. I've never heard the details, but I think it has something to do with the way he got started on his empire. It was here in Bodrum, I believe."

"Not exactly the seat of power," said Levent. "Or great wealth in those days. If you can find out some details, I'd like to know."

"I suppose I could," said Eren. "We'll call it my bribe to the authorities."

"That's the kind I like," said Levent. "Information."

Their waiter had just brought the meze—a bean paste with a fine onion, pepper and garlic sauce—when Levent came across another information infusion. Metin called with news that he had just heard from the employee who rented the Peugeot. He was not as excited as he might have been, saying the man recalled little—"the lazy bastard barely remembers his name"—but Levent took the number for a call back. He excused himself from the dinner table to raise Fethiye.

In the small garden, pacing and looking to the parking lot with its afternoon memories of heat and nothingness, Levent finally heard the voice of a man who was obviously young and on the short side of hostile. His parents said that he should go through life with the name Efe.

"I talked to the Jandarma," he said. "Told them all I know."

"But you won't mind another round," said Levent. "You've had time to think, and it's important to have a description of the man who rented the car."

"Tall," he said. "I remember that. Beyond six feet."

"How far?"

"I can't say."

"You were with him for several minutes," said Levent. "Did he go outside to examine the car before he accepted it?"

"Probably."

Levent was thinking that Efe had been out on the water all day and into the raki. His voice sounded slurred, control elusive. "He found no damage because he took the car. Did he have a bag with him?"

"Might have," said Efe, slowing his response time. "Now that I think of it, he opened the trunk and put the bag inside after I left him with the keys."

"It was a large bag," said Levent, trying to work back in Efe's memory for a key. "Did he have trouble lifting it into the trunk?"

"Not that I recall," he said. "But I didn't help him. It was large, though, and not the usual black thing. Something designer. Louis whathisname."

"Vuitton," said Levent. "So he was an upscale traveler."

"Not otherwise," said Efe. "I remember now I marked that. He could have had the 306, but wanted the 406. Not cheap."

"So he asked specifically for a Peugeot," said Levent. "I take it you have several other models of cars on the lot."

"Two kinds," he said. "Top of the line Opels and Peugeots. Neither are cheap. So he was well-to-do, sure."

"Well dressed?"

"Not for an evening party," he said. "This is Fethiye, you know. If the tourists get out of their bathing suits before night-fall, we like to think there must be a funeral in town."

"So he rented the car early in the day."

"Not so early," said Efe. "In the afternoon, maybe on the late side."

The rental slip might show the time, but Levent was concerned with concentrating Efe's mind. That seemed to be happening slowly. "He probably came in on the bus from Dalaman airport, wouldn't you say?"

The silence told Levent that Efe had finally made his way back to the day of the rental, albeit on a leash. His brighter voice confirmed it. "You know, I think he got out of a taxi. Yes, he did. I recall because the driver came into the office at the same time.

He wanted to change euros for the fare into lira. We do that for a small fee."

Levent bet the difference went immediately into Efe's pocket. Nothing worked on the memory like a commission that never hit the books.

"Did you speak to the driver for long?"

"Of course not. But it was a big fare. Twenty-five euro, so he must have come from Dalaman or some place far off."

"Did you know the driver before he came in to change money?"

"At one time I'd have known all the drivers in this area," said Efe. "Now there's too damned many. He was probably a stranger." A pause came across the line, like a strike on a fishing line that was in the water all day. "You know, I recall he had a harelip. Some kind of impediment."

"A strange look about his mouth, then."

"Could have been plastic surgery for all I know," said Efe. "People do almost anything to get out of military service, but I never heard of one who disfigured his face for it. This one shouldn't have had to. He could have gotten a pass for being so damned ugly."

"So his face was memorable."

"And his smell," said Efe. "I've never been close to anyone who stank so of cigarettes and sweat. It was a hot day, but I like to change my shirt once a week. His fare—the Peugeot 406—stood at the end of the counter upwind. I don't know how he survived the drive, but maybe it was because he was smoking, too. He filled my ashtray halfway while he waited and filled out the form."

"A chain-smoker."

"Long chain," he said.

"What brand?"

"A small packet," said Efe. "No filters. Maybe the pack was blue. The cigarettes had a strong smell. Like burnt dung."

"Local?"

"No."

"Foreign?"

"I think so. I'd say Gitane or Galois at a guess."

"We're beyond guessing," said Levent. "You're doing well working back."

"That may be true, Inspector, but I can't remember much about that man. I don't see him, but I can smell those weeds he was smoking."

Give the French cigarettes time to work. Efe had entered the past through his sense of smell—the most powerful for recollection. An addict seldom switched brands, so the man would find it hard to replace them in Turkey. Both brands were rare in the stores. And rare belonged to Levent.

"He was tall," said Levent. "Strong, too, hefting that large bag into the trunk. Was he wearing sunglasses when he went outside?"

"Yes," said Efe as if he had discovered something. "Big ones. He put them on from his pocket when he went outside. So he was wearing a shirt, not a T-shirt. Blue, I think. Dark, like his hair."

Dark blue shirt, dark eyes—the stranger was coherent. "What about his eyes?"

"The usual number," said Efe with a snort of a laugh. "I think they were brown."

"His accent?"

"We spoke English," said Efe, as if he wanted Levent to appreciate his versatility. "You have to do that here or you'll never rent a dry cow. I couldn't tell you what kind of accent he had, but it wasn't like the usual British we get."

"Continental, let's say. Did he ask for a map of the area before he set out?"

"No," said Efe. "He seemed to know where he wanted to go. When he was at the counter, he asked how far it was to Marmaris. Yes, he did. I'm sure of that now."

Marmaris was the next real city along the Aegean Coast from Bodrum, not quite halfway to Fethiye. The entrance to its bay was a long promenade through grand mountains, and the marina in the city center large.

"You told him the way to Marmaris?"

"I must have," said Efe. "Something about friends sticks in my mind. Friends for sure. He said he wanted to go to Marmaris to meet them."

"Did he mention a boat?"

"I don't remember that," he said. "Maybe he did."

Efe's voice stopped dully on that point. Levent looked through the fence toward the pale white masts in the harbor. A purple-striped two-masted ship. Was that all he would ever see? There were plenty of places to dock a ship in Fethiye, but the man wanted to know the way to Marmaris. So his friends were probably there. Then.

"Are you finding anything more in the memory bank?"

"Not a thing, I'm afraid," said Efe. "What was there was probably more than there should have been."

"You're going to sleep on this," said Levent. "You might recall more about the man later."

"You're pretty sure about that?"

"You'll call me if you have anything to report."

Levent hung off thinking that when the alcohol wore off, and sleep took over, Efe would journey. Where he landed might be problematic.

Levent had missed the first two dishes of meze when he returned to the table, the raki was half gone, and Emine was wearing the face that said he had been absent far too long. He sat back down at the table with his friends, holding the picture of a tall, strong, dark-haired brown-eyed man who smoked French cigarettes and might have gone along the mountain and valley roads of the coast for Marmaris.

This was the best vacation that Levent could remember. Had he really been bored all those years in Bodrum?

Part Three:

The Name of the Devil

CHAPTER 11

Levent took his coffee out to the terrace again in the morning as the sun streamed off the water in fierce horizontal sheets. The white *sites* across the bay took the glare as if it was the way they communicated with the world. Someone unloaded bright wind-surfing sails from their berth and set them out on the dock. Two sailing vessels anchored outside the swimming buoys turned slowly in the current.

The stillness was interrupted by a distant rhythmic sound as a fire helicopter rattled over the hill on the opposite shore. Carrying a long cable from its belly with a huge bucket of miracle fiber at the end, the chopper swung toward the water, dipping its Bambi bucket for a long scoop of sea-water. The operation took only seconds before the chopper turned and raced to the north over the abbreviated sand beach of Bitez. Somewhere on this quiet morning, a fire had started in the woodlands. Fire on this very dry and very scattered peninsula was always a serious thing.

Levent was glad not to think of that, or the summer rains that never came, when his cell phone rang. It was the commandant.

"The first piece of news I have for you is negative," he said in a tired voice that probably meant he had wrestled with paperwork half the night. "Passport control has nothing on this man Francois Gaspard. Either he came into the country with the bilge water or he's using other ID."

"We might have expected that," said Levent. "He may not be a professional, but he's behaving like someone who knows how to hide."

"It makes sense for a drug runner," said Metin. "The lab got back to me with a report on the heroin. It's as pure as anything they've seen in this district. You'd think they have a lab here to process the drugs, though I doubt it. That's the second biggest industry in Istanbul, and it wouldn't take much to ship the goods down here."

Processing heroin was not the second biggest industry in Istanbul, but it was the first in profit margins. Drugs did not run across the country without organization and the cooperation of the authorities, especially in the east. There, the Jandarma was the main arm of the law. And that was not all the overhead the commandant had to buck.

"They probably shipped the goods from the lab in a car," said Levent. "Thousands of cars every day and no one to stop the flow."

"I really like those numbers when I'm short of time," said Metin. "I haven't even been able to check the weapon we found in that car. It didn't seem like a priority since it was never used."

"There can't be many dealers here," said Levent. "Tell me the one you'd go to if you wanted to buy a weapon quietly."

"Yilmaz," said the commandant. "He's been around the longest and he's the best thief. If you want to jog over there, his shop is not far from Bitez on the main road."

"I'll try to stop by today," said Levent. "You must be under pressure to close this case out."

"If you're telling me we caught the whirlwind in a jar, I won't disagree," he said. "What we got off the prints yesterday is disturbing, too. They belong to a man who took a drug bust in London several years ago. The British are still looking for him."

"Really?" said Levent, trying for surprise. "Has the lab compared the prints with the victim's?"

"They had a hell of a time with all the damage to the body, but I heard back late last night," he said. "They say the prints match. At least they're close. The technician said they had enough points for a match on the thumb."

"I suppose you ran the prints through our records."

The commandant made a noise that began far off but ended too near. "He's not really in the system, Onur. Here we have a drug runner who was never brought before the law for anything in this country. He's a fifty-three-year-old virgin who shows up in England dealing serious weight under the name of Nadir Panter, then drops off the map like a ghost. The only way we know he's a Turk is that he entered military service in 1985 as Yunus Harman. Of course, when we queried his military records, we got back a truly shitty notice saying that the information on Harman was under classification. I've only seen one thing like it since I've been here. A couple of years ago, we were told that the manager at Yalikavak marina was off-limits when we put him through the system. I heard later—let's say informally—that he'd worked for MIT for years. They didn't want the connection known."

If Levent needed confirmation that Harman was Deep State, he had it. That Harman's records were protected was enough to prove the link. If MIT—military intelligence—was involved, nothing would ever come out.

"You don't have a choice except to back down," said Levent. "Make too much noise and you could be reassigned to the eastern mountains in time for winter."

"I figured that out myself," said Metin. "But I don't like it. It means someone is protecting the memory of a drug runner. The next call I get will tell me to look *for* the killer, not *at* the victim. I don't want to think about where that call will come from."

"You'll never know where the call is coming from even if you know the man who's calling," said Levent. "Did you get anything from Rehber's phone records?"

"He only made one call that night," said Metin. "To a business in Istanbul called Yelkenli, Inc."

The incorporation made no sense, though the name Yelkenli made more. It was the village where all the workers came from. "I may have something on Yelkenli later," said Levent. "In the meantime, I had an indication from the rental agent last night that Marmaris might be a good place to look for the ship."

"You mean you actually got that prick to focus?"

"It wasn't easy," said Levent. "But after the raki wore off, he remembered that the man asked something about the way to Marmaris. Check the marina there for records on the ship in the past three weeks. It's possible she went there when she sailed yesterday."

"We'll get on it," said Metin. "I hope the captain is a marina type of woman. If not, there must be fifty different coves at Marmaris where a ship could put in."

For practical purposes, that was endless, too.

* * *

When Emine awoke, and after her duty breakfast of one slice of toast with coffee, Levent drove her to a chain grocery store on the upper road before doubling back to the gun shop the commandant had said was the best place for Harman to have bought his pistol. Yilmaz Gun World was a small place with the usual noise-makers propped in the display window on mounded boxes of ammunition.

The owner sat at a tall workbench with his back turned to the door, where he worked on a shotgun that he had broken down into two large and several small pieces. By the mirror on the wall, he knew someone had entered the shop, and by the radar that all gun shop owners had, he was sure he would be talking to someone unfriendly when he turned around.

"Help you, pilgrim?"

Levent said nothing. He moved to the counter and around it to the workbench, wondering how a man as old as this still had the eye for close work. Yilmaz looked more than seventy, though raki-wear could have added ten years to the count. His face was as full of moving parts as his products, with brown eyes that did not linger long on anything and a mouth that twisted to the left side as if it knew no other direction. Only his hard shell hands said he was steady enough to be a survivor.

"I have a question for you, sir."

Yilmaz looked at Levent at a distance of two paces without wondering who he was. "I don't do nothing illegal here," he said. "You want a gun, show me a permit. Otherwise, there's the sun on the street for you."

"One question," said Levent, who had dealt with gun dealers more than he liked to remember. "Answer truthfully and I'll be a happy Inspector of Homicide. Tell me a lie and I'll close this place down."

"Homicide," he said.

"Istanbul Homicide," said Levent. "I'm working with Commandant Comert of the Jandarma. You might know him."

"If I wanted to remember that prick, I'd say yes."

"You don't have to remember him well, Yilmaz. I'm interested in knowing if you sold an HK nine-milimeter pistol to one of your customers recently."

"I don't carry HK. You could special order one, but it would take a few days."

"If I went into the back room, I'm sure I'd find any number of special orders," said Levent. "I'm also sure that a good portion would be contraband. You don't want to push me on this."

Yilmaz shrugged. "You think I'm stupid enough to deal in smuggled weapons?" he said. "You want me to tell you how long I been in this business?"

"I'm listening."

"Twenty-five years," he said. "You don't get past the first two if you attract the wrong kind of attention. At least not in a town as small as this used to be."

Levent sometimes appreciated lies when they were artfully given. Yilmaz undoubtedly sold more illegal weapons than the other kind. Probably half of the guns sold in Turkey were illegal. Many came in from HK's Germany with Turkish workers returning home.

"I don't care how you got the pistol," said Levent. "I want to know if you sold an HK nine-millimeter to Nadir Panter."

"Don't know the name," he said. "What did he look like?" Levent noticed that Yilmaz used the past tense for Panter, but he probably deduced that. From the front fatigue pocket of his shorts, Levent produced the picture of Panter that had come in yesterday from Erol Akbay in Istanbul. Because it was slightly wrinkled, he smoothed it down on the workbench.

"He looked like this," said Levent. "You might add half a dozen years to the photograph if it helps your recollection."

"He seems familiar," said Yilmaz, whose left eye began to twitch. "Didn't know his name was Panter. The first time we met, he called himself something else."

"What did he call himself then?"

"Nothing I remember," he said. "I told you I been in business a long time. For longer than I care to think about, I was the only gunsmith and seller in this town. If I sold a pistol to this man, it would have been the second time I did it."

"You sold him two pistols?"

"If I sold him one, I sold him two. That's the way I might remember it."

"What was the first pistol you might remember?"

"It wasn't an HK. A Glock nine-millimeter, if I'm not wrong."

"So he bought two pistols here," said Levent. "Did you sell him the ammunition for either?"

"The first time, I did. The second, he wanted hicap mags. They're illegal in a lot of places. I don't have any and won't for a while that might last the rest of my life. I told him that. He didn't seem worried. It was like he knew another place to get them. For the Glock, well, he wasn't so particular about his loads in those days."

"In those days?" said Levent. "When did you sell him the Glock?"

Yilmaz threw his head back as if looking at the red calendar on the wall. It was an odd thing, ceramic and static, with each month permanently engraved along the sides and the bottom. The logo said Ruger, so it was probably a gift from a supplier that could be used as an ornament when its time was done.

"It might have been twenty years ago," said Yilmaz, who looked at both hands as if they did not have enough fingers. "Could have been longer."

"Are you saying you remember a pistol that you sold twenty years ago?"

"I remember guns, not names," he said slowly. "I remember them damned well and a repeat customer does things for my recollection. As a matter of fact, I told him that when he wanted the HK. So how you been for the last couple decades? He didn't seem to want to recall the old days, and I didn't press for a friendly drink."

Twenty years ago. The late eighties. Rehber at South Beach said that Harman knew a lot about Bodrum as it once was, but this was the first time anyone had put him in the past in the flesh. Levent could have said it meant nothing to the present. If he had not spent so much time in homicide, he would have meant it.

"What was he like in the old days?"

"You think we were friends?" said Yilmaz with a smile of broken parts. "He had a permit then and he had one now. That's what I know."

"Yilmaz, if I tell the commandant what you said, he'll put you against the wall until the rest of your teeth fall out. Talking to me is easier."

"It doesn't seem like that."

"It will," said Levent. "Soon."

Yilmaz looked at the ceramic calender again as if it might be correct again in twenty years, or twenty years into the past. Levent did not mind anything that moved him in the right direction, and he did not hurry the recollection.

"I used to see him around town then," said Yilmaz, "and it might have been twenty-five years ago. You couldn't help come across people in those days. There were four bars downtown where there's forty now. There wasn't any of those gigantic cruise ships coming in to double the population in an hour—and not many of the little ones either. Some people ran boats to the islands and over to Gocek Bay, but they were the kind that didn't mind starving to death as long as they had enough in their pockets for raki. That was cheap in those days. You could buy a case of raki for what a bottle is now."

"I know. Tell me about Panter."

"That's all of it actually," said Yilmaz. "I used to see him around the Old Town in the bars. He used to run with the divers. The ones that put Bodrum on the sponge map. They were a rowdy bunch, and I never had nothing to do with them."

"Except to sell one of them a pistol," said Levent in his warning voice. "Tell me when he came to you and why."

"If he was a gun I could tell you," said Yilmaz, who seemed to be straining, and honestly. "That's the way my mind runs. It ain't much good for remembering anything else these days."

"Think, Yilmaz."

"Won't do no good," he said. "People come here to buy a gun because they want to protect themselves. That's the first kind. The other kind you can sense with a little experience. They're the ones that want it to deal with a problem that can't wait."

"Which kind was Panter?"

"The first," he said without referencing his memory. "Not a man on the hunt. A man who might think he was hunted. It's always something from the past that turns into another thing in the future. Isn't it?"

* * *

Levent rejoined Emine at the chain store. It was such a large place that Levent did his liquor shopping while Emine took in the groceries. She swore that she would cook at the apartment soon, though Levent had never suggested it.

He never would suggest work on holiday except to those people who loved what they did to an unhealthy degree. That was a working definition of Levent.

He could not help thinking that Panter-Harman had seen his future written in French characters. Somehow, he had known the name Varan-Vardan and sensed danger from it, even going so far as to tell his estranged wife that he had money hidden in Switzerland. The danger had come sooner than expected from a young man with dark hair who drove a green Peugeot. The results were all consuming.

He had been struck on the head, perhaps with a bottle of raki like the one Levent had in his hand. The inspector was still comparing prices—all the raki was expensive, the result of the taxes the Islamic government kept larding onto the top end—

when his phone rang. Levent was expecting several calls, but the one he received had the most familiar voice.

"Tell me you're sitting down, Boss."

"Is it that good?"

"When a man puts me on the trail, he has to be ready to field all the take," said Detective Erol Akbay. "The first thing you should know is that most of the things I found on our man Harman don't come from our departments. We seem to have a disliking for his name. I'm going to leave it to you to decide why."

"The records have been scrubbed, Erol."

"I'm glad to agree," he said. "The first thing I found on Mister Harman was a bulletin put out by the American DEA. That's their drug enforcement administration. They had Interpol, us, everyone in the greater Mediterranean area looking for Yunus Harman in early 2003. A bad man, they said. They wanted him for laundering money in Cyprus. It was casino money mixed with drug money. This was our part of Cyprus—the north. Kyrenia to be exact."

"That fits with the situation here," said Levent. "Drugs are involved. Very pure heroin in good weight."

"Everything seems to fit and that's the problem," said Erol. "I went backward from that point and found out some things through a detective in the department down there. It seems the Americans presented a mountain of evidence that one of the local banks, together with one of the gambling halls, were running black money through their operations."

"Sounds like the normal day-to-day," said Levent.

"That kind of thing is normal in Cyprus," said Erol. "Everybody knows it. But for some reason the police moved on this operation. It must have been a political decision—the government trying to show the Americans they were against corruption, at least when their relatives aren't involved. The upshot was that they arrested the bank manager and the man who ran the casino operations. In fact, they arrested his whole staff. One of the men they took in was Yunus Harman."

"I'm guessing he got away," said Levent. "The bulletin says that much."

"Sure he did." Erol liked to paint himself as jaundiced by every event. "The DEA is still looking for him. Their office in Cyprus says Harman was a serious outlaw, and believe me, they were delighted to hear he was dead."

"I wonder when he assumed the name Nadir Panter," said Levent. "When was he arrested in England?"

"It's close for timing," said Erol. "The English bust was a year-and-a-half later. So Yunus Harman was reborn in a related business as Nadir Panter. The DEA said he was a bit more than he seemed in Cyprus. The manager of the casino was a dummy in an expensive suit who met high-rollers at the door and handed out the keys to the whorehouse. The man who ran the money laundering end of the business was Harman. The Dolphin, they called him. The Americans don't like real names for scum. Animals, insects, that's different."

"I'd like it better if they called him Fish."

"Why's that, Boss?"

"Apparently, Harman's friends called him Fish if they were really his friends," said Levent. "But Dolphin is close. I'd like to hear more about the money trail. Where were they shipping the cash?"

"They sent it out to banks in Turkey mostly," he said. "They favored a branch of the bank in Cyprus, but they didn't care that much. Any bank that liked deposits, which should be all of them. This information comes from the casino manager, who didn't get away. Sometimes, he said, they body-packed the cash off the island if they thought the paper trail might be too easy to trace. The hands-on approach was Harman's area. He ran mules for every season and a big stable of them, too."

"I'm sure he wasn't the boss of the operation," said Levent. "Everything I've found says that's unlikely. Who was behind the operation in Cyprus?"

"DEA was confused about that," said Erol lightly but with some follow-through. "They're good at chasing paper trails, but the rational approach usually breaks down in this country. At least, that's what my boss taught me. Or that's what it does when someone higher up wants it to. The casino is owned by a holding company in Turkey—an Istanbul address—that seems legitimate. The name is Desenli Logistics. You probably heard of them or seen their trucks on the road. They're in transportation basically, but plenty of other things, too. I'd be surprised if they didn't make the cigarette I'm holding in my hand."

Levent thought he had passed several of their trucks on the way to Bodrum. It seemed as if he had passed every truck in the western part of the country. The name Desenli was not much otherwise. It meant filled with designs. But patterns were what homicide lived for.

"The ownership of the casino seems straightforward, Erol."

"Seems so," he said. "Until we learn the legitimate company is owned by another company that's just a mailbox. That's what the DEA found when they investigated. They tried to push back the veil, but the dark things pushed back. No one could tell them who was behind the parent company."

"What's its name?"

"Yelkenli, Inc."

Levent tried not to let his conclusions jump so fast. Yelkenli was a common word any place near the sea and almost as common inland. But Yelkenli was the village where Turan's family came from. Yelkenli, Inc. was the number Rehber had called on the night Panter was murdered. It seemed they were making progress on the paper trail.

"Anything else, Erol?"

"There is," he said. "I asked the Americans if the reward was still good for Yunus Harman. They said they thought so, but they'd check. So I'm wondering what we should buy for the office. They'll let us keep some of it, won't they?"

"You're out of the research area now," said Levent. "You're dreaming."

CHAPTER 12

They had gotten the groceries in and Emine was dressing for the beach—not a small thing—when Levent received a call. He went out onto the terrace to take it as the voice of Sultan Kara crept close and seductive in his ear. She had devil's feathers, too, of the female and equally dangerous kind.

"Inspector, how was your morning?"

"It's been interesting," said Levent. "Biography is to me."

She laughed, and that, too, was seductive. "I wish I knew what that meant, but something tells me I'll find out."

"We find out the things we need to know," said Levent. "It could be called experience, but it's usually known as survival."

Sultan laughed and took up the dare. "Do you know Crystal Beach, Inspector?"

"I could see it if the hill tended the other way," he said, looking from the head of the bay to the beach halfway along. "Why do you ask?"

"I'll be there in half an hour, and I'd very much like to talk with you."

"You have the information I requested?"

"As promised."

"Then we have a date," he said.

Levent came back into the rooms, where Emine modeled her latest swimsuit in the hallway mirror. She looked wonderful, her breasts mounding in twin crescendos, her legs as darkly tanned as a mirror allowed. He wondered why she did not look even better, while understanding that everything was relative.

"You're not dressed," she said. "What have you been doing?"

"I took a call from a young woman."

"Young," said Emine, but not to the mirror. "Is she very pretty?"

"Beautiful," he said, enjoying himself for a moment that he knew would pass into regret.

Emine smiled. "Then it's business."

"I'm afraid so," he said. "I have to run down to Crystal Beach, but you should take the car. I'll find you later. It's Green Beach today, isn't it?"

"I was thinking that, yes."

It was part of the summer promenade, beach to beach to beach on a rotating and unpredictable basis. Levent never knew what prompted the changes, since the water was the same, and the chaise lounges and the food, but Emine always knew where her friends, who maintained the same feverish rotation, would gather. They ranged the length of the peninsula, sometimes at long distances, to enjoy the show of themselves and the pageant of others.

"I shouldn't be late," he said, kissing her on the shoulder and having the notion that he should not stop there. "You enjoy yourself in the meantime."

"That means you won't be there at all, Onur."

"Not so."

"Liar."

* * *

Levent carried Emine's accusation on foot the half kilometer to Crystal Beach, knowing it was true. The pursuit of the truth was fascinating, and the things that were false were often the most alluring.

Sultan Kara had chosen plush surroundings in which to present herself, a beach shelved on rocks and covered with bleached wooden planking like a temple raised to the sun. Crystal Beach was known as such because of the massive cushions in white-gold canvas that were flung everywhere. Its huts and umbrellas were of tropical thatch, and its beer fifteen dollars a bottle. It was all cinematic and tribal, but the water was the same.

Sultan was the same, less her clothing. Levent would have said that her body was perfect but for the mole high on her left buttock that only the most daring woman would bare to the world. Her bikini in all its parts would not have filled one hand of a dwarf. Her sunglasses were larger than the small cups that held her breasts, and her nail polish, fingers and toes, was exactly the same color as the cushions around her. Preparation. Seduction was not the same as distraction, though it seemed so in the midday sun.

"Inspector, you haven't dressed for the beach."

"I'm sorry, but this is a work day for me," said Levent, as he took the hand she offered. "I had the impression it should be for you."

"I could find a better place to interview a new manager," she said as she swung her long legs to the teak deck and removed her sunglasses. "But not nearly so pleasant. Can I offer you a drink today?"

"A beer," said Levent, sitting on the matching chaise lounge in the area that Sultan controlled. "Something imported."

"At once."

She called the waiter with the same gesture as she had summoned the help in the hotel. The new one appeared at the same speed, his sandals clicking like hooves on the deck. Levent thought the young man should not have looked so long, and longingly, at her cleavage, but it was clear that Sultan had nothing physical to hide.

"The last time I was here," she said, after the waiter walked away, "he gave a twenty percent discount on the bill. I wasn't really grateful. I thought it was a bit light, considering."

"He almost swooned," said Levent. "That should be worth something."

"Less than you think," she said, adjusting her bikini carefully but not casually. "It's always the men I'd like to impress who are immune."

She was damned good and would have been good if she had been in a headscarf and veil. Of course she was veiled. It was Levent's intention to see her real face, if that could be done.

"I'm impressed by the truth, Sultan."

"Aren't we all?"

She waited to address the most elusive thing in her life until the waiter came with the drinks, placing her pomegranate mojito and his Heineken side by side on the small table. Taking a long sip of the blood-red drink, she lowered it back to the table like another thing that could hold its place in line.

"Actually, Inspector, I owe you a great deal of thanks," she said, touching his hand across the table. "Regardless of what people think, no one in a position of responsibility can be happy when they badly misjudge one of their employees."

"You did that, Sultan?"

"I'm sorry to say."

She was doing something else with her fingers on his wrist, the underside of it, that could not be said to be fair. A head-strong man of the tribe would have taken her to his hut already.

"We're speaking of your general manager now," he said. "The corpse."

"Yes," she said, tapping his wrist as if she was done with therapy. "I simply wasn't aware of the mess Panter made down here. I knew the profits weren't there, but in real estate patience is everything. So I thought. But you were right when you said that Panter knew nothing of the business. When I looked at the books, I came to that conclusion. You misstated nothing, In-spector. What happened at South Beach is appalling."

"Have you been out to the *site* to see it first hand?"

"Not yet," she said. "One catastrophe each day is all I can bear."

Levent thought that Sultan had a reason for not visiting the *site*, and that it had to do with heroin. "You're not confident about the prime location any longer?"

"I've lost my confidence about anything having to do with DenizKum," she said. "I'm afraid I may have to stay on in Bodrum until things can be put right."

"Summer's not a bad time to be here."

She smiled and picked up her drink, which had turned a blurred red in the sun. "So if your general manager contrives to

be murdered, he should have the manners to do it in high season. That's very droll, Inspector."

"Yunus Harman had manners," said Levent. "They were bad,
but he had them."

Sultan understood that the name of one devil had been spoken. She could not ignore it. "Harman, you say. So he had another
name?"

"Nadir Panter was his other name," said Levent. "When his
mother looked at him in the cradle, she called him Yunus. People
who knew him well called him Fish. Have you ever heard that
name used for him?"

"Something about it's familiar," she said as if she had to give
Levent a morsel. "When I was here in the spring, I think I heard
a man call Panter that."

"What man?"

"No one really," she said as if she would like to withdraw her
observation. "He was someone we saw at Yalikavak marina. It
was a kind of orientation tour for us. The man waved as we passed
on the boardwalk and came over to shake hands with Panter."

"And called him Fish?"

"Yes," she said. "I thought it was strange. He stopped for a
minute and didn't say much before he disappeared into one of
the buildings."

"The administration building?"

"I really don't know." Sultan decided that she had said enough.
She had decided that Levent's interest might be too much.

Levent thought it might be just enough. The manager of the
marina, according to the commandant, had been another man
whose records were tightly kept. He was MIT's eyes in Yalikavak,
it seemed.

"Harman was well known around Bodrum," said Levent. "This
wasn't his first pass at the place. He lived here when he was younger.
In the eighties."

"I'm constantly amazed by your resourcefulness, Inspector. I
wasn't aware that you knew very much about Mister . . . Fish."

"I didn't know much about him yesterday," said Levent. "But twenty-four hours is a long time in a murder investigation. I'll know more by tomorrow. You should try to help me, Sultan. Being asinine is not the way."

He had slapped her hard instead of throwing her on her back where she was most comfortable. Her face flushed the same shade as the mojito. "I told you that I came here to help," she said. "What do you want to know?"

"I want the name and phone number of the first manager you sent down here to oversee South Beach."

Sultan did not beg off. She reached for her enormous purse and brought up a notebook bound in morocco leather. Turning the pages and tracking for a minute, she finally said "Ah" and tore a sheet from the binding.

"Thank you."

"I can't guarantee he'll talk to you," she said. "He left us in a hurry and may want to keep his distance."

Levent nodded as if the problem were hers. "People talk to me sooner or later. The first question I'll ask this man is why he recommended Harman. He must have known he was furthering the career of a wanted criminal whose only talents were washing money and dealing drugs. Those are related skills in case you don't know."

"If that's true, he won't to talk to you. You should let me find out what I can."

"You'd like another day for that?"

"Less," she said.

"Dinner at your hotel tonight?"

"If you wish."

"In your room?"

Sultan did not answer. Her first bout of executive anger filled the space between them like a second sun. But much darker.

"It's not this man I wonder about," said Levent. "When a company hires an employee to an important position, they usually check his background. If you'd done that, you would have known that Harman was nothing but a clever thug."

"Of course we checked," she said quickly. "But I wasn't aware of his real name. You should believe that because it's true."

Levent might believe her, but if she had been unaware it was because she had been told to be. "There are other things you might have known, Sultan. Harman lived well. He had a nice apartment in town and had bought a unit at South Beach. He drove a Mercedes. But that was the part that showed to the world. He had millions of lira in his bank accounts."

"Are you saying he embezzled from us?"

"I don't think he had to," said Levent. "Harman was sent here to cool. The law in several countries wanted to talk to him. The question is, who sent him to you? It's easy to put words of recommendation into a man's mouth. I think that was done before the name Harman became known to your manager."

"It's possible," she said. "I heard his name spoken in a meeting, but not as if he was a stranger. It was as if he had been known for some time."

"What meeting?" asked Levent. "At what time and at what firm?"

"It was at a board meeting at Desenli Logistics," she said, putting annoyance behind her with an effort. "Three months ago."

The name of the firm was the same as Erol had found by talking to the American DEA. "Exactly what is the relationship of your firm to Desenli Logistics?"

"They're the parent company," she said. "It's a complicated corporate structure."

"Complicated because it's meant to be," he said. "But the parent of the parent is Yelkenli, Inc. What's your relationship to them?"

"It's a holding company," she said lightly. "Obviously."

"In this case, there seems to be no difference between holding and hiding. I'd like to know who makes the effort to hide their ownership. I know why, of course."

"Then you know more than me," said Sultan with a decisive change in her body language as she drew back into the cushions.

"I was hired by the management at Desenli to run Bozkurt's operations. We have three companies under our umbrella—DenizKum here, the Fantasi Hotel in Kemer, and Perge World in Antalya. They're all in the tourism business. The last two are large hotel complexes."

"That's quite a responsibility," said Levent. "The other businesses must be profitable. Do they offset DenizKum's losses?"

"And a bit more," she said. "They were expected to take up the slack until South Beach got well underway."

"Planning," said Levent. "There's been plenty of it and none honest. It's clear that no one was very concerned with South Beach's financial condition. Yunus Harman was hired to make sure the future didn't arrive too quickly. There was too much money to be made dealing drugs in the meantime. You might want to know that we confiscated heroin from his apartment at South Beach. It's more than an addict should keep around the house."

"I didn't know that," she said quickly, taking her sunglasses into her hand as if they might protect her from more than the sun. "Not at all."

That might be true. Sultan was the pretty face Yelkenli kept to protect itself from discovery. They might be prepared to let her go down with the ship at DenizKum.

"You seem amazingly unaware of what's happened in your subsidiary," he said. "In that case, you may want to resign your position before we bring charges. It's late for that, however. We've arrested the sales manager at South Beach. He's held out so far, doing the job you paid him to do, but he'll give up everything when he's brought before a magistrate. You should get your cooperation on record beforehand."

When Sultan looked at Levent, he thought she might for the first time be looking to her survival. If she made that breach, the rest would follow.

"It seems like an option I should consider," she said.

"Mister Rehber called Yelkenli before he broke into Harman's apartment looking for your drugs, Sultan. This is more than an option for you. I want to know the name of the man at Yelkenli. The boss. Your boss. Harman's boss."

"What if I had him contact you, Inspector? I promise this will happen before the day's out."

"I might settle for that," said Levent. "The fact, not the promise."

She took up her mojito as if it was her last work of the day. It was pink now, bleeding out in the heat. When she had taken it down to the leaves of mint, she put her sunglasses back on and turned to Levent.

"You can arrest me if you like," she said, reflecting everything, including her fear. "But I've given my guarantee. You'll have what you want."

Levent thought it was too easy, but he knew Sultan was frightened. She would call the man in the shadows and perhaps he would step into the light. There he should be vulnerable, like all creatures of night.

CHAPTER 13

Levent made it to Green Beach long enough to visit with the friends who had gathered for the day. They were playing scrabble and backgammon and making bets on whose daughter at the next patio had gone in for surgical breast enhancement, and Levent would have called it making up with Emine if he had not taken the car when he left.

This case was different than any Levent had worked. The only man who could have been charged with serious criminal activity was the victim. The men who were most culpable could be found in every major apparatus of business and government. Levent thought he might locate one of those in the man who called Yunus Harman "Fish" one spring day in Yalikavak while walking with Sultan.

Levent would get used to the drive, which was nearly the same as he had made in the last two days, until finally he would not see the parking lot of the convenience store or the road leading to the Jandarma post. He kept on into the crooked little town of Yalikavak and did not stop until he reached the marina arched to the sea.

The complex covered a large area at the western end of the old port. Yalikavak had a great sheltered bay and harbor, and the marina matched its progress with a promenade of bars and restaurants and boutiques that ran along the shore. Huge expensive pleasure vessels were tied up at the front, and smaller but still expensive pleasure vessels sat at docks that ran well into the bay.

Levent found the marina office on the short second story of a strange orange building with porthole windows that overlooked the harbor. The name in antique brass on the door said: Oral Orhan.

The man sat at his desk with his feet on an open drawer and a cell phone in his ear. Was there an advantage in not using the phone on his desk? Who might, or might not, be listening to his call?

"Oral Bey, good afternoon."

He started in his chair. He seemed surprised that anyone would call him by an honorific, closing the phone abruptly and kicking the drawer shut. "It's a very good afternoon, sir." He got to his feet, as if he had carried off a complicated maneuver. "I'm sorry, but have we met before?"

"I doubt it, sir," said Levent, taking the large hand that was offered. "I've only just come down from Ankara."

"Ankara can be hot in the summer," said Orhan. "Hot and uncomfortable. And so damned cold in the winter."

"Hot and cold politically, too."

Levent felt they were talking in a code that neither understood, though Orhan did not sound confused. His deep voice seemed thrown. The luggage-weight bags under his eyes and heavy jowls were evidence of cares that had found their way to the bottom of the raki bottle on a steady schedule. The look of Bodrum, as it were.

"Are you keeping a boat here?" he asked.

"Not yet," said Levent, as if he was leaning in that direction. "A friend of mine told me I couldn't do better than Yalikavak Marina. I looked around and have to agree. I've never seen any marina with so many boats in foreign registry. By the scrawl on their sterns, Delaware is the place most of them call home."

Oral smiled with nested, chaotic teeth. "We have a deal with a company there," he said, waving his hand. "Delaware's south of New York, I understand, and a center of creativity. These people write up the ships up for a fee, but our customers save a lot of money anyway. Delaware charges a thousand dollars a year to keep a ship in registry. In Turkey, the same thing can run a thousand a month."

"I'm aware of that," said Levent, who was now. "I just bought a place at South Beach. I suppose I could get the same deal at the marina in Turgutreis, but my friend told me not to bother with the second rate. Get over to Yalikavak, he said."

"I won't argue with sound judgement. He must be a good friend."

"Fish and I go back to the beginning," said Levent. "New York in the old days. He was married then with a couple of kids, but you wouldn't have known it. We closed down a lot of bars."

Orhan looked at Levent closely, his long face stern. "When did you talk to Fish?"

"Last week as soon as I got in," said Levent. "I'd have been here earlier, but I had to run over to Antalya for a couple of days."

"Then you haven't heard."

"What haven't I heard?"

"He died several days ago," said Orhan. "I thought everyone knew by now."

Levent sat down in the chair to accept the blow. He was aware that he should not overdo his grief in light of Harman's character, but he took the time to shake his head and reflect on those shared nights in New York.

"How did it happen?"

"He was murdered," said Orhan, who had studied Levent's reaction carefully. His furtive eyes, a strange color of brown like rye bread, kept to their target. "I understand it was a brutal end. His car was set afire."

Orhan's intelligence was good, as Levent expected of a sometime MIT agent. There were more than one in every port on the coast. They were expected to keep their ears to the ground and report things of interest to the military. The channel worked both ways, though not equally.

"This *is* bad news," said Levent. "I wonder what he got himself into this time. It must have been a hell of a thing."

"You'll have to ask the Jandarma about that."

"Fish, my God," said Levent, as if invoking his spirit. "You never really took care of yourself." Levent turned to Orhan. "He used to walk around New York like the king of the city. Some hard case with a grudge could have come out of the shadows at him any time. He never minded his back."

"You seem to have known him well."

"We were at Folklore together for a couple months," said Levent. "I mean, we took some rogue Turks down. Every illegal in the city had us for companions."

"That sounds about right," said Orhan slowly, as if he had begun to take Levent for a player. "Fish was a legend. I think I heard all the stories over a bottle of raki. If not the first, then the third."

"Damn," said Levent. "What about the wife? The kids?"

"I'm sure they're taken care of," said Orhan. "Fish was never careless with money. He would have provided."

"I know that," said Levent. "But he still owes me some . . . consideration."

"A debt?"

"Call it that," said Levent, looking at Orhan in the same way Orhan had looked at him. "I was supposed to take some product off his hands. A unit or two. Price to be decided. God, this is really bad news."

"The worst," said Orhan, moving to sit in the second chair before his desk and beside Levent. "What business are you in, Mister—"

"Onur," said Levent dully. "This isn't a good time for surnames. I'm in transport. Trucking, mostly from the east."

"Well, you can present a claim to his estate."

"I'd like to do that," said Levent bitterly. "I'd like to walk right in and pick up the money I fronted. But that wouldn't be a good idea. Not at all."

"I see. There's a question about the debt."

"If you knew Fish, you knew there would be," said Levent. "He wasn't a man for paper except when he was running money out of Cyprus."

"That part of his life I know nothing about," said Orhan as if he would like to. "Ask me about Fish and Bodrum, I'll turn you a tale or two."

"I'd like to hear them some time," said Levent. "Over a bottle."

"We can go downstairs to the bar," he said. "They have all the raki we'll need."

"They may not have enough today," said Levent. "But it's a good idea. I'm on holiday, believe it or not."

* * *

The things Levent did in the line of duty were sometimes beyond the call, but he knew after fifteen minutes with Orhan he should be considered for a medal. Drawing the man in the right direction, which meant into the past and away from his raki, seemed like a dream of lost destinations. Orhan was not only boring, but his voice had no variation in delivery, as if he depended on the instrument to sing the song of his life but had forgotten to tune it. A matter of pitch.

The most interesting thing he said, when coaxed from his third drink, was that he had seen Harman on the day he died. It had not been much of a visit, several minutes at best, then he was on his way. Harman seemed in a hurry, but gave no indication that he knew what would happen to him later. They were supposed to meet the next day to go over their arrangements. It was too bad about that. Levent thought so, too, but at least he knew why Harman had been on that road and out of his way when he stopped for his cigarettes and ice cream bar.

"Burnt alive in his car," said Levent, bringing things back to the beginning of his acquaintance with Harman. "The Mercedes?"

"The Silver Arrow," said Orhan. "He told me his ex-wife bought it for him after he screwed her for three hours straight."

"He was a champion," said Levent wistfully. "Had a whole stable of women in Kyrenia. He provided good service for every one before he strapped them up with hundred dollar bills and sent them down to the ship. He never heard a complaint no matter what the numbers." Levent cocked his ear as if he had heard something from the distant past. "I wonder what he did for hygiene around here?"

"Well, I know he wasn't getting together with the ex-wife," said Orhan. "She has some yoga sort of thing going on now. You couldn't fuck her unless you stood her on her head first."

"That's what Fish said?"

"Exact words," said Orhan as if his memory could never drown. "He said he was glad he only got horny twice a week these days. Careful planner, though. Kept a woman to take care of the twice-a-week over in Turkbuku. He didn't like having to drive so far for it, though."

"This was a serious thing?"

"I don't know what to call it," he said. "Pussy is an unbelievably serious thing when you need it."

"What's her name?" said Levent aggressively. "Someone should go over and break the news to her. I mean in person."

"You bastard," said Orhan with a smile that hung from his wide mouth in a leer. "I can read your filthy mind. You want to go over there and console her. What I mean is, put the meat to her."

"I wouldn't do that," said Levent. "What do you think I am?"

"I know what you are," he said. "You're a friend of Fish."

"What's this woman's name? C'mon, Oral. You can't hold back just because you want to pay her a visit yourself."

"I *can't?*"

"I'll let you know how it works out," said Levent. "Prepare the ground for further ventures, so to speak."

"You randy bastard," he said again, his voice filled with admiration. "Melanie won't have a damned thing to do with you. You're not her type."

"Melanie," said Levent. "She sounds exotic. Foreign and to my liking. Now the last name. Address. Phone number."

Orhan took out a small address book from his pocket and handed it to Levent, after taking a moment to mark it at the correct page. It was a nasty thing with the entries in atrocious handwriting. It had obviously seen many bouts of drinking and probably some wenching.

"You're lucky I have the key to your future in a blonde-haired woman," he said with the raki climbing in his hand again. "Fish never used to keep his damned cell phone turned on. I got the number so I could contact him at her place."

"You two must have done a lot of business together."

"Not a lot," he said, belching demurely behind his hand. "But it was important when it came around. You'd be surprised how important direct access to the sea can be for some people."

"Direct," said Levent. "You mean unimpeded."

"Something like that."

It was something like smuggling and no doubt for high value product. "I'd guess you must have been able to expedite some items for Fish. Seaborne items, you being the manager of the marina and all."

Orhan shrugged. "You really don't want to know about that."

"Yes, I do," said Levent. "I have some special items I might want to send and receive without consulting normal channels. It would be worth something to me."

"Something," he said.

Levent thought he should bring in a figure that roughly tallied with the money that had been burnt up in the trunk of Harman's car. He leaned across the table, though there were only two other people in the bar at a table near the door.

"Let's say I could go ten thousand lira for small packages. A bit more if they have extra weight."

"And if I could arrange that?"

"I have to know the ship," said Levent. "Turkish flag?"

"A couple of those," he said. "I've got one American, too. Turk with a green card. He's as good as done for anything up to and including Malta."

"I'd have to talk to him," said Levent. "It doesn't have anything to do with me trusting you or the other way around. I want to know the man who'll handle my goods. I have to look him in the eye just like I'm looking at you."

"That's scary as hell," said Orhan with a sharp burst of laughter. "But I might be able to manage what you want. He puts back in tomorrow. At least he should. This man is a full-bore rakici, but reliable for all that."

"What time tomorrow?"

"Call me in the late afternoon," said Orhan. "I'll want to talk to him first, then we'll see if he wants to talk to you."

"Fair enough, Oral."

"You can call me Double O," he said with a smile. "All the boys do, you know."

CHAPTER 14

As Levent drove away from Yalikavak, he tried to sort the sequence of events that had brought Harman to his flaming end. He had left DenizKum after enquiring about a Frenchman named Varan. Driving to South Beach—not an unusual part of his day—he visited his apartment to check on the heroin. He then drove up the coast road to Yalikavak Marina. He spent a short time with Orhan, probably arranging for the heroin to be expedited from the country aboard ship.

Harman's last day was now a progression, though knowing its parts did not tell Levent enough. Somewhere, Harman had picked up a green Peugeot that followed him the three kilometers from the marina to the store. It did not make sense that the young man who was probably French waited for his victim in the parking lot. He might have seen Harman at the marina, since the killer had proven access to a ship.

But Levent doubted that. Spotting Harman at the marina meant luck had played a key role in the killer's plans. Not as likely. Harman had known something that told him to be wary of a French connection. It was more logical that the killer tailed Harman's Mercedes from a place he knew Harman would be. Routine was the thing that favored the ambusher. That suggested the DenizKum office or South Beach.

As Levent turned from the main road onto a smaller one that led into the mountains on a steep grade, he began to see South Beach as the starting point. Harman, an experienced man, would have been alert for a car tailing him. A car following all the way from Bodrum would not have been hard to spot, but the distance from South Beach to Yalikavak and then to the convenience store was closer. The roads were hilly, allowing the Peugeot to keep back, hug the rises and be less easily seen.

Levent's theory did not have to be correct. The killer had friends who could have acted as accomplices. Two cars switching off a tail were much more effective than one. Recruiting another man off the ship could explain how Harman had been handled so efficiently.

Harman had spent so little time at Yalikavak that he was not befuddled by raki. That was more than Levent could say for himself. He had nursed three drinks while Orhan threw off what seemed like his usual five.

The road he traveled was better than the one that had led him to Reema, paved with asphalt, but erratically. The surface had been patched too many times and the rocks that found their way down the slopes were a menace. Constantly winding and switching back, Levent gave the road complete attention. Even so, he almost ran headlong into a large herd of goats as he came out of a turn two-thirds of the way up the mountain.

Big animals as dark as night. Big wild eyes and man-like beards. They did not want to give way to a vehicle, but the goatherd talked them aside. He was a dark man with wild eyes and trousers that had been patched so often they told the history of his travels on the mountain.

"How far to Yelkenli?" asked Levent.

"In a car, I can't say."

"Let's say walking."

"Two cigarettes," he said, holding up one finger. "Not more."

"Who's the head man up there?"

"It don't take much to look after the village these days," said the goatherd. "But you can ask for Yeter. About this time he's at the coffee house. At any time, I'd say."

No last name. Those were unnecessary in a village. Levent said thanks and waited until the man passed to roll up the window. The stench of the goats was so penetrating that the first breaths he drew did not clear the air.

Levent did not roll down the window until he reached the top of the hill, where the mountain air cleansed itself.

* * *

Yelkenli was the heartland in miniature, a village much larger than Zamir, where tradition ruled before it came to be called Islam. It was a substantial settlement, forty houses, with a general store, what seemed like a small mill, and a coffee house. The women wore headscarves, but not as a political symbol. Most of them still wore the wide pants when they went into the fields to work after they had worked the morning feeding their families. The head of the family, after he was fed, repaired to the coffee house to settle the affairs of the world.

That the world paid no attention to the decisions reached at the coffee house did not matter. It was the place of the man to rule, and if he became bored by his rule, he headed to Bodrum or another city, where he took a job. Even so, he kept his position as the arbiter of all decisions. This was the reason for the rise of the Islamic parties in the land of Ataturk. The ways of the village would be brought to the city by hook or crook and the vote.

The men in the villages were used to big families because that was the way it had always been. If the first wife gave out, they found another, so the breeding continued. It had a purpose when multiple sons were needed to work the land, but now the numbers mounted without reference to time or machines. Sometimes, when the crops were lean and the wife proved more fertile than they had thought and the house was overrun with children, they called a halt to the family. The last child could be called many things, but he was often given the name Yeter.

Enough.

Levent found Yeter at the coffee house as promised. He was a small wizened man of sixty years with more gum than tooth and ears as big as hands. He sat alone at one of the tables to receive pleas from petitioners, and he did not doubt that Levent was one of those. Everyone had seen the Honda pull up at the cafe. If there had been a bigger event in Yelkenli this week, they pretended not to notice. So did Yeter.

"Will you have something to drink?" he asked, throwing his gruff voice around the tables like a dare. "I'm sorry we have no alcoholic drinks here, Onur Bey."

"Coffee," said Levent. "No sugar."

"A good choice," said Yeter, who had blinked mightily when he shook Levent's hand. "You should not drink raki so early in the day. It's bad for the prostate. You'll be pissing all over your shoes before you know it."

"I keep a good stream to my piss with pumpkin seeds," said Levent, who seemed to remember that as a remedy. "My work sometimes gets in the way of my good health."

"Drinking alcohol is work?"

"At times."

"There are many people who would like such a job," he said with a smile that showed more stumps than teeth. "What do you inspect as an Inspector?"

"Usually it's murder," said Levent. "But I'm on holiday."

"We never had a murder in this village," he said as if he would not permit it. He would also never ask Levent's purpose in coming to the village. With a show of pride, he looked around the tables at his neighbors, all male. "We had a suicide last year." Yeter sniffed. "A woman."

Levent looked around the tables at their neighbors. All the men were the age of Yeter within a decade. They did not seem ever to have been young.

"Suicides are a problem in villages," said Levent. "I think it's because the women find no men to take up with. They don't see a promising future."

Yeter nodded gravely. He lit his second cigarette since Levent sat down and began to work on it with vigor. "The young men leave the villages," he said. "We used to say whenever we had a terrible event, like an eclipse of the sun or a great storm, that the young men in the village were fucking farm animals, especially the sheep, which may have offspring that favors neither. But we don't say that any more. The young men go to the cities to find animals to fuck."

"And to work."

"For wages," said Yeter with scorn. "Wages they spend on whores when they should be marrying the young women here and making them pregnant. That's what you need to know about keeping women happy."

"I understand the drain on manpower," said Levent. "But the loss from Yelkenli seems worse than most. Where do all the young men go?"

"Bodrum," he said as speaking the name of the devil. "Look around these hills, Onur Bey. They were once covered with trees and the next mountain, too. Bodrum took them for ships. To make the wind ships. They took them until there were no more trees, and then they took the young men who no longer had work in the trees."

While the waiter brought the coffee, Levent looked around the village as if to confirm. He had seen some small trees coming in, and some trees and bushes around the village, but trees of the size that could make ships he saw none.

Maybe one. It stood beside the antique sawmill. He was glad one mystery was solved. Yelkenli had cut the wood that made the sailing vessels until there was no more. They should change the name of the village now. It should be called Bad Coffee.

"When was the last time you cut wood for ships?"

Yeter shook his head. He pulled on one of his huge ears as if it was the luck that had deserted him. "Twenty years ago," he said. "It may be more."

"*Twenty* years?"

"At least," he said twisting the ear again. "I remember my youngest son was born about that time. He's twenty-six years now. Or twenty-five."

Or eighteen. Levent was determined to narrow this down. Every time he looked into the past he found something that only led him further on, but at some point it would end. And make sense, too.

"I'm told most of the men go to Bodrum to work for one firm. DenizKum."

"That may be true," he said. "Two of my sons worked for them at one time. But now they're with another firm. This one doesn't pay as good but they pay on time, which I hear was a problem with the other."

"It wasn't a small problem," said Levent. "Did the man who ran the firm come up to the village to recruit workers?"

"No need for that," said Yeter. "They knew where to go. The old woman sent word up when men were wanted. And they answered."

"Old woman?"

"Valide Hanim," he said scornfully. "She was born and raised in this village until her husband came and took her out like a load of green wood. He was a big operator, an engineer for the ships that robbed us of our birthright. But still I was glad when he used her up and went with another woman."

What Levent was hearing sounded remarkably like the family history that Eren had told about Turan. His mother had been a village woman whom his father divorced. When the father's work gave out, which may have been the time Yelkenli went bare, he married a woman from Istanbul. The son, of course, would not leave his mother. There was no way a Turkish mother could be left behind.

"So Valide was responsible for the young men leaving," said Levent. "She never really abandoned the village. She provided, so to speak."

"She provided cheap labor, that's all," said Yeter. "The old bitch lives in the big castle on the hill with her rich son, but that ain't enough to satisfy her. I'll wager she was getting something for every head she brought in from this village. She always took what she could as long as she could, and that was as long as she had an ass to shake without knocking the whole tree down. But she was a fine-looking woman when she was young. I remember."

Levent listened closely, because Turan lived in a castle on a hill outside the city and his mother was still alive. "It's not every engineer who comes to an out-of-the-way place like this to find his bride."

"Like I said, we wasn't so out of the way for them that wanted what we had. And her man wanted it. More than anyone, he was the one who stripped this mountain bare. After that, his son came up to do the same thing."

"His son Turan."

"He has to have a name and I guess that's his," said Yeter as if he was speaking of a thief. "He was the captain of a ship, too. One of the last cuttings we had went to him for his boat. He was a man who dreamed—I'll give him that—and what he got from God's green pasture was that there was money to be made in diving. He made some for a while around Bodrum, then went on to other places. I don't know exactly where, but it was Arabs he went with. They made a fortune, some say, in the sand-sea. That's what Arabs call the desert, you know."

Levent wondered what he meant by Arabs. Probably, it was anyone with money who was not a Turk. "They weren't drilling for oil, were they?"

"They made no holes in the land," said Yeter as if speaking to a dunce. "They was divers in the water."

Sand sea. DenizKum. Levent knew this oaf had said something he did not quite understand. The past never seemed to die completely with these people. They carried it with them in name if not deed.

"About what time would all this have happened, Yeter?"

"The year my youngest son was born," he said. "I told you that, and I think you should listen to what people say."

The gunsmith had said that Panter ran with divers when he was in Bodrum twenty-some years ago. This information seemed to fit. It might fit better if Levent found another old man who knew the town from the modern beginning.

"Do you know anyone who could fill me in on Bodrum in those days," asked Levent. "It was a long time ago."

"I don't know anyone who ain't pissing on his shoes," said Yeter, looking at his cheap new sandals. "A man goes down to Bodrum with a thirst, and it turns into raki every time. I shouldn't have to tell you that."

"I need a name," said Levent. "I'll take him into the toilet and shake him down myself if it comes to that."

"You're a desperate man."

"I'm an Inspector of Homicide. It's the same thing."

"You should learn to relax with your life," said Yeter, sitting back as if he would go nowhere for the rest of the day. "Finish your coffee so as not to insult the cook. Have a smoke. I've told you all that any man can."

* * *

Levent left Yelkenli feeling that Yeter had told him useful things, but perhaps not the most important. He could have supplied the name of a man with a memory as good as his own— if he had wanted. He could have spoken more directly to Levent's questions. Village philosophers were as common as village idiots, but if the past was the key to understanding the present, Levent had fallen short.

Going down the mountain and nearly at the halfway mark, the cell phone rang. Levent pulled off the road before he took the call, knowing that at this point attention to the road and the case were the same.

A stranger's voice came over the line in a noisy way that blamed isolation for its problems. Levent let the car drift at the side of the road until the noise on the line cleared and he found that his caller was Ali Berman. He was the man who had preceded Harman as general manager of DenizKum.

His voice was cheerful enough for a man who sold second homes in a good market, though he may have been trying to make up for not returning Levent's previous calls.

"Mister Berman, I suppose you've heard about the death of Nadir Panter."

"Yes, I have."

Levent did not ask from whom. "I'm calling about the recommendation you made that put him in your place as general manager at DenizKum."

"Yes," he said. "I did that."

"You must have known Panter well."

"Indeed."

"Then I don't understand how you could have recommended him," said Levent sharply. "Are you telling me you knew him well enough to overlook the fact that he was wanted for drug trafficking in England?"

Silences were easy to fill with images of wonder and surprise. Levent's ran the gamut before Berman's voice returned with less than half the cheer.

"I didn't know that," he said. "Not anything like that."

"From where did you know Mister Panter? It wasn't England? Could it have been Cyprus, where he's wanted for money laundering and fleeing an indictment?"

"Not there either," he said.

"New York?" asked Levent. "He was there for some time, blackmailing his countrymen who forgot to renew their visas."

"No," said Berman quickly. "I knew him in Istanbul."

"As what?"

"A friend," he said.

"Friends like that can lead you into deep water," said Levent. "He was associated with criminal elements in Istanbul, too. Was he your neighbor, perhaps?"

"Yes," he said. "In Florya."

"Mister Berman, I'll give you a chance to reconsider. If I keep hearing lies, my next call will be to the Jandarma. They'll pick you up and hold you in jail until I get there to question you. I'm not sure when that will be, but not for several days."

Another silence. When his voice returned, all the salesman's cheer was lost. "I was only trying to help," he said.

Was trying. That was not the same as is trying. It was better. It was almost as good as cooperation.

"Are you saying that you were trying to help when you made the recommendation to hire Panter?"

"Yes. I was trying to help him."

"Not because he was your friend, Mister Berman. Tell me what he was to you, or what he was to someone else."

"This is not easy," said Berman very quietly. "I know you're the police, but these people are more than the police."

"Who are they?"

"I don't know them and I don't want to," he said. "I was having dinner in Oludeniz yesterday after being out at a *site*. I was dirty from climbing around the construction and when I came into the restaurant I ordered a drink, then went to the men's room. Two of them followed me in, and I knew I wasn't going to get out of the stinking place unless I agreed to what they wanted."

"Tell me what that was."

"It was a couple of things and none of them very much," he said. "It's just not worth your life, or even a beating, to say no to people like that over something so small. The one was as big as the door and the other kept mumbling, telling me how no one ever said no to them and everybody worked with them because they were the right sort."

"You mean the right animal," said Levent. "The wolf."

"I'd say so. Those animals were in that shit house with me. So I agreed to say I'd recommended Panter as my replacement."

"But you really didn't do that."

"I never met the man until he showed up to take my place," said Berman. "I can't say we became fast friends in a week."

"What else did you agree to say?"

"It wasn't much. A negative. They wanted me not to talk about the company."

"Gray Wolf?"

"No," he said. "The other. Yelkenli. I told them not to worry. I didn't know anything about it."

"Were you telling the truth?"

"Pretty much," he said. "I really didn't have anything to do with them except for one time."

"What happened then?"

"I received a call that was switched from Sultan at Bozkurt to a man at Yelkenli," he said. "I'd been up to the village called Yelkenli that day, asking questions out of curiosity, but I especially wanted to know why all the workers had to come from there. One toothless old fellow told me it all had to do with a ship that burned out in Bodrum harbor one night. Burnt all the way to the water. It seems there was a scandal connected with it."

Now Levent knew why he had been stymied in Yelkenli by a toothless old man named Yeter. "A scandal?"

"A scandal in my business is anything that distracts a buyer from his wallet," said Berman. "This fell in the same category. That man on the phone was convincing when he said I should keep my mouth shut. Forget what I heard in Yelkenli. I wasn't even sure it was serious until he made it that way by insisting."

"As if it was serious to him?"

"Yes."

"So the vessel and scandal were important," said Levent, knowing it could be important to the case. "When did the ship burn? Was it recently?"

"No," said Berman as if he was sure. "It was a while ago. Long before I got to Bodrum, probably twenty years in the past. I suppose you could find out if you really looked into it. I tried until I got that call—and probably that was the reason I got it. I didn't want to push anything after that. Talking to that man was the closest I came to being scared—until last night."

CHAPTER 15

Levent was down the mountain, passing through the out-skirts of Gundogan, when the commandant called. Metin's voice touched excitement like a combat boot, something that Levent had never heard before.

"Onur, I have news. We put reports out to everyone at sea about that purple-striped ship, and we just had our first buzz. The captain of one of the ferries to Rhodes thinks he might have seen the vessel in a cove near the head of Marmaris Bay when he was coming in."

"How can we be sure?"

"I have a helicopter coming in ten minutes," said Metin. "We're going out at once, but I don't know if we can fly into the cove directly. It's rugged in that area, sheer cliffs. We might have to take a boat in."

"As long as you don't let that ship get away."

"Where are you?"

"Coming in on the road to Turkbuku," said Levent. "You'll have to go airborne without me."

"Seems a shame if this is our target," he said. "With all the work you've done, you should be there to handle the cuffs."

"It's your case, Metin. I don't like helicopters, and I have an appointment in twenty minutes to interview Harman's mistress."

"He had one of those, too?"

"That's what I was told," said Levent. "I was also told that an event in the past might have some bearing on the case. It hap-pened some time ago. A ship burnt out in Bodrum harbor."

"I heard about at least one," said Metin. "But it happened long before I came to this post."

"A lot of this investigation seems to be heading that way," said Levent. "All I'm sure of is that it will have a bearing on this case. A strong one. But I need someone to fill in the details."

"I'll look around for a source," said the commandant. "There's got to be someone still alive who wasn't buried with his Yeni raki by now."

"I'd be grateful if you can find a live body," said Levent. "You'll be sure to keep me up with the chase."

Metin hung off promising to relay anything of importance. Levent hated missing the end game more than he would admit. Credit for the arrest did not matter, but being there to close all the doors was another thing.

Levent was thinking of the things that could go wrong—and the ship that might not be the right one—as he made the lazy turn into Turkbuku. Coming again to the place was like taking his memories through their paces. Slow holiday paces.

Years ago, he and Emine had rented a house here within yards of the shore, which in those days was two docks jutting into a quiet bay. It was a Blue Flag Beach, if anyone bothered with colors then. These days, Levent could not afford the rent on a small hotel room or apartment in Turkbuku. It was a strange how the place had come to be what it was, but these things followed a pattern of novelty and discovery, moving outward from the city to the most distant point of the peninsula.

There were no more places to discover since Bodrum had filled completely with tourism. Turkbuku, a tiny village, was now a busy town with cushioned beaches, venues for entertainment, and valet parking, too.

It also had a traffic jam that Levent avoided by referencing the past, turning up the hill to the *site* where Melanie Porcher had her home. He flashed his badge as he passed through the gate of the gated community, and found an illegal parking space not far from the number that was hers.

* * *

The woman who answered the door was not the most attractive Levent had seen this day, and that included the village women. Melanie Porcher was in her late forties, he guessed, though he could have been wrong by a decade. She did have blonde hair that seemed natural, but life had deserted it, and her complexion had taken on the same wan tone. Perhaps she had been crying.

Her face seemed puffy, though not chafed. Her pale blue eyes were surprisingly frank.

"You're the inspector," she said slowly, still holding onto the door. "I must say I'm surprised they sent someone around."

She had not been surprised to hear that Panter was dead when Levent called to set up an appointment. Pinar at DenizKum had told her about it when she enquired after him. That made her the only human being who noted his absence with enough curiosity to pick up a phone.

"Onur Levent," he said, offering his hand and receiving something warm but less than vital. "I'm investigating Panter's death, though the Jandarma have control here."

"Rather have you," she said. "I've been in this country five years coming and going, but my Turkish isn't where it should be."

She moved away from the doorway with careful steps, leaving Levent to follow her inside. The front room of her apartment was an open plan more European than Turkish, but the furnishings seemed more Turkish than any native would have, especially in Bodrum. A long divan close to the floor, bracketed by two small end tables, made it seem like a village house. She had even hung a kilim on the wall between a ceramic plaque and a ghastly painting of Bodrum harbor by night. In it everything that was not black was flame red.

She sat down on the divan under the painting. On the table stood a tumbler half filled with whiskey that had once been taller. Levent hoped his coming had not caused her to go into the bottle too far. Whatever her state of mind, she did not offer to share.

"Sit down," she said, taking up the whiskey and putting a long measure down. "I haven't had a chance to tidy the place. Actually, I had plenty of time, but didn't do it. Housekeeping's not high in my priorities today."

"I understand," said Levent, sitting in an armchair to her right. "This must have been a great shock to you."

"And if I said no?"

"I'd be interested in hearing the reason."

"I told you I've been in this country a while," she said, her voice slightly slurred. "I know how things are."

"How are things?"

"This isn't a third world country," she said as she took another drink. "I mean, you're not on the official UN list of basket cases."

"I'm not sure we shouldn't be," said Levent. "Someone might have made an administrative error."

"That's funny," she said, carefully putting her glass on the table as if it was still full. "Fish always said Turks had a sense of humor if you got past the mustaches. He was right about that and some other things, too. Shave the damned thing off and what do you find but a human being under it."

"I'm sure he was considerate with you."

"Inspector, I like you, even when you're wrong. But don't think you have to spare my feelings. If you a question, ask."

Levent thought about that, but the best beginning he could find was eccentric. "Do you know why he was called Fish?"

"Sure," she said, slurring through the word like a brush fire. "He was a diver, the best diver in the Aegean when he was young—and not bad now. The people who went out with him called him Fish. What else could you call a man who was better in the water than out?"

Levent did not want to tell her about the name Yunus, or disturb her perceptions, but he wondered how many men could be the best diver in the Aegean. He was gathering candidates.

"He must have been a fine athlete," said Levent. "There are certainly some very good ones around here."

"Kids," she said with scorn. "If you're talking of a mature man, Fish was what you'd like to have. He could go down forty meters and still keep his air."

"He must have learned to dive early," said Levent. "Not many pick up skills like that when they're his age."

"He wasn't *that* old, Inspector." Melanie shook her head hard. "Of course he learned to dive when he was young. He was one of the original Libyan Pirates, if you must know. They started out in Bodrum, taking what they could out of the water, then went to every place in the Mediterranean where they could get a visa. That's not such an easy thing to do for Turks."

"Fish seemed to have confided in you a lot."

"Inspector," she said wearily. "Do you want to ask me if I killed him, or do we just go on like this?"

"Did you kill him, Melanie?"

"No," she said. "I wanted to from time to time."

"Why?"

"His attitude," she said, tipping her glass to Levent. "We were not Romeo and Juliet—too old for that—but we found some space to play with the idea. Fish didn't want to play after a while. He was a man. I'll never forgive him for that."

"Melanie, you're not supplying enough reason for murder."

"Are you sure of that?"

"I'd like to think so, or we're all in trouble," said Levent. "Who were the Libyan Pirates?"

She shook her head as she looked deep into her glass. It was suddenly empty. She seemed to realize that with an electric start. "I wish I could tell you who they were," she said. "Really. It was a name Fish used when he talked about his friends in the rip-snorting salad days. I have to think the Libyan Pirates are not exactly the same as Angelina Jolie. But I could be wrong."

"I think you're not," said Levent. "I'd say Fish came to Bodrum, where he spent his early years, and that brought back memories. I'd say when he found you he relived those memories. Same place, a different love. A better one, I'm sure."

"You're in gold medal territory now, Inspector. I like this."

"Did he talk about other places?" asked Levent. "Other than Bodrum and Libya, that is."

"I don't know if the Libyan Pirates ever set foot in Libya," she said, rising and turning her back to him. She did not continue talking when she reached the small sideboard on the opposite wall and poured the glass half full again. He did not know why she stopped at half unless it was an alcoholic's way of limiting the take. As long as she could rise to the sideboard and pour a consistent amount, she was sober in her mind.

"Do the Libyan Pirates ever have to have been in Libya?" she asked of no one. "That's a deeply troubling question, Inspector. Fish always tried to impress me with how sophisticated he was. I suppose that's another way of saying he was a man. It's certainly a way of saying he was a Turkish man dating a foreigner. You never know what lies really are until you've been in a tangle like that."

"I'll apologize for him," said Levent. "How did you manage to get together?"

"A summer party," she said without referring to her drink for memory. "My neighbor across the way had one going for the solstice celebration. She's English, too, a committed witch. The Wicca kind and the solstice is their high holiday. I'd like to say the festivities got out of hand, but they didn't. We were sitting around the barby with our hands full when this big-shouldered Turk showed up as if he had been invited. I think he had been, but barely. A couple of days before, he tried to talk Cecile into one of those disastrous places over in Gumushluk, but she had the good sense to walk away. He had the good sense to keep her phone number."

"I see."

"Don't see too much," she said, taking another drink that moved the glass closer to the bottom again. "Fish was good enough to talk himself into my phone number, and patient enough to wait a day before he called. I was surprised. It was the first time I'd met a Turk in Bodrum who had a steady job. So that was impressive. Fish had money and he spent it without looking at the checks. We closed the marina restaurant down and stayed on for the music. Fatih Erkoch, I remember. He had a repertoire of old songs that went from the forties all the way to the zeroes. Just the thing for us."

"It wouldn't be the first romance Fatih started," said Levent. "Usually they're his own."

"That's absolutely the most charming thing about this country," she said with a smile too broad. "People *want* so to be in love."

"Even if they know better, yes."

She laughed too loud. "That's the first time you really sounded like a policeman," she said. "I suppose we can't get away from what we are."

"That's true," said Levent. "Panter did a lot of things. Some were not as useful as they might have been. Tell me, did he ever give you anything to hold?"

"I don't know what you mean," she said. "He gave me several presents. That rug on the wall, for instance."

"It's handsome," said Levent. "But I was thinking of something quieter. A package that you weren't supposed to open?"

"No early Christmas presents," she said. "You seem to be comfortable with the idea that Nadir was doing something he shouldn't have outside the law."

"Not necessarily," said Levent. "Policemen like to push the limits to see what topples over. Did you ever meet any of his friends?"

"If he had one, that would have been a crowd," she said. "I was disappointed that he didn't introduce me to anyone he knew. I would have liked meeting other Turks. It's not as easy as everyone seems to think."

A mistress was what Harman wanted, and all he seemed to want. Levent would like an opening to Europe. "Did he ever mention Frenchmen? Or women?"

Melanie tipped up the glass to look into it as she yearned toward the sideboard in decision mode. "French in this lifetime, no, but he did talk of Paris as if he knew it. As if it was home ground. Marseilles, but especially Paris. I'm sure it was mixed up with the Libyan Pirates. They were international. Nadir told me that at some point in their travels they anchored a houseboat in the Seine. From what I gathered, it seemed like an important party boat. Every loose woman in the city found her way on board."

"Really," said Levent. "That's interesting."

"For you, Inspector. Not for me. The numbers that Nadir threw out were truly Turkish. In the thousands. Of women. He was trying to impress me again, and he didn't think I'd mind the company. Or the talk of money. There were piles of it that the Pirates made. I couldn't understand what they were diving for. Shellfish? Sponges? Sunken treasure? Whatever it was stuck to their hands. They took the booty to Paris and spent it. Yes, that's very definitely the way it was."

Levent did not think that Harman ever spent it all. If he was a party animal, the party ended at the teller's window. Was his time with the Libyan Pirates the key to anything more?

"Did he ever mention any names from his days in Paris?"

"No," she said quickly. Then she corrected herself slowly. "Wait. I'm thinking of something. It's maybe Sevim. Yes, I remember that name. Nadir mentioned it one night when he was drunk. Very, uncharacteristically drunk. He seemed to love Sevim as only a Turk can love another man. Like a brother's brother. But he was sad when he talked about him. I guessed that Sevim was dead. Or had died. Possibly in a diving accident, but certainly before his time."

What Levent had was another name. A new one that apparently belonged to a dead man. Sevim did not mean anything, but it could mean—my love. It was hard to reconcile that concept with Harman, even while sitting with his lover.

"Did Panter ever mention anything about a ship that burnt in Bodrum harbor?"

Melanie rose again to the whiskey bottle, walking to the sideboard with exaggerated precision. She kept her concentration on the act of replenishment, half full and no more, until slowly she moved the focus to the divan and the painting that hung over it.

"No," she said. "Nothing like that. Nadir didn't even like the painting. He wanted to take it down and buy another. I told him no. I'd bought it at an exhibition at Yaghane and was attached to it."

Of all the things she had said, Levent found that hardest to accept. Fondness for that painting spoke of a moribund imagination, but the woman who had loved Harman might have snakes in her head. Disliking that painting was the first thing the victim and Levent agreed on.

"Did he tell you why he didn't like it?"

"The colors," she said, hefting the whiskey glass. "They're all wrong, he said. Bodrum harbor never looked like that, even on its darkest night."

CHAPTER 16

On his way back to Bodrum, Levent took a call from the commandant, who said they had found the purple-striped ship that flew the tricolor of France from her stern. Metin had talked the helicopter pilot into putting them down on a narrow strip of land near the base of the big mountain, something that he regretted.

"I know what you mean about helicopters now. I was damned sick before we got on the boat that took us out to the ship. It may be a coincidence, but that's where things went wrong."

"You mean it's not the right ship?"

"It is, Onur. But the man we're looking for isn't on board. He was never aboard, according to the ship's owner. She's a decent-looking woman who isn't decent in any other way. She didn't want us searching the vessel for a stowaway, but we insisted. She's still screaming about all the things she'll have her embassy do to us."

"Arrest them," said Levent. "Diplomats exist to explain away mistakes. And we know this isn't a mistake."

"But we've nothing on the woman or her passengers," said the commandant. "As far as we know, the Jeune Revanche is a sea-taxi."

"The idea is to get them to talk, Metin. That works best when they're taken out of their normal environment into one we control."

"Jail will only work for a little while, Onur. The thing it's guaranteed to be is a career ender. And I won't have the helicopter for transport back to Bodrum."

Metin really was wary of arresting foreign citizens. The Minister of Tourism must have given specific instructions about that. "We can make all that work for us," said Levent. "Pile them in a Jandarma van and make sure your men carry automatic weapons. Drive them fast over the worst roads and bring them to Bodrum."

"That's at least three hours," said the commandant. "I can't do it faster and I won't know how to explain to my superiors why I kidnapped these people."

"They're suspects in a drug investigation," said Levent. "The vessel has been impounded until a search is done down to the keel. Your people will understand that it can't be done in minutes. And don't worry about getting our prisoners here quickly. Slow but ragged is better. Don't answer any of their questions. Don't ask any. Make them aware that they're not on the same planet as they were until today. Let them be uncertain about what's ahead."

"And if I say yes?"

"You can say anything you like, Metin. It's your case."

"What I mean is, you'll be there when we come in."

"I'll be in the city soon."

It took more persuasion for the commandant to move over the line into administrative rebellion, but that happened as Levent entered the four-lane straightaway into Bodrum. Metin also had one good contact to share before he hung off.

"I found a man for you to talk to about the old days," he said. "He's a sea-captain, retired to his home on the hill by the military barracks. Actually, I just about retired him and he's grateful he didn't see the inside of a prison cell. If you can get to his place before night falls, he'll probably be sober."

That was good news and convenient. Levent could swing into the city without fighting early evening traffic. Coming out, he would be on his way to Bitez and his wife. He had called her twice, reporting his movements to the only person who mattered. Her tone was friendly, something that Levent did not understand until he learned she had a special outing planned for tonight—a large dinner party with most of their friends. He was expected to show.

Levent would make an appearance, knowing that divorce was an expensive option. Emine agreed to meet him at the restaurant and would find a ride with Zekeriya Tek. Levent was happy when things seemed to break right. It would take Metin all of three hours to find his way back with his cargo from the ship.

* * *

Enis Kutman lived in a small *site* on the brow of a hill over-looking the western side of the city, so Metin had probably not taken a piece of the money the captain had put away for his retirement. That was encouraging.

Kutman answered the door himself, though Levent saw a maid in the kitchen as they passed by, beginning to prepare the evening meal. The captain was a man of sixty-five with a grey beard and a head of hair stark white and tied back in a high ponytail. He was not happy to greet Levent, but warmed measurably when he learned his visitor did not come from the Jandarma. The hand he had given to Levent was still strong and his movements vigorous.

"Commandant Comert called," said Kutman. "He didn't go into details. I really don't know who he wants me to put to the shit house this time."

"We're not doing that today, Captain. I'd like to borrow your knowledge of old Bodrum for a while. That's all."

"You're lucky," he said with a grin that closed down on itself. "That's most of what I have in my head these days. Ask me what happened last night and you won't get a good answer because the deck's been shuffled too much."

They came out on his balcony, which like most in the south was wide and deep and meant for display. In the distance, dusk began to slip over the city, transforming the huge castle at the head of the harbor into a figment of the medieval. The masts and antennae of the marina sprung up before it like spears carried into battle. Far off but much too near, a bandwagon passed blaring rock music, summoning the faithful to one of the discotheques.

"We won't be talking about any of this garbage, I hope," said Kutman, waving the back of his hand toward the city below. "It grieves me to see what they've done to this town, though we all knew it would happen some time. I spent most of my life thinking it never would, but wishing in my black heart for god's gift of tourists. I just wasn't prepared when the shit came down so fast and hard."

"The city was different in the eighties," said Levent. "I remember. Nothing but fishing boats—maybe yours was one—and others that went out diving."

"Not too many of those," he said.

"I'm thinking of one in particular," said Levent. "The Libyan Pirates had a ship. They were the pioneers in sponge diving, I hear."

"Not really," he said. "We had bell divers here in the sixties and seventies."

"Let's say we move into the eighties," said Levent. "Free divers."

"We didn't have any free divers then," he said. "Those were still the days of a locked-down economy. Not many tanks could be bought anywhere, and those you could find were hell to refill. It made for a strange business. We had a garage owner pumping oxygen in the tanks for a while. It worked fine until one day he sucked up some carbon monoxide by mistake."

"So how did the Libyan Pirates dive?"

"Surface air pumped down through a tube," he said. "It works. Restricts your movement, but you can stay down a good while. The Pirates dove the waters around here before they were known by any name. Then Sevim had the idea of building his own ship to his own design and sailing to virgin waters."

"Sevim?" Levent pulled the reference from Melanie's nasal voice when she told of Harman's secret guilt. "He was the leader of the Pirates?"

"In his way," said Kutman fondly. "Sevim was young but smart. He'd been to college in Istanbul, but he didn't put that over on anyone. I remember he used to whistle tunes no one knew. Classical music. Hell of a man in spite of that. I never heard a bad word said, and you'll never hear one from me."

"So he built a ship in Bodrum. Special order."

"It was that," said Kutman. "After Sevim had the wood brought down from the hills, he put it in a bakery to dry out over the winter. You had to adapt in those days. No seasoned timber; make some."

"The timber came from the mountains," said Levent. "From Yelkenli?"

"As I remember, yes," he said. "Best place for timber, those days. When they finally put the boat together in the spring—nice design, double ender—they did some diving around here to see how she bore up. The Meltem ran fine. So when they got their documents together, they set sail for Libya."

Meltem—the breeze from the sea. In the Mediterranean it was usually benign—the sailor's friend.

Levent waited while the cook came with coffee for him and the first raki of the night for the captain. Or what seemed like the first. Kutman did not have the glow of alcohol around him, but his cheeks had the leathery texture that the sun and raki brought on until skin could best be called hide. He greeted the milk-white drink in the tall slim glass with ceremony, taking a long appreciative draught.

"So that's how the Libyan Pirates got their name," said Levent. "They went to North Africa."

"It was a hell of a silly name considering that they never did any diving in Libya," said Kutman as he put his drink down on the table. "When they got there, they found that the government wasn't about to let foreigners dive in their waters. Couldn't buy a permit. The way I heard it, they almost starved to death trying to wait Qaddafi out. They were begging on the streets, stealing, whatever. They were Turks. They knew how to survive. Then Sevim had the idea of sailing out for Tunisia. That was the key. They talked to the government and got everything they were supposed to have in Libya. They even talked the Tunisians out of some dive boats. All they had to do in return was promise to train the locals to dive."

"They did that?"

"I suppose," said Kutman. "But they worked those waters for several years, and they always took new divers from here when they went out again, so I don't know about the Tunisians. The important thing was, they were making money. Those really were virgin waters for sponges. Sevim and Turan cleaned up."

"Turan," said Levent, who was beginning to see the end of this now. "Turan Yoruk?"

"None other," said Kutman, grimacing as he took up the raki like medicine. "They were partners in the ship from the beginning. Sevim was the lead diver and the man everyone liked to follow. Turan was the one with the business head."

"He still has it," said Levent. "It's bigger now."

"That's what I hear," said Kutman. "I try not to hear too much about that son-of-a-bitch. Even an old man can get pissed off."

"You don't like him?"

"I didn't like him then, and I didn't like what he did later."

"What did he do?"

Kutman's hand pulled his ponytail. "He murdered Sevim."

Levent was not sure he had heard the captain correctly. He had spoken succinctly, but murder was something an Inspector of Homicide took as his work from the streets of Istanbul. This was too close.

"Tell me how he murdered Sevim."

"In a way he wouldn't be caught," said Kutman, who had been caught at least once. "He and Sevim weren't much for staying in an Arab country during down times. When winter came, they used to take their sponges to London. After they cashed in, they took themselves to Paris. They were young—we were all young then. They had a load of fresh cash. They partied as long as their money lasted, but Sevim never knew how to keep anything but his dick in his pants and he didn't do that nearly enough. I went up to Paris that last year to pay a visit and get some of the good stuff for myself. I was sure there'd be plenty of the good stuff—and I found as much as I thought. But that houseboat was sitting in the River Seine, and it was a wreck by then. No head, no kitchen, just a five-ton water tank and an engine. Turan had already branched out into better fields. He'd bought a damned pig farm not far away and fermented his own Calvados brandy from the orchards. I could tell they were never going to use that houseboat for another year of partying, and not long after I left, it decided to die. When that happened, Sevim left Paris with a couple of French girls and sailed back to Bodrum."

"Did you ever meet a man named Yunus Harman in Paris?"

"No," said Kutman. "Not there. I saw him around Bodrum, but he'd had enough of diving by then. Someone told me he went to New York later. I couldn't believe that. They told me he'd come back to Bodrum lately, too, but I didn't believe that either. It would take more nerve than he had."

"I believe he found some in the meantime," said Levent. "Harman was here under an assumed name, working as a manager of a construction company until someone set his car on fire in the parking lot of a convenience store. He died there."

"Set him on *fire?*"

"Yes."

Kutman put his hand to his face, stroking both corners of his beard slowly with his fingers and thumb and finding it in the place where it had appeared in the morning mirror. When he finished his dry shave, the captain asked a question in the same slow rhythm.

"Why didn't I hear about this?"

"It was a grisly death in a public place," said Levent. "The Jandarma were told to sit on the news."

"And you're their quiet man," he said in the same slow way.

"I've never been called that before."

"What if I said it was a compliment?" Kutman's face brightened in the way that many men's darkened. "What if I told you that for once justice was done."

"You'd have to explain that, Captain."

"That wouldn't be necessary if you knew how Sevim died. I'll tell you about it, and then you tell me if it makes sense to you."

"I'll give you my opinion."

Kutman drew up his chair, holding the glass of raki with both hands. "Sevim came back to Bodrum, but didn't stay long. I guess he wanted to bring the ship back rather than leave it for the Tunisians to ransack. He went back to Paris for what I don't exactly know. Let's say I do know, but never got her name."

The captain put his glass down on the table again with a long centimeter left in the glass—his way of controlling intake. "He was in Paris for a bit before he came back to Bodrum again. While he was here, he stayed on the boat most of the time, going out on charters in the day and sleeping in the cabin at night. But he was still on a party and drinking a lot—raki first thing in the morning to steady his hand and raki the rest of the day to forget what the morning was like. He never thought he might be in danger, and he wouldn't have known he was anyway. He couldn't hear a thing by that time. All that diving took his hearing, and if you wanted to say anything you'd better come up from the right side and speak real loud. So there were a lot of explanations for what happened."

"There was a fire on the ship," said Levent.

"He burnt alive one night," said Kutman quietly. "It was over a holiday and no one was on board with him. Even if he screamed, no one would have heard him. And he might have been so drunk that he couldn't scream until he was ablaze."

Kutman left the image for Levent to compare. Two deaths by fire separated by twenty-odd years. The symmetry was strong, but could be logically disconnected. The intelligent man often left his mind in the bottle. The deaf man usually slept a drunken sleep. From the west, night filtered over Bodrum harbor as the tourist lights in the castle came on. There was less light in those days when fire consumed the ship.

"Did Sevim smoke cigarettes?"

"Everyone smoked in those days," said Kutman. "Ask me if he ever set himself on fire before."

"But he should have been able to find his way overboard," said Levent. "Water was all around the ship."

"He would have," said Kutman, who put the last of his raki down. "Sevim didn't love that boat half enough to go down to the bottom with it. The only way it made sense was if he couldn't move."

"You think someone made sure of that."

"I know it," he said. "I knew Sevim, so I know it."

If that was true, the symmetry was inevitable. Two men immobilized as the flames took them. If it had been done once, it had been done twice in the same way. Levent waited while the cook appeared with another raki for her captain. He had not called for it. She knew his pace as well as she knew the ingredients of the eggplant salad she placed on the table.

"Did the police investigate the incident?"

"They investigated his death," said Kutman. "After they put their heads together—there wasn't much for brains here in those days—they decided that sure enough he died. They had a list of things that could have caused the fire, but it seemed at some point the bottle gas blew. In the end, they called it an act of God."

"But you don't believe that," said Levent. "You have motive in mind."

"I might have believed all of it if his partner didn't have the boat insured to the limit," he said. "Turan hadn't been around for weeks until he showed up a couple of days before the fire. But he left the day before it happened. And left himself clear."

"Was there bad blood between them?"

"There was always some of that," said Kutman, holding his thumb and index fingers apart, as if enmity could be measured. "You can call it competition, if you like a bigger word. If it was a woman—or who could stay down longest—they came at it as if they were the only two men in the world who had a chance at the prize."

"Who usually won?"

"I wasn't keeping score," said Kutman as if he had done exactly that. "But Sevim was a hell of a good-looking man and a natural athlete. He did things without thinking about them. Turan had to work at it hard. You don't know how that grates on a man unless you are that man."

"Do you know of any specific trouble before the fire?"

"I heard they had a fight about going back to Tunisia," said Kutman. "Turan wanted to keep working the sea, but Sevim had had enough. Diving is hard on the body, all of it, not just the ears. Sevim didn't want to go near the water ever again unless he was on top of it."

"He used the ship for charters," said Levent. "Was there much money to be made in those days?"

"Not a lot," said Kutman grimly. "You don't want to ask me how I came by my retirement. The answer wouldn't be that I made it running tourists out to Black Island for the day. I'd be surprised if that was Turan's idea for getting rich."

"Did he have another idea?"

"He always had ideas for making money," said Kutman, as if that was good but bad. "If you ask me, there was only one way to turn a real profit on that ship. It was the sudden way—the insurance way."

"But he was out of town when the ship burnt," said Levent. "If the fire was set, who do you think did it?"

"I didn't know until today," he said.

That was plain enough. "So you think it was Harman?"

"He was here, and I never knew the reason why," said Kutman. "Always close with Turan, that one. I saw him around town, and I can tell you that a man I know saw Harman at the docks that night. He saw him getting out of a boat before the fire. Then he was gone."

"He left Bodrum?"

"As far as I could tell, he wasn't even at the funeral," said Kutman as if this was the worst accusation. "Of course, I might have missed him in the crowd. A lot of people came to pay their respects because everyone knew Sevim. If they knew him, they liked him. No, they loved him."

"Did Turan come to the funeral?"

"Not that anyone saw," said Kutman, as if offering more proof. "I don't even think the police questioned him. One thing that man always did was put money around with your people. He was a businessman, like I said, and he was moving up in the world at good speed. He sold that pig farm outside Paris for a good price, but not enough to put him over. He wasn't running no charters out of Bodrum. If I knew what his bunghole buddy Harman was doing then, I'd tell you. It was a lot of nothing, we thought."

"What if I told you I had a lead in Harman's death," said Levent. "It points to a young man who should be French."

Kutman had no quick reaction to that statement. He ran his hand through his beard again around the mouth, as if wiping the worst taste of the past away. When he pointed one finger at Levent, he had found something.

"I told you when Sevim came back from France the first time he had a couple of women with him." Kutman shook his head. "One of them was a serious thing, but they both stayed on board the ship. That's more than I'd do and more than they could stand after a while. It wasn't a week or two before they decided they could find better quarters back home."

"Everyone loved Sevim."

"Everyone," said Kutman. "Two women were about what he needed for comfort, but there was only one who showed up at his funeral."

"The serious one?"

"Yes, sir," he said. "Late coming in on a flight and missed everything, including me putting down my three shovels of dirt at the cemetery with the biggest hangover I ever had. The thing we had in common was that this woman was supposed to be sick, too. I didn't see her, but the man at the hotel where she stayed told me it was morning sickness. She was pregnant."

"Do you know her name?"

"Give me a minute," said Kutman, who liked to talk his way back into his long-term memory. "I saw her when I was on the houseboat in Paris, and when she was here for those couple weeks on the ship. As far as I know, Sevim never ran with anyone else when she was around. He was good to her, and I think the other girl there was her cousin. He'd run the boat over to Bardakchi for the day just so they could get their toes wet." Kutman tapped his finger at Levent again. "I wish I could say this for sure, but I think her name was something like Suzanne."

"Suzanne Vardan?"

"Might be," he said. "Not much in this head would hold up in court, but that sounds like what I remember."

"They weren't married, were they?"

"No, and there was something about that, too."

Levent waited until the captain seemed lost in his recollection. "The name Vardan sounds like she could have been Turkish," he said. "An emigrant, possibly."

"She spoke a little Turkish," said the captain. "It was a foreigner's Turkish, but it didn't sound like something a French woman should have." He snapped his fingers quick and loud. "Armenian. That's what she was. That's why she and Sevim got along so well in a mangled language and that's why they were never married. A Turk was too much for her family. When they left this country—and I think they were jewelers in Istanbul—they never planned to return."

"Do you know if she delivered the child?"

"No, Inspector, I don't," said Kutman. "But I'm pretty sure that you do."

CHAPTER 17

With little transition, Levent found himself at the dinner Emine had organized. The restaurant's terrace hung over a quiet bay like a private rampart to the night sky. A giant moon rose slowly over the hills before it began to accelerate. A sailing ship glided toward the dock below, its lights reflected in the black water as if two vessels were approaching. The reflection was the better, incandescent and trembling.

Two long tables had been placed together to handle the crowd of Emine's friends and all were occupied. This was what they had come for. The raki flowed, including Zekeriya Tek's clear and straight up. The meze, always superb here, arrived on the shoulders of waiters in a procession that would only end when the main course of fish was grilled to perfection.

"That's Federico's boat, I'm sure," said Emine, turning her eyes from the husband she had forgiven to the sea. "I don't know what he's doing at this restaurant, since he has his own cook on board ship."

"Italian?"

"Arab," said Emine. "They can be trained to Italian cooking— or any other kitchen—if you're patient."

"This one came trained and house-broken, too," said Eren, who had taken textile design to a new height with a green shirt emblazoned with blue parrots. "Turan had him sent over with a ribbon pinned to his ass. A gift."

"Turan's familiar with Arabs," said Levent. "I understand he spent time in Tunisia when he was young."

"Don't know about that," said Eren, who sat opposite Levent with grilled squid on his fork. "He still does business in North Africa, that's for sure."

"What kind?"

"Foreign trade," said Eren with an insider's smile. "I know he locked in an oil contract with the Libyans last year. Everyone said, 'Oh, you're overpaying at sixty dollars a barrel.' Now that oil is twice the price, Turan looks fine. He's carting it away in his own ships, so he makes a profit twice and most of it hidden. He's reselling the oil, including some to our government. And they're grateful."

"That's how to keep on the good side no matter who's in power," said Zekeriya, again at Emine's side. "This government thinks that if they pray to Allah, they'll be sent a Turan every time. They don't understand he was sent by the Other Guy."

"They'll never understand that," said Levent. "No one does. If we knew who we were dealing with, a lot of the mystery would be gone from life."

"I think I can solve some of the mystery now," said Eren, dropping his voice so it did not carry far. "I talked to a man I know about what you asked yesterday. He seemed knowledgeable. He said that Turan hadn't been allowed to show his face in Bodrum until two years ago. They put a ban on his aging ass, which is remarkable considering all the money he has. The prohibition lasted through several governments. That makes it more remarkable."

"Why the ban?" asked Levent.

"Something that happened years ago," said Eren breezily. "Turan had been partners in a ship with a man who was killed when the ship went down at sea. Or something like that. No one knew that this fellow—"

"Sevim," said Levent.

Eren barely noticed the correction, though he accepted it. "No one knew Sevim had made over his half of the ship to Turan if anything should happen to him. Happen to either, but it didn't happen to Turan, lucky devil. Anyway, Sevim's family was outraged by his death and probably more by the insurance settlement. And they were not without resources. Since they had no proof that Turan had a hand in Sevim's death, they went to one of their cousins—a strong man in Mugla politics. He saw to the ban."

Levent did not believe anyone could be forbidden to enter a city even if it was as medieval as the castle in the harbor. But it would be easy to keep Turan from coming to Bodrum and entering the public eye.

"I wonder what changed?" said Levent. "Turan is obviously back."

"It goes about as you imagine," said Eren. "When the politician died five years ago, Turan began to agitate for his return. After all, Bodrum was his home. Some of his family is still here. But it wasn't until Sevim's mother died last year that things changed. No one was around to keep up the roadblock. It seemed Turan was simply homesick, at least in the summer months."

Levent looked to Tek. "That was about the time when he started work on his castle on the hill, wasn't it?"

"Believe so."

"And that should have been about the time South Beach broke ground."

"Around then."

Levent looked to Eren. "Do you know if Turan is involved in a company called Yelkenli?"

"I think so, yes. I've never had dealings with them, but I heard it was one of his. He shuffles them like cards. Hard to keep track."

It was hard and deliberately so. Levent had no doubt that other holding companies controlled Yelkenli as Yelkenli controlled the most visible branch, Desenli Logistics. He was sure as he watched a small boat put out from the sailing vessel—the yelkenli—toward the dock. The mother ship had anchored close, fifty meters or less. Four or five people had gotten into the small boat.

"Do you know if Turan has a piece of the Yalikavak Marina?"

Eren shrugged. "He likes big projects, but I don't know if he's in that one. I might be able to find out."

"Please, do."

"I like it when the police say please."

"Onur," said Emine in that special tone. "You promised no business tonight."

"And I never lie," said Levent. "This is curiosity."

Because she knew that was a lie, Emine withdrew with a brief nod. She looked over the water at the small boat that had come to the dock, bumping against the pier with a sound that carried over the water.

The passengers began to climb the short ladder onto the carpeted dock, assisted by two waiters who rushed down the stairs. First out was Federico, the captain on this journey. The second was a woman Levent had seen at the beach last week—a handsome Istanbullu who must be Federico's date.

The third passenger was a broad-shouldered man that Levent remembered as the bodyguard he had seen at the beach three days ago. At that time, he had been assigned to Tolga, the MIT man. Now, apparently, his services had been parceled out to the needy.

And that was Turan. Levent hardly recognized him in light evening dress as he mounted the ladder to the dock. Turan waved away the waiters and put his arm out to help the tall lithe woman all in white who was last from the boat.

"Who's that creature?" asked Eren.

Everyone looked if they had not already. Zekeriya, who looked longest, said, "You mean the crispy-crunchy hand-in-hand with our exile?"

"That's exactly who I mean."

Emine laughed, but not loud. "That's Sultan. His mistress."

CHAPTER 18

When Levent received a call from the commandant saying that the van was ten kilometers from the city, their passengers on board, the Inspector excused himself from the gathering. No one protested, not even Emine. He had been uncertain company since Federico's party came ashore.

The five people from the ship had come to the table to say hello, nodding and smiling and making talk so small that no talk would have been larger. They demurred on the offer to join the dinner party that was well underway, but did not return the sense that they would not be lowering themselves by accepting. The presence of Sultan made even rejection seem gracious. She was the morning star of the evening. The dress that Levent had thought was white was really an iridescent silver that bared her cleavage most of the way to her navel.

The presence of the bodyguard did not go unnoticed, though Levent was sure he was the only one who understood why an armed man should appear at a social function. When Federico's party moved to another table overlooking the water, the man posted himself by the wide steps that led down from the parking lot. The entrance was now secure. Perhaps they would feed him.

Levent made a point of stopping at the king's table as he left the restaurant. Everyone pretended to be surprised by his early exit, though Sultan was the only one who seemed happy.

"We'll miss you," she said. "I hope you're not working on such a fine night."

"I'm afraid so," he said. "We had a breakthrough on this case."

Rarely had Levent known such attention to his words than the table gave. Sultan literally held her breath. Turan pretended to drink his wine to a depth that should have gagged him. Only the Italian was unaffected.

"Must be a genuine pain in the ass," said Federico. "Vacation and all."

"More than you know," said Levent. "But there's some satisfaction when the pieces finally come together."

"Primal," said Federico. "Man is the puzzle-solving creature. Well, we might include chimpanzees to be fair."

"Solving puzzles can lead to conclusions," said Turan. "You'll keep us informed."

He had made the request sound like an order that came to the front lines from a general officer in his headquarters. Maps on the walls with flashing lights indicated even the most distant points—and Levent was one of those.

"We were supposed to talk tonight, but I'll settle for tomorrow," said Levent, as if the rest of the table were eavesdropping. "We should have a better conversation after I talk to the people Sevim left behind in Paris."

Turan gave away nothing. He had several ways of addressing his audience, and he slipped into the ironic. "So you're traveling, Inspector?"

"A short way," said Levent. "It seems that Paris came to us. I'm sure you had some indication of that already."

If Turan remembered Paris as anything but the capital of a European country, he did not show it. He watched the waiter refill his glass with white wine before he spoke. "I'll be at my place after one, Inspector. You can be sure I'll put by a baguette and brie for lunch."

"I look forward to it." Levent pointed toward the bodyguard who stood with his arms crossed to hide the bulge in his suit. "Good idea, that man."

Levent quickly walked up the stairs to his car. He was surprised to see Turan's Mercedes convertible parked in the lot beside his. Close coordination for the rest of the evening ashore, he supposed.

The chauffeur had just gotten out of the car. He gave a short greeting to Levent, as if he remembered him. "Going down for a bite to eat," he said.

"The food's good."

* * *

Levent was still on the road but closing fast on the Jandarma post when the commandant called to say he had arrived with his prisoners. "We're waiting for you, Onur."

"Put our guests in separate rooms," said Levent. "Don't make them comfortable, but allow them to smoke."

"If that makes sense."

"Did you recover any weapons from the ship?"

"No," he said. "Except a flare gun. Not a weapon unless you're close."

"We won't be able to keep up the drug trafficking angle for long," said Levent. "What about cell phones?"

"Two," he said. "But only one that works in this country."

"Put a man on the second," said Levent. "He should make a list of the last calls made and the directory of contacts."

"Right."

When Levent arrived at the post five minutes later, each of the four prisoners had been placed in a separate white room that was clean and brightly lit, but so sterile that it could never be confused with creature comfort. Levent wished he had all his suspects in a place so inhospitable to any human intercourse except confession. A monk's cell should have the same aura.

"Numbers One and Two told me they're man and wife," said Metin. "They say they're hired members of the crew and would like to be in a room together."

"Conjugal privileges have to wait," said Levent. "What about the other two?"

"Number Three is the owner of the ship," said Metin. "Suzanne Vardan. She's about as tough as any sea-captain I've come across."

"Number Four?"

"He's used to this kind of treatment," said Metin. "Hasn't said a word, and he's been smoking like a forest fire since we separated them."

"Gaulois or Gitane?"

"Gaulois."

"Have all these people been fingerprinted?"

"I had it done in Marmaris," said the commandant. "I sent the prints to Istanbul, and they just got back saying that some of them match up with the garbage you took off the vessel."

"Are there any unidentified prints from the garbage?"

"Yes," he said. "One set."

That meant the fifth person was the missing man. Levent had to find out where he went before the French Embassy made a rescue attempt of their wayward citizens.

"What about the fingerprints off the gas cap? Do we have anything like a match with Number Four?"

"I spoke to Mahir," said the commandant. "If you want him to lie a bit, he'll say the prints are very close. He can do a lot with whorls and points and other things to make it sound scientific."

"But he thinks they're a match?"

"He didn't say that," said Metin. "He said he could tell a story if it helps."

"Let's hope he won't have to," said Levent. "What about a passport?"

"Right here," said Metin, reaching to the desk and handing over a burgundy red passport with a metric stamp on the front. "His name is Achille Bodoin, but if you're looking for a hero, you should look in a better place."

Mister Bodoin had been born thirty-seven years ago on May thirteen in the city of Paris. The passport had no visa stamp, since none was necessary for travel to Turkey, but it had been recently issued—less than three months ago. That seemed to mean that the document was mission specific. Levent wondered how the proposition for murder in a foreign country had been put to Achille, and who had supplied the bogus credit card he used to rent the car.

"I'll talk to this one first," said Levent. "I'd like to do it alone."

Metin shrugged as if he did not mind being excluded from his own interrogation. "He's all yours, Inspector."

When Levent entered the room where Achille was held, he carried the passport open to the photograph. It showed a different man than the one who sat in the left seat of three yoked chairs. The features were the same however—a dense low brow that would never speak of intelligence, a damaged nose that had never been reset, and small brown eyes too close together. Only the straight coarse hair compared well.

"It's really a terrible photograph," said Levent, sitting in the chair on the right side of the yoke. "I have a better description of you from the car rental clerk in Fethiye."

Achille said nothing. He looked somewhat at sea in the calf-length deck pants that seemed to be de rigueur in Bodrum. His shirt was open two buttons to display a deep hairy chest and a bright red rash. His shoes were topsiders, and he sat strong but wire-taut in the chair. Two cigarette butts and a shower of ash littered the concrete floor where he had stepped them out and a third was in his hand. The commandant should have provided an ashtray.

"If you speak English, this conversation will be over with quickly," said Levent. "If not, an interpreter can be found. But we will talk."

Achille seemed to mull the offer. He had undoubtedly heard bad things of people who found themselves in the custody of the Turkish police. He had been given a sample in the rough ride from Marmaris, but had every right to be puzzled by the indifference shown afterward.

"I have nothing to give for you," he said. "I have done nothing to bring the police. This is *mauvais*."

Wrong. Mistaken. His accent was definitely French, but his English could not be called broken because it was too bent. The only consistent thing was his bad attitude.

"You're lying," said Levent. "That's not what I consider co-operation."

Achille shrugged in the universal language. He took a long drag on his short stinking cigarette. He was convinced that he would have them forever.

Levent reached for the cigarette that Achille held between his third and fourth fingers. Tossing it to the floor with the others,

Levent stepped it out. He stepped on it again deliberately and put his hand in the front pocket of Achille's shirt for the packet. Half full. Good. Levent put the packet in the front pocket of his shirt.

"These French cigarettes aren't even made in France any more," he said. "Spain, I believe. Nothing much is the same these days, but the tobacco's still Turkish. For an addiction, Turkish can't be matched."

Achille said nothing. He might have sulked.

"You should get used to doing without them," said Levent. "The new laws say that smoking is illegal indoors."

Achille looked at the butts on the floor for the lie. "*Merde*," he said. "The new laws is that. Shit."

"You can smoke if an official gives you permission," said Levent. "I'm an inspector. If we get along, I'll do what I can do for you in that way and others. You should understand that you need friends in this country. If you don't, you soon will."

"My passport is *allouez* for ninety days," he said. "I do not stay longer."

"Ninety days is forever in this case," said Levent, speaking slowly so the English would be clear. "The automobile you rented was used to facilitate a murder. You know that, but I'm sure you don't realize that the Peugeot was caught on video tape as it left the convenience store after the murder."

"*Non*," he said.

"You can't disagree with facts," said Levent. "We're current in this country. I'm sure you didn't know that, and I'm sure your friends wouldn't tell you."

Levent made two areas of interest with his hands held apart. "The petrol station is here, across the road from the convenience store, there. Cameras monitor the traffic that passes in the road. I'd be wrong not to tell you how unfortunate this technology is for the rest of your life. Believe me, you won't find Turkish prisons to your liking."

He stirred in the chair for the first time, shuffling his feet and rubbing the fingers of his right hand where the cigarette wanted to be. He almost started when Levent rose and walked toward the door where the Jandarma guard stood. Levent stopped before reaching the guard and turned back.

"We compared the fingerprints left at the scene of the murder with the ones that were taken from you a few hours ago," said Levent. "They're close enough for a match. They're good enough for a Turkish judge to set you aside for trial."

Achille said nothing, but he shook his head slowly.

"You shouldn't shake your head in disbelief," said Levent, wagging his finger in the same rhythm as Achille's long no. "You should do it with bitter resignation for the life you'll never know again. We have a very good video of the car that you rented leaving the parking lot of the store in a hurry. We have your fingerprints on the gas cap of the same car. We don't really need more."

"You will not have more," he said.

But his voice had altered slightly when he went to his automatic denial. It was a small thing, but interrogations sometimes turned on less.

"You don't have time to make your decision," said Levent. "I'll talk to the others. One of them will talk to me. I'm sure their version of events won't do much to implicate them. They'll shift the blame to you."

"You don't know what you say."

"I know that the man and woman—the couple—are hired hands who came on the ship without any idea of what would happen. They aren't so stupid that they'll stand for having their lives ruined for the sake of you or Mrs. Vardan."

Achille did not stir again in his chair, but Levent sensed movement in another part of that big head with the heavy hair. It was nothing but a feeling that Levent had fought against having in his job. The first fifty times proved him wrong. When a man went inside himself like that, he had made the decision to fashion a story. The details made the wheels grind silently.

Levent hesitated as if waiting, then quickly stepped out the door and began to walk down the hall. He was nearly to the commandant's office when he heard the noise that the guard made.

"Inspector," said the guard, who was the same man with the slick sleeve Levent had seen on his first day at headquarters. "I think this fellow has something to say."

* * *

What Achille wanted to say was that he was innocent.

What he had done was to rent the Peugeot in Fethiye. That only. It was why he sat in this white room accused of God knows what.

But gradually Achille expanded his story with the help of several meanly distributed Gaulois. He said he had flown from Paris to Dalaman airport alone by plane. He had taken a taxi from Dalaman to Fethiye, where he rented a car, drove to Marmaris and then to a house on the Datcha Peninsula farther along. He had waited there for two days until he met the ship, which anchored offshore in the bay.

All these things were arranged by Suzanne Vardan, who supplied Achille with an identity and credit card in the name of Francois Gaspard. It was Achille's reputation as a man who knew his way around corners that had recommended him to Suzanne.

He had once been involved with some young men in Paris who formed a gang that was finally broken up by the police. Just before that happened, Achille had married a woman with enough fortune that enabled his retirement from that kind of edgy work. He had not known at the time that his new wife was a second cousin of Sevim Verbanian.

Achille's wife—from whom he was now estranged—liked to advertise her relationship to a family as wealthy and well-connected as the Vardans. They were jewelers who owned a splendid shop on the Champs Elysee and a factory in a town outside Paris. Sevim was Suzanne's son by a previous marriage, a young man still in his twenties. Achille did not know how Sevim acquired a name that was certainly not French. The name did not come from the father, Fernan, who headed the household but frequently worked abroad with his job in the foreign service.

Sevim took the name of Verbanian from him, though that was nearly all he borrowed from his stepfather. The times when those two got along could be marked on a calendar of years and the benefits of separation. Sevim had grown up ungovernable, an unmotivated student, but an excellent amateur soccer player who could have turned professional if he had the incentive to earn money. In the Vardan family that condition did not arise naturally. Their origins may have been Armenian, and the family trade in jewelry, but they were thoroughly Parisian and privileged in every way.

The holiday in the Mediterranean was put to Achille in a similarly continental way. He would come along to enjoy a Mediterranean cruise while keeping an eye on Sevim, who was always a problem when left to himself. His relationship with his stepfather had been bad enough, but his behavior seemed to worsen as he grew older. Sevim had smashed up the car that he had been given when he graduated from lycee and had gotten at least one young girl pregnant. He was said to be like his blood father in the bad and to have received none of the good.

Achille agreed to the cruise even when it became clear that he was to do more than chaperone a headstrong young man. The change occurred slowly but emphatically. Sevim, who had been sent to a sailing school to learn how to handle a ship, came back from Brittany a different man. The first time Achille saw him afterward he would not have recognized the young man for the look in his eye. Even the cadence of his language was supercharged with new vocabulary.

Revanche was not only the name he attached to the boat, but his dominant idea. This young man who wanted for nothing had found something to pursue. A targeted life was what he had lacked. All the things that had been awry could be righted by redeeming his honor. He would do this by confronting complete evil. Sevim was so focused that the amphetamines he constantly took hardly affected him.

Sevim had need of a chaperone to keep him from his worst instincts, but Achille never suspected that anything like serious violence would take place in a foreign country. It was decided in a gradual and casual way that Achille would go ahead to Turkey to rent a car under an assumed name and prepare for further duties.

Those had not immediately materialized. Achille settled down to a cruise in Aegean waters after he turned the car over to Sevim at Datcha. The complement of four sailed to Marmaris, then to the island of Rhodes and the waters around Bodrum without seeing Sevim. Achille was sorry he had brought along more than bathing trunks until the evening at Yalikavak Marina when the third version of Sevim showed up.

He was wild that day, steaming and hyperactive on a non-stop high. Achille had seen other men behave like that when he had run with the gang in Paris. It meant they had done a job and gotten away. It also meant they were worried about what might catch up with them when their grab became known to the cops.

The ship left Yalikavak Marina the next day without Achille on board. He was told to find a room in a hotel and not draw attention to himself. He would drop the green Peugeot at Bodrum Marina on the following day without returning it to Fethiye. Achille did not question the instructions. He understood that there would be a good reason for the anonymous drop.

"So the ship waited at the marina until you got there."

"Of course," said Achille. "They would not leave me behind in this place. They could not."

But that was what Levent would have done with this dunce. He might babble as he was doing, but the rich, back in their country, shielded by their lawyers, feared extradition not at all. That they had waited for Achille in Bodrum was mildly surprising.

"Where did you go after leaving the marina?"

"We went to Datcha."

"To the same place?"

"No," he said. "We left Sevim to the town. The rest went to the house to have a proper shower and change of clothes."

"Where did Sevim go from there?"

"I don't know," said Achille. "I do not see him since he leaves the ship. The next day, *voile prendre la mer.*"

"You set sail."

"Yes."

"For Marmaris."

"That was the intend," said Achille very precisely. "But we found problems with the *voile* as we came into the bay. The wind was too great. We made our way to a good place to stay for the night."

It was there that the afternoon ferry from Rhodes had spotted the purple-striped ship. Shortly afterward, the commandant came down from the sky. The time that had elapsed after the ship left Bodrum seemed accounted for. Most things, except those that implicated Achille in a brutal murder, were accounted for.

"Where do you think Sevim went?"

Achille considered his answer, thinking that Levent would not like a quick reply. "I cannot truly say."

"Tell me that you think," said Levent. "I value your opinion. I understand you have no special knowledge of his whereabouts."

Achille went through his motions of thinking, scratching the rash on his chest before giving his reply. "I think he will go to Bodrum," he said. "To Bodrum again."

"What makes you think that?"

"I think he went there to finish his business."

"What business?"

Achille raised his hands, palms up, and looked into them. He did not speak.

Levent could think of no unfinished business in Bodrum other than the death of Turan Yoruk. Any approach to him would require resources and time to prepare unless Sevim had done that already. And he might have.

"Does Sevim have a weapon?"

"Perhaps."

"Do you think he'll kill again?"

"I have no idea what he will do," said Achille slowly. "It may be so that he has no idea. But we were in the way of Bodrum when the ship found the high wind. We should be there in the morning were we free."

* * *

"What did you find in the cell phone?"

"Two calls were made about the time we landed in the helicopter," said Metin. "The first was to an Istanbul number. I checked it against the consulate number, but it's not the same. It could be the private number for one of the consular officials."

"Possibly," said Levent. "And the second?"

"A local cellular number," said Metin. "Mugla district. I thought of ringing it up to see who answered, but thought I'd leave that to you."

"Don't call that number," said Levent. "It might be her son's and we shouldn't alert him. Have the Jandarma check the house at Datcha. It's near the sea and not in town. You can get a better description from Achille."

Metin took up the receiver from the battered assembly on his desk. "But you don't think we'll find this man in Datcha?"

"I think he's on a mission," said Levent. "I may have a better idea of what that is after I talk to the mother."

"Good luck," he said. "She hasn't moved since we put her in the room. Hasn't asked for anything, even a drink of water."

"I like hard cases, Metin."

But Levent knew he had misspoken when he entered the room where Suzanne Vardan sat in a hard plastic chair. Her feet barely touched the floor, dangling but tucked under the chair. That put her an even five feet tall. She had straight black hair that was probably dyed and dark brown eyes that looked upon her captivity with the patience of a solitary hunter. When Levent searched for the remnants of a young girl who had found her way to houseboat parties on the Seine, he found no sign of frivolity but some of daring. Her fine browned legs in shorts had not changed. Her large breasts strained containment in their brief red halter. This was sailing gear for the sea of vengeance.

Levent took the second chair in the room and set it facing her. She did not react except to assess the danger he presented. Levent thought that he had never seen a suspect less impressed.

"My name is Inspector Levent," he said. "And you've ruined my holiday."

"I'd say you returned the favor."

She had spoken in good English in a subdued tone that she controlled completely. It was clear she had controlled this violent descent into the past and provided its support. If a stone man on the road to Yalikavak had not seen a green Peugeot passing his shop, she would have gotten away with everything. If Levent had not followed the directions of a prophet, he would not have found the car at the marina. There were always many "ifs" in an investigation, but this one seemed to run toward a monopoly.

"I'm sorry not to get around to you sooner, Mrs. Vardan, but I was busy talking to Achille. He confessed his part in this affair. I'm sure the things he told me are a study in falsehood, but even so they're damaging to your case."

"You must have frightened him," she said, as if she had anticipated Levent's words. "Achille's a hard man—but not strong."

"My advice is to get your story on record," he said. "The procedures followed in criminal trials in this country are exact."

"The procedures followed in criminal trials are exact in France, too," she said. "That's where I plan to be tomorrow."

Only the rich could say things like that. Levent was sure they would send an official from Ankara on the first plane. Fortunately, there was no consulate in Bodrum, or their servant would have been banging on the door already.

"Your consulate hasn't called," said Levent. "When they do, they'll be told that a murder investigation is in progress."

"An investigation is not in progress," she said. "I've done nothing and won't say I have."

"Mrs. Vardan, I could make a case against you with less than I have from Achille. Or let's say, I could make a case against your son. A very strong case."

"Then perhaps you should talk to him."

"I will," said Levent. "All points of exit from the country have been covered. Your son will be found."

"Bravo, Inspector."

Levent wondered where she found her nerve, but that must have been with her even before she took up with a Turk in defiance of her parents and bore a child out of wedlock. She had buried her first love and would bury another if necessary. Love was insanity when it carried past the grave.

"He's Sevim's son, isn't he?"

"He was named after his father," she said. "You don't know the father or the son, and I assure you that you won't."

Levent rose from his chair and walked to the window that overlooked the parking lot below. The lights of Yalikavak were visible in the distance. They had probably laid their plans for Harman's murder as the water lapped against the ship in the marina.

"I wish I'd heard what you said to your son when you told him who he really was, Mrs. Vardan. Everyone thinks at some point in his life that he's grown up in the wrong house with the wrong parents. Every time something goes badly, he's more certain of it. When he finally has an explanation for all the things that bedeviled him in his life, the confusion falls away. It must have been easy for you to motivate him. All you had to do was tell him the truth."

She said nothing.

"His father was murdered," said Levent as if it was an accepted fact. "His murderer was never brought to justice. I understand how you must feel, and I sympathize with your anger. You were carrying Sevim's child at his funeral. A thing like that can never be forgotten."

"Inspector, what you know is absolutely nothing," she said with a sharp rise to her head. "You're a voyeur looking into the lives of others. If you weren't Turkish, I'd tell you how sad that is."

"In this case I'm glad to stand at a distance," he said. "The man you killed was not worth the blood on your hands. He was human filth who fed on filth. The people behind him are worse. I'd gladly let you walk away from this if I could."

"You can," she said calmly. "I'll tell you how."

She was remarkably confident in speech and manner. Nothing seemed to have affected her and nothing seemed as if it could. "Please go ahead, Mrs. Vardan."

"Achille can survive a Turkish jail," she said as though working out a lengthy equation. "When you declare one of those periodic amnesties that turn all the human filth back out on the streets, he'll simply join that procession. He'll be compensated for the time he spent away from the family that he doesn't really have. He'll say yes to these conditions because he wants to return to France when everything has passed. Now, the question is: will you say yes?"

"How can I say no?" said Levent. "What you propose will happen anyway."

"The captain and his wife are to go free," she said, phrasing the statement like a demand. "They're not involved."

"I might believe that."

"My son will return to France," she said. "He'll continue to enjoy the diplomatic immunity he has now."

"Immunity?" said Levent. "That's a twist."

She did not hesitate to repeat. "Diplomatic immunity is inviolate. It's extended to all members of the immediate family of a diplomat. My husband was posted to Turkey early this year. He works with the consulate in Istanbul."

This time Levent was silent. What was the way to parry a man who had sanction for murder? By having equal sanction. As evidence of her connections, the claim was supreme. Levent could not longer doubt Suzanne Vardan or the source of her confidence. An immediate member of the family of a diplomat could walk away from anything, even murder. But this was Turkey, and it would be best if he fled the country before invoking the privilege.

"Tell me where I can find Sevim."

"I don't know where he is," she said. "That's the truth."

"You could call him."

"He won't answer his phone," she said. "I told him not to."

The destination of the two calls from her cell phone were obvious now. The first went to her husband in Istanbul, the second to her son in this area. She had calculated everything, including emergency procedures. It was only his years in police work that told Levent not everything could be calculated.

"Tell me what Sevim plans to do with the rest of his holiday."

"That's his business."

"It's mine, too, unfortunately," said Levent. "Will he try to avenge his father by murdering Turan?"

"I don't like the word murder," she said. "You should know that obligations rule in a case like this. That much Turks understand."

"I'm more worried about what will happen to your son, Mrs. Vardan. Turan knows danger has moved close to him. Perhaps he always knew it would. His house is a fortress. He has security around him at all times, along with a man who's one of the best security advisors this country has produced. Having a young man, an amateur, attempt to take his life is not a good idea."

"So I'm to put my trust in you, Inspector."

"Yes."

"You'll excuse me if I find I can't do that."

"I may excuse you," said Levent. "But when the time comes, you'll find that Turan Yoruk will be very unforgiving."

"I don't expect he's changed," she said.

CHAPTER 19

"You were late last night."

"I thought you were sleeping when I came in," said Levent to his wife, who sat across the table on the balcony at breakfast. It was her breakfast, which meant it was later than it seemed. "I thought you were deep into your dreams."

"I heard you," she said. "I always hear you come home in Istanbul, even in my dreams. It's not a serious thing. You occasionally take the form of a pickpocket on the street. My husband, the thief of time."

"I'm sorry," he said. "We should be back to Bodrum time shortly."

"We've only five days left of the holiday," she said. "I hope so."

"Emine, I do apologize," he said, taking her hand across the table. "This case is anything but normal, and I could have used your help. Why didn't you tell me that Venus—pardon me, Sultan—was Turan's mistress. It would have shortened my day."

"You didn't ask," she said. "You tried to be so coy when you said you were meeting a beautiful woman yesterday."

"I'll learn not to tease," he said.

"Is that what you were doing?"

He should have told her he still had no idea what he was doing. He knew almost everything about this case, past and present, with no idea of how to alter the future. Last night, he had thought about calling Turan and alerting him to the danger of a man on the loose with harm in mind. But he had not.

Levent took another slice of white cheese on his knife and spread it gently on the toast. "I'm supposed to have a talk with Turan today," he said. "His place."

"My advice is to watch your tongue," she said seriously. "I've heard some disturbing things about our friend. They say that as well as being a leader of industry, he's a leader of smuggling in the area."

"That's no surprise, Emine."

"But it seems he may even be involving Federico."

"That isn't good," said Levent, knowing how much she liked the Italian. "But I thought Federico had money. He has a big boat."

"A very fine and expensive boat," said Emine. "That may be the reason why he'd listen to promises of illegal money—to keep it."

"There isn't anyone's affairs that Turan can't mend," said Levent. "Except his own. He made a mistake long ago that could bring him grief now. I don't know how to stop the past from catching him, and the odd thing is I don't know if I want to try."

"You're serious."

"I think I am."

"Onur, I've never heard you say anything like that before."

"Probably, I never have. It's what happens when you start to think of fate as a beggar at the door."

But an insistent one. Levent had never heard of any so circuitous. When he had questioned Mrs. Vardan about the reason why she had chosen this week or month to right the past, he received no reply. She said nothing further while she waited for her husband to arrive from the airport. He had flown from Istanbul on a private plane that was almost as quick as the taxi ride from the distant suburbs of Bodrum.

Fernan Verbanian seemed like a decent sort in no way overawed by the police, his wife, or the truth. He was as bald as a sausage and as polite as his leather shoes, but adamant about the immunity that was his by right of his country's sovereign existence. No government on earth dared to deny the godlike status of diplomats, and he was certain that Turkey would not fashion itself as a criminal state in this case.

Perhaps Verbanian would not have been so certain if the commandant had been free to deal with what he had not known existed—legitimized murder from a diplomatic pouch. Metin called the number that put him in touch with God's representative in Ankara. And even he stood aside.

* * *

Levent was in the shower when Emine opened the bathroom door and shouted over his singing. "You have a call."

"Answer it."

"I won't go that far," she said.

Wrapped in a towel, Levent found his cell phone and returned the call that had come from the commandant. Metin answered quickly, his voice filled with the grit that had been with him the last three days. The hoarseness was new.

"I thought you'd like to know that our guests are up and around," he said. "Husband and wife Parisienne. They took a walk in the garden, then spent some time renting a car from the front desk—not a Peugeot this time—but haven't decided to use it. When they do, we'll be following."

"Keep your distance," said Levent. "Tell me when and where they stop."

"We have two cars on them, so that might do the job," he said. "You'll also want to know that we heard from the Jandarma about the house in Datcha. No one home, but they had the good sense to make a thorough search. They found an empty ammunition box in the trash. Rifle ammunition. 7x57 Mauser."

"A powerful cartridge."

"Not what you'd use for shooting rabbits." said the commandant.

"He wouldn't have trouble finding ammunition here," said Levent. "I wonder how he got hold of a rifle."

"If you think Customs searches incoming vessels, you're in for a surprise," he said. "They don't have the manpower unless something arouses their suspicion. I can tell you a boatload of tourists in a prime vessel doesn't appear on their radar. A cannon could have been hidden on board that ship."

"Did your search of the ship find places where large things could be hidden?"

"Not really," said Metin. "But we were looking for small spaces where drugs might be. At least, we were pretending to."

"Could you go back to the search team and ask?"

"I can, Onur, because I'm a patient man. Now do you have some idea what they should have been looking for?"

"It would be good if they checked for residue of weapons," said Levent. "And any traces of gunpowder-like substances—ammunition, explosives, etcetera."

"They've got a dog that can do it as fast as a crap," said Metin. "Chemical analysis will take a lot longer."

"I suppose we have the time," said Levent. "I'm just not sure how time applies to this case. It seems to be lost."

"Onur, that's too poetic for me this morning. We're going to catch this prick and close the case on his young ass. I'm sitting here hoping he tries to resist. That would be the best answer."

Levent did not disagree as he hung up. The best solution would be if Sevim and Turan killed each other. Levent could not see that happening, but if Metin followed the car to a promising destination, the cycle of violence might be broken.

Otherwise, they were looking at a sniper who could kill at long range. Sevim must have given up the idea of symmetry and decided one blast of fire was enough. That made for a serious complication. Protecting a man from ambush was nearly impossible if the target exposed himself, and Turan liked showing off in plain sight.

Levent looked at his watch. If he left for Turan's castle on the hill now, he would arrive an hour early. Bad manners. He decided on a consultation first.

* * *

Yilmaz at his small Gun World pretended not to recognize Levent as he entered the shop. The gunsmith kept up his conversation with a customer about the benefits of the German-made Ruger versus the German-made Walther PP Super in nine-millimeter pistols while Levent examined a rack of rifles that hung on the wall to his left. Only after Yilmaz had made the sale—a Ruger, like the ceramic advertisement on the wall— did he turn to his nemesis.

"I'll ask what I can do for you today," he said. "Not that I want to know."

"You shouldn't take that tone," said Levent. "I know you told me a little about Yunus Harman when you could have said a lot. I have to wonder why."

"I can't think of a reason," he said, reaching behind him for the stool at his bench but deciding not to sit.

"Was it because you knew that Harman killed a man by setting his boat afire?"

"Actually, no." The mouth that twisted left twisted heavily. "I said he ran with divers, and they were a wild bunch. Some of them are still around, unlike him."

"You mean Turan Yoruk."

"That's a good guess," said Yilmaz. "Everyone knows he was behind the fire, but they don't want to know. That fire got him the money to be what he is today, sitting on the hill like a king that can't be touched by the law. It's odd how he and Harman showed up back in Bodrum together."

"But not at the same time."

"That's the way they move," he said. "Slow. They always make sure they control the ground before they come down on you from above."

"So you know that, too?"

"I know what I need to stay in business," he said with what even he recognized as understatement. "If you really want the truth, I was expecting some business from them, even though I know the wolves have their own ways to guns."

"I'm interested in ammunition today," said Levent. "I'd like to know if you've sold any rifle cartridges to a young man in the last two weeks."

"I told you about my memory and I wasn't lying," he said, twisting his mouth again hard. "Near term it ain't worth a shit."

"But you remember your products," said Levent. "This young man would have bought at least one box of 7x57 Mausers."

Yilmaz shook his head. "I'm not the only gunsmith in this town."

"Let's say you are. Your shop is on the main road and visible."

Yilmaz corrected the twist on his lips. "Two boxes," he said finally.

"When?"

"I'd say it was about a week ago," he said. "Could be less. But don't hold me to that."

"Tell me about him."

"I don't remember that much," said Yilmaz, whose eyes held Levent's steady. "He was young, sure. He spoke English for sure. And you don't need a license to buy ammunition, so we didn't get into a serious discussion about ways and means, and I didn't put a lecture to him."

"Describe him."

"Tall, over six feet," he said. "Looked fit. He had dark hair cut like the young ones do nowadays. A coxcomb, I'd call it. That's all I get back on him."

Levent believed that, but not all of it. "Mauser 7x57 shouldn't be your most common call."

"They're not," he said. "The cartridge drives a 139 spire point bullet on a fairly flat trajectory. Just right for the occasional hunter who's not too sure of himself."

"What did he say he wanted the cartridges for?"

"I don't think he did," said Yilmaz, who was trying to claim less ground. "He knew what he wanted and asked for it, if I remember right. 7x57 is not something I'd suggest. There's cheaper and not really worse."

"What would you use that cartridge for?"

He pointed to the poster of a rampant bear that hung on the wall near the rifles. "Bringing down a big animal," he said. "As far as I know, there's no game that big around here."

"Except one."

"That one I don't know anything about," said Yilmaz, who understood exactly what was meant. "What they do with their cartridges is none of my business."

"But you suspected he might hunt the forbidden thing," said Levent. "Man."

"Bear, wild elephant or man, he'd probably take the shot from above," said Yilmaz, moving his hand on an arc toward Levent. "The flat trajectory will give you a bit better chance of compensating for elevation."

"A shot from above," said Levent.

"Just a guess, Inspector. There's lots of things we don't know in the retail business. I don't think we're meant to know them frankly."

CHAPTER 20

Southern Cross, the grand monument to Turan's ego, occupied one shoulder of a stern mountain eight kilometers outside the city of Bodrum. It reared above the secondary road like a fortress in red and gray stone, commanding a view of the sea that was three kilometers away.

The entrance was guarded by a middle-aged man who carried an automatic weapon. Unlike most, he was alert and serious as he signaled Levent to wait outside the gate. By a hand-held device, he spoke with the house before allowing the Honda to pass. Even then, he insisted a quick look at the trunk of the car.

The slope of the driveway was so steep that Levent had to replace the emergency brake while the guard took his look. On the go-ahead, the Honda labored up the slope, whining in first gear all the way. The summit came in a circle of stone that stood before a small house that was obviously the guards' quarters. A garage lay left next to it. Several vehicles were inside—Sultan's BMW rental, Turan's Mercedes convertible, two small cars and a van to ferry supplies for the household.

A second uniformed man, as professional and as well armed as the first, looked Levent over as he got from the car. He spoke without disrespect or respect as he said, "Follow me."

They circled the guardhouse by a stone path and climbed fourteen steps to the second level—the living level—of the complex. Though impressed by the rustic but not primitive architecture, Levent looked for gaps in security. None were obvious, but as they reached the grand articulated entrance to the main building, he stopped. Yes, from above. The mountain continued its climb in back of the house and its satellites, rising more than two hundred meters higher.

The summit was invisible, but its ragged edge was an expanse of large boulders that loomed over everything below. Still, the distance was probably three hundred meters or more. A man with a rifle, regardless of his cartridges, had to make a lucky shot. Only if he managed to scale down the jagged rocks and move closer to the complex could he be sure of his target. The only other chance was if he commanded the V-point of a long crevice—a sudden indentation—in the rock face. That was closer.

But it was not likely given the steep rugged grade. Levent was sure the master of the house had factored it into his plans, and if he had not, Tolga, the MIT agent, had. Levent saw Tolga watching the new arrival from the upstairs window that was probably his room in the castle keep. Turan did not come to be where he was without professional advice. He had it in every part of his life, but most spectacularly in the woman who stood before the front door.

"Welcome, Inspector."

"Well found," said Levent, using the proper form. But he was thinking that it would be impossible to find Sultan badly. She wore jeans and a too-open blouse. In her hand she held a single rose on a long stem.

"I didn't know you were a gardener."

"I'm not," she returned. "But this place brings out the villager in me."

Southern Cross was big enough to house a village. The main house rambled in at least two wings that followed the curve of the mountain to its end in an abrupt precipice. There, the drop was sheer in tightly mortared stone, adding another degree of difficulty to intruders. Levent kept to Sultan's side as she shunned the path toward the drop, veering around the side of the house.

"It's the most beautiful place in the country." She cast her arm wide. "Really. *Architectural Digest* has been dying to get in here for a shoot."

The grounds were planted in flowers in every color that liked the southern sun. The view was magnificent, rolling down the foothills and valleys to the sea. None could be better. Every wanderer since Odysseus had called it his own until Turan shut the gate and closed in his dominion. He might have known that some day he would need its natural fortification.

"You're staying here now, Sultan?"

"Yes," she said. "I was graciously invited to share."

Then the charade was over. The elaborate investiture of the hotel had been for Levent's benefit, as was everything afterward. He felt they could start anew.

"You know, they say the gardens outside the old walls of Istanbul have the best vegetables in the city," said Levent. "No one knows why, but I'm sure it's because so many armies left their blood and bones to enrich the soil."

"That's interesting," she said. "I'd almost say charming. I never thought of it at all before."

"You should have," said Levent. "From what I learned in the past few days, Turan's fortune was built using the same fertilizer. A man died a horrible death of fire on a ship in the harbor so he'd never have to look back. But of course that's all he does, since Harman died in the same way."

She stopped abruptly as they came to the back of the house. Its centerpiece was a large swimming pool that did not quite exhaust the space behind the house or the water supply of the district. It was meant to be reached conveniently by all the buildings in the complex, of which there were four. Two more houses—guest houses—rose in canted tiers toward the top of the mountain.

"I don't understand," said Sultan as she gave the eternal objection of a mistress. "Turan's a gentle man. I can't imagine violence in him."

"He had it done," said Levent. "He delegates. You know that."

"Inspector, I appreciate the fact that you're trying to warn me—"

"You can take it as you like." Levent watched Turan come from the house down a set of stone stairs toward a table that sat in a nest of chairs under a wooden pergola. "My advice is not to stay here for the summer. It wouldn't be good for you, Sultan. The man who killed Yunus Harman is hunting for Turan."

She looked bewildered, like any peasant with a rose. "You can't stop him?"

"He's a machine," said Levent. "His clock was set at his birth."

"But you have to do . . . something."

"I'll do what I can," said Levent. "You saw the success I had in talking you around. Imagine the same scene with Turan."

Levent walked away. He hoped as he measured his steps to the table that he would do what he said without prejudice. He had been foolish with a beautiful woman. Sultan was nothing but a suspect who had lied about everything when she was not lying about the specific. The only lead she had given him—the manager of Yalikavak Marina—was inadvertent.

Turan sat among his teak furniture that was placed at a suitable distance from the fierce glare off the pool. He seemed momentarily distracted, cocking his head to listen as the breeze snapped the canvas awning in the rafters above his head. Levent did not expect him to rise from the chair, but Turan did, putting his hand out to his visitor.

"Onur, I'm glad to see you."

Levent took the hand, but said, "Why?"

Turan's smile was good, his teeth mastered from a perfect mold of technology. "I like very much having guests up here," he said in a low thrumming voice that Levent had not heard before. "When I put this place together in my mind, I imagined it as a small world. I populated it completely. Relatives here, friends there. But it hasn't turned out like that."

"I understand why you haven't thrown open the gates," said Levent. "I understand the reasons better every day."

Turan could have risen to those words, but deflected them. "I could give a list of reasons why things haven't gone as I wanted. All my burdens. But whatever the circumstances, I know I've brought them on myself."

Levent recognized that this was a newly engineered Turan. He should have encouraged the phenomenon, but was confident it would continue. "It isn't every man who knows that. Congratulations."

"Sit," he said, indicating another portion of the teak forest. "What would you like to drink?"

"Beer," said Levent. "Imported."

Turan did not appear to rise to an order, but when he motioned toward the house, a servant came across down the stairs at a quick walk.

"Two beers," said Turan. "The imported."

The servant turned around immediately, but did not return to the house. He moved toward a separate smaller building that should be the kitchen. Turan waited for him to vanish into it before he spoke in the same come-hither voice.

"This should be an open session between us," he said. "Nothing hidden."

"The main thing about you that was hidden is the past," said Levent. "I've managed to decipher most of the information from others."

"And that would be?"

"I know about the ship," said Levent. "About Sevim."

Turan waited until the servant returned with two bottles of Becks beer on a silver tray, meting them out with lager glasses like precious goods. He did not leave a wake when he passed, nor did Turan as he leaned closer to Levent in his chair.

"I won't tell you that didn't happen," he said, using the same low soft voice. "I will tell you that I lost the best friend I ever had when the Meltem burnt in the harbor. No one knows what we shared, but it was everything that two young men never had before they knew each other. We set out from this port like pirates on the high seas. This country was a closed society in those days, a closed economy, and we knew that something better lay across the water if we could find it. We did. We made more money than we ever dreamed. And we spent it like a sailor's dream."

"In Paris."

"Everywhere," he said, still purring. "This is still a country where men go to concerts to watch a woman do things with her microphone. Suggestive things." Turan rolled his hand like an entertainer, inviting in the man's world. "But we weren't watching. We were doing. And there wasn't one damned thing we missed."

Levent realized that he felt like entering Turan's world, carried on the timbre of his voice. It was an instrument for seduction, man or woman, laying out the good things that could be had for the asking. The asking, of course, had to be done of Turan. The devil's feathers were his.

"Yunus Harman was there in Paris, too, I understand."

"Part of the time, yes."

"And in New York."

Turan did not dodge that crucial addition. "That was a different time, Inspector. We were working with the Turkish Folklore Council. It wasn't quite as it sounds—not much on folklore and more toward illegal immigration that both countries wanted to shut down. But I was happy in the city. There are advantages in getting to know the financial capital of the world. I learned some things in New York."

"The value of blackmail," said Levent.

Turan laughed, and that was feathery, too. It could not be called natural or good, but it led him away from the harshness of the truth. "Let's say I learned that blackmail turns this world. If it's mixed with a bit of legerdemain, there's nothing it can't do. I met a man at a party one night who told me he had invented a new field of investment. It all had to do with tax evasion, but it wasn't presented that way to his clients. Depreciation of oil pipelines was the thread. The government never called him on his idea because they didn't understand it. His clients didn't understand it. But they made money and everyone was happy for a time."

"Until someone figured it out," said Levent. "A clerk in Washington."

"No," said Turan, smiling and purring. "The price of oil fell to nothing in the nineties. The companies eventually outlived their usefulness in producing revenue. So there's the lesson. The government can't decide on what it doesn't understand. The market did in time."

"I'd like to know what our government had to do with your work in New York."

Turan smiled again. "Not a great deal," he said. "The military liked to keep its hand on the ones that got away into fool's paradise. They had the idea that anyone who left Turkey during the eighties was a traitor."

"But you didn't think so?"

"I was an opportunist looking for opportunities," he said, including the rest of the human race in the assessment. "I still am. I won't apologize for that."

"I'm surprised you took Fish along to New York," said Levent. "Was he blackmailing you?"

"Fish was a Libyan Pirate," said Turan as if that was enough explanation. "We were all pirates in those days. Raiders. New York was the place for corporate raiders. I can't tell you how inventive they were in those days, and I don't think they've stopped today. The newspapers keep talking about the way mortgage instruments were structured to work until they failed. Sounds pretty much the same to me."

"I've heard that you had a head start on the process," said Levent. "Insurance money that came your way when the Meltem burnt."

"Let's say I was looking ahead," said Turan lightly. "I learned that, too, but not in the way you think."

"The way I think is the way a lot of people do," said Levent. "All the ones who remember, that is."

"You've been listening to rumors," said Turan. "No one proved anything then, and no one can do it now."

"But someone saw Fish in the harbor the night the ship burned," said Levent. "He disappeared and didn't return to Bodrum until lately. Until you did."

Turan nodded. "He came back here to work for me."

"Smuggling drugs."

"I'd know nothing about that."

"It's a good thing," said Levent. "I'm not sure you could talk your way out of a heroin bust that goes from DenizKum to Yelkenli and ends with the American DEA. They're not easy to shake, the Americans. They don't bribe as easily."

"Then I suppose losing an old friend has it uses." Turan's voice lost a little of its purr, but quickly recovered. "I sent Fish to Bodrum as general manager of DenizKum. I knew he wouldn't be our most honest employee. He'd been in trouble in Cyprus. And some in England, too. When he came asking for a job, I told him he'd have to leave that part of his life behind. He assured me that he would, so I sent him to Sultan with a recommendation. She knew nothing about him, so we can't blame her for my mistake."

This man was the best at admitting mistakes that Levent had encountered. Correcting them was another matter, and he had never done that. The idea of justice did not apply to the very rich. Excuses, yes.

As if to prove the point, Sultan came down the stairs to the table with her huge beach bag over her shoulder. She still wore her jeans, but had changed her blouse for a diaphanous wrap of clinging black. And Levent envied his host. The envy was stronger for knowing how close they were.

"Sorry to leave, Inspector, but I'm being the beach bitch again today."

She leaned down to Turan, placing a kiss on the back of his neck. "I think I'll go to Calimera," she said. "Do you mind if I take the convertible?"

Turan removed a set of keys from his pocket and handed them to Sultan by an oversize Mercedes emblem. "I may join you later," he said. "We're thrashing it out, the inspector and I."

"Be careful," she said. "I wouldn't like to see you in jail."

"He's being very careful," said Levent. "Don't worry."

Turan smiled. "Excuse me for a moment, Inspector?"

Levent watched them walk across the lawn together. They were lovers, yes, but familiar with the routine of their duties. It would be Turan's job to provide the surprises that broke up their day. Sultan tied her hair up as she walked, wrapping it in a tight ball around her head to keep off the wind in the convertible.

When they reached the head of the stone path, they stopped and moved closer together, as if conspiring. Yes, possibly no.

Turan's arm moved behind her back and they kissed. From Levent's distance, with her hair tight around her head, it seemed as if two men were kissing.

He looked away, thinking he should prepare his questions better. Three that could easily become thirty came to mind. He was arranging them in order of importance when his cell phone sounded out Benny and the Jets.

"Onur, I just received a report from the team that searched the boat," said the commandant. "You'll want to know they found traces of explosives."

Levent heard himself say nothing in reply. Should he have been so surprised? "How do they know that?"

"I told you they have a dog," said Metin. "He doesn't even have a name that I know of. They just call him The Nose."

"He sniffed out the remnants of explosives on board ship?" said Levent, knowing that he was repeating himself. "Are they sure?"

"As sure as they can be." Metin made a noise that could have been his notes riffling. "There's a market for explosives, as we know, and the buyers think they're being anonymous when they put their money down. But all the manufacturers these days put taggants in the explosives. It's one of the few things to come out of 9/11 that's of real use. This taggant is known as DMDNB. It's a chemical marker, and I'll never be able to break down the components for you. The smell can't be detected by human beings, but a good dog can identify as little as one part in a billion. The Nose is even better, because he sniffed out the taggant even when the explosives were gone."

"Give him a bone," said Levent. "What kind of explosives are we dealing with?"

"They haven't narrowed that down, but it's the plastic kind," said Metin. "It could be any of the Cs from 4 to 6. These people are Europeans, so it might be Semtex, too. Semtex is orange, the Cs white, but they all make the same big noise."

As he watched Turan walk back across the lawn, Levent tried to place the new information in context. He had worried about a rifle shot coming from the mountain before deciding it was a long chance. But even that seemed controllable now.

Distance was irrelevant with explosives. A remote detonator could work from far off. If the explosives were placed well, they would be hard to find. No one would know where they were until that was all they knew in the last seconds of their life.

Still, the explosives had to be placed. If Turan was the target, he was as secure as he could be with every entrance and exit controlled and his personnel hand-picked. Tolga was as good as could be found in identifying danger.

But Levent knew he would have to tell Turan of this new vector. To warn him. That did not sit well with what Levent considered his conscience. The man who moved to sit at the table might be the most evil that Levent had ever known. He was the most evil because he was the most good at every wretched thing he did.

"Now where were we?" he asked, taking up his beer again.

That was the last thing anyone said before the good mountain air filled with the awesome power of fire.

CHAPTER 21

Because the top had been down, the blast severed her body above the waist and scattered it over the lower part of the driveway in bloody rags. Bright gouts of blood had been blown in ways that the eye did not want to follow.

Levent did not stop to examine the things he saw on the driveway or on the bare ground or hanging, scorched, from the branches of the oleander and bougainvillea and the thorns of rose. He recognized the ring she had worn, a single black stone set in gold, but not the finger on which it had been mounted. As he paralleled the wreckage, Levent veered and ran down the driveway on an angle, vaulting onto the wall to keep clear of the tangled inferno that was the Mercedes.

Smoking, sizzling pieces of things had been thrown for fifty meters in every direction but basically to the right. The passenger's side. Much of the rear of the car had been torn upward by raw force and consumed by fire. The deck was still burning, the plastic melting and stinking, the bumpers and struts and sheets of metal twisted with no reference to shape.

The gate was slightly ajar and seemed to have come down from above like that. The roof of the guard station was askew, but the man who had looked into Levent's trunk less than an hour ago was alive, sitting on the ground with both legs extended onto the berm of the road.

Levent jumped down onto the first part of the road, moving back toward the guard. The man hardly responded when he saw a form before him, but he looked up belatedly. Good. He did not seem to be bleeding.

Levent did not think the bomb had been detonated on a preset timer. That was too uncertain. The killer must have watched his moving target from somewhere in the area. He had seen the Mercedes clutch down the steep driveway but not been close enough to tell that a woman sat in the driver's seat. Black blouse, hair tied back, he might have been close enough to see Sultan but still not know she was a woman.

Sevim had done it again in a way that mirrored the past with precision but the wrong victim. Levent should have known. He should have reacted the instant he heard the word explosives.

Levent crossed the road and the three meters of rough shoulder that ended in a long gradual drop down into the valley. There was only one way out of here. One road. He felt the heat moving against his back as he shaded his eyes from the sun and scanned the poor switchback asphalt.

Three cars. Three, dammit.

He could discount the first one, he thought. It was too far along, swinging into the straightaway that led into the turn right to Yalikavak, left to Bodrum.

The second car in sequence, two hundred meters back, was a small white van. It seemed to move leisurely, not careening or braking hard as it swerved into a long turn, so he might be able to eliminate that one, too.

The third vehicle, the closest, followed the van by a hundred meters. He gained on it. He was driving fast, not dangerously fast, but seemed to be moving urgently. The distance was too great to make out the model, but it was small, a hatchback, black.

Levent had his cell phone in his hand, the number last received redialed, but the commandant did not answer. Five rings, six, until the voice arrived and said he could leave his message now.

* * *

Metin returned the call three minutes later, but the black car had vanished. Levent could not tell which way it had gone because the crossroads were invisible from the top of the mountain. Nor could he pursue with the driveway staunched by the ruins of the Mercedes. Unless they got lucky, the killer had escaped.

Climbing back up the driveway was harder than going down. Lacking outlets for water, the household staff had joined several garden hoses and run them down from the pool, coaxing water, fire, and burnt things into a rank mud. Levent tried to ignore the things in his path and succeeded but for the flowering bushes at the side of the driveway. Some were in bloom while others had been burnt black, turned toward the sky like the prayers of the damned.

Turan, king of the damned, sat in the driveway ten meters up the slope from the wreckage, looking at his hands in his lap like a beggar at his coins. No one seemed to mind him, and he did not react when Levent came near. He did not seem to be capable of doing anything that called for focus.

Levent went down in a crouch beside him, speaking softly to his grief. "It's dangerous here, Turan. We still might have secondary explosions. Get up now. Come with me."

He obeyed. Although Turan refused the hand that Levent put to his arm, he rose and staggered a step down the hill toward the flames that were beginning to gutter.

"No, this way," said Levent. "To the house."

Turan listened to Levent's voice with a violent lean of his head, as if momentous words had been spoken. He blinked, turned slowly, and began to walk away from the wreckage. He seemed to understand that this was the way it would be for the rest of his life—walking away from the flames and the things he had left there to be consumed. He had taken several labored steps when he saw Tolga standing near the head of the slope, directing more hoses to the fire.

"*You!*" Turan shouted in a voice filled with discovery. "What happened? What did you allow to happen?"

Tolga was one of the few men who had witnessed things like this before, and had probably made things like it happen. His face lined with heavy vertical creases did not show confusion or surprise.

"This is not the time," he said. "We'll find out how it was done."

"You'll make a report," said Turan, his voice breaking badly. "Be sure to use my computer for the work."

Tolga said nothing.

Turan stepped closer, looming. "Why don't you tell me the woman I loved died in that car? Say *something!*"

Tolga spoke almost inaudibly, "Don't worry. Someone will pay."

Turan's hands were already in fists, but he when he brought the right one across Tolga's face it struck as an open slap. The sound of flesh meeting flesh was surprisingly feeble. Anything would have sounded feeble after the tremendous roar that had crashed across the mountain.

Tolga's head moved to one side, then moved back into place, every gray hair in place, as if he was a device with limited motion. He could have blocked the roundabout, but he was a professional who knew that amateurs spent emotion to right themselves.

"If you won't be needing me any longer, Turan."

"I want you off my property," said Turan, who recognized everything but his impotence. "Tell them to send me another man. Damn it, I want someone who knows what he's *doing!*"

As Tolga turned away, he looked at Levent as if to pass off a burden. Levent nodded, though he was more concerned with what Turan had said. *Them.* Tell them to send me another man. He had not spoken of an employment agency.

"He's a legend," said Turan to Tolga's back. "A legend! I'd rather have a man by my side any day."

Tolga stopped his climb, but only to tell Turan he had heard the slur. When he knew Turan would not speak again, Tolga resumed his pace up the driveway toward the house.

Turan shook his fist at Tolga, making a strange tingling sound. Levent saw that he had a key chain lapped over his fingers. "She gave me this, you know," said Turan, shaking the chain toward Levent now. "It's the key to a rented BMW, in case I wanted to run down to the village. It's what I have left."

"Did the keys to the cars circulate freely in the house?" asked Levent. "It might be important."

"No," he said belatedly, heavily, as if he had been slapped. "Of course not."

"If it was me, I'd worry more about how my security was breached," said Levent. "The same thing could happen again."

Turan shook the image away by shaking his head. "I can't imagine it."

"Was the Mercedes out of this compound at any time after you returned home last night?"

He shook his head again. "No."

"Then the explosives were probably planted earlier," said Levent. "I saw your driver go down to the restaurant for food. It might have been done then."

Turan was thinking, but not well yet. "We drove home last night. Nothing happened. Nothing was wrong."

"You wouldn't have noticed anything wrong," said Levent. "The killer apparently didn't want to destroy a car with innocent people in it. He had a specific target. You."

Turan wheeled his head by moving his whole body around. "Me?" he said. "That isn't me scattered all over this mountain."

As he spoke, the first Jandarma van arrived, wheeling into the lower driveway. It was not Commandant Comert, but another van from the closest post to the mountain. At least someone had the sense to call them. Probably Tolga.

"He thought it was you driving the Mercedes," said Levent. "He wasn't close enough to know it was someone else."

"He?" said Turan. "*He?*"

"Sevim's son," said Levent flatly. "He killed Harman by fire. He wanted to kill you the same way. You can see that. If you think for a moment, you'll see it."

Turan saw it, because he had known it, too. But he could not bring the past close enough to himself to admit his complicity. "You *know* this," he said. "How long have you known it?"

"Since last night," said Levent. "Late last night."

Turan found another focus for his anger in the man before him. "When were you going to tell *me?*"

"If you'd been direct with me, you'd have known already," said Levent. "Last night we impounded the ship he came into the country with. We arrested his mother. Suzanne Vardan is quite a woman. You knew her in Paris, I'm sure."

"If I knew her, it was because I was last in line at the mattress," he said angrily. "What in the hell are you talking about?"

"You didn't go to Sevim's funeral, did you?"

"And I don't remember why," he said.

"You should have gone, Turan. You'd have seen her there. She was pregnant with Sevim's son."

Turan saw it now, and how much of it he knew was his secret. "This piece of shit will die," he said. "He won't live one more day."

"We'll take care of him," said Levent. "His time is ours now."

Turan had his manner back from the flames. He spoke calmly. "I'll want to know when that happens," he said. "I want to know *first*."

Levent said nothing.

"First," said Turan, his voice turning where it went when he found his feathers. "You'll do that because you know that the rest of your life will be taken care of. It will be a generous life, Onur. You know it's nothing I ask but justice. You owe that to me."

Turan was done delegating. He wanted the feeling of blood returned for blood. Levent watched as the fire wagon came into the driveway fast, the driver shouting for the Jandarma van to move aside. Another Jandarma van appeared on the road. It was the commandant's.

"What you're asking is a lot, Turan. It's more than you know."

"It's not," he said in a tone that had gotten more aggressive even as it grew smoother. "It's not more in any way."

Levent nodded to Turan as if they had made a bargain. "My advice is that you keep clear of this investigation. Stay in the house and don't go outside for any reason. I'll be in touch."

"You have my number," he said. "Use it and you'll prosper."

CHAPTER 22

"I have to say we didn't expect a response this soon," said Metin, as they walked at the side of the road and down the hill. "You must have had quite a start."

"It was a finish," said Levent. "A sudden one."

"That's what comes of letting those bastards loose, Onur. We could have milked them for everything if we'd been left to do our job."

Levent continued to walk in the dust at the side of the road until he reached a wider place where cars had worn a bald area as they reversed after missing the turn into the valley. On the ground were a set of tread marks that looked recent. The constant wind ripping along this side of the mountain said they were.

"He could have watched from here," said Levent, pointing to the tread marks. "Small tires made these marks."

"Possible," said Metin. "But that black car isn't the only small one in the area. It's just the one nobody can find."

"He watched from somewhere," said Levent. "He didn't work off a timer, or the car would have blown up in the garage or last night at the restaurant."

"There's one problem, Onur. You seem to think this animal wouldn't kill other people if they got in the way."

"I do. He wanted Turan, not his mistress."

"An unlucky girl."

"She was lucky for a while," said Levent. "Anyone who has anything to do with Turan Yoruk prospers for a while."

"I'm looking for a lesson in this," said the commandant, turning his arm back toward the house. "It's too bad I can't put it in my damned report."

Levent wanted to tell Metin the things he had kept back, because he had learned to trust him. What Levent could not trust was the structure behind Metin. The Jandarma were close to the military, close to MIT, and the things that clustered around Turan. The Deep State was a shadow, but not insubstantial. It was more powerful for being dark and always at the threshold of vision. Tek was right: the only thing that betrayed it was the smell. It was here on the road, traveling all the way from the compound.

"Do you have anything on the parents yet?"

"Nothing large," said Metin. "The woman went to a shop in town after their late breakfast. She bought a new cell phone, so we can assume she plans to use it."

"To get in touch with her son."

"I can't think of another reason," said Metin. "After she got back to the hotel, the diplomat went down to the Internet on the first floor and stayed ten minutes. Checking his mail, I suppose."

"Did he wait long after his wife returned before he went downstairs?"

"You're thinking cause and effect."

"He could have relayed the new phone number to the son," said Levent. "Ten minutes is not a lot of browsing time. What did they do afterward?"

"Nothing unexpected, but they're on the move," said Metin. "They took their car—a red Renault Megane—and drove out to Yalikavak Marina for a late lunch. They're still there at last look."

"How many men do you have on them?"

"Two," he said. "I put them in plainclothes, but they still look like Jandarma."

That made for convergence. If the parents were at the marina, and Levent had an appointment with Oral Orhan, triangulation was possible. The son might try to contact his mother, and it could work the other way, too.

"If you can spare another man, put him on them, too," said Levent. "I'm going to shake these people as hard as I can. With some luck, they'll jump for contact."

Metin shrugged. "They didn't the last time, but all right. I'll go myself."

"Can you spare one of your digital cameras from the van?" asked Levent. "That should be my best weapon."

* * *

Levent drove into Yalikavak in fifteen fast minutes. It would have been another five to the marina, but he halved the time by parking in the boatyard. Metin would see to his men and reconfigure their surveillance.

"I have one stop to make before I talk to the parents," said Levent. "Keep your men out of the way. Remember that Sevim has a rifle."

"And a license to kill."

Levent headed toward the office of Oral Orhan without taking that into account. When word circulated among the police that a young woman had been blasted to meat from ambush, diplomatic immunity would not do much to protect Sevim. Levent would have cautioned the commandant about that if he thought it would do any good.

Double O had a visitor in his office, a young man in his early thirties whose face was burnt dark by the sun and hair lightened by the same. Oral rose quickly when he saw Levent.

"This is the fellow I told you about," he said, pointing to the young man. "Green Card Harry, we call him."

Levent nodded toward Harry, but did not put out his hand. He looked directly at Oral. "I'd like to speak with you privately. It's urgent."

"No problem, Onur."

Green Card Harry moved like a sailor from the room in a rolling stride, as if he had just come off a long cruise. "Later," he said in English.

When Levent was sure the young man had moved on down the hall, and made a point of making sure, he asked Oral: "Is this office secure? I mean, is there any chance we'll be overheard?"

"I sweep this place myself," he said. "The last bug will be the first."

Levent moved to the window that overlooked the harbor where no vessels seemed to have left for the sea or changed position in the last day. Oral would not be distracted from his second job with MIT, or his raki, for long.

"There's been a serious incident," said Levent. "You know Turan, of course."

"Of course," he said with no hesitation.

"There was a bombing while I was at his house on the hill," said Levent. "It happened not more than an hour ago. A young woman was killed. Turan, well, if you know him you understand that he never loses control."

"Absolutely."

"He's lost control," said Levent. "Absolutely. He was close to the young woman, as close as can be, so it's understandable. Still, it's a volatile situation. We don't have any indication of who planted the bomb, but you know—"

"Kurds," said Oral. "Who the hell else uses bombs but those PKK bastards?"

It was best to let others suggest their fantasies, knowing that they usually chose the most convenient one. Turan might have been on the PKK short list, along with Tolga, Harman and others.

"We can't jump to conclusions without knowing more," said Levent. "Right now, I'm concerned about Turan. He blames everyone for falling short on security, including the men immediately around him. He attacked his bodyguard in front of everyone. He says he wants help from your people. That's not a good idea right now."

Oral nodded in agreement, his heavy jowls trembling. "What you're saying makes sense. Having him go off the deep end would be the worst thing. But I don't know what can be done about it."

"I'd like you to put in a call to your people," said Levent as if he knew exactly who they were. "I won't tell you what to say, but explain the situation. Tell them to ignore any requests for personnel or other assistance that come from Turan. Just for a day or so. Until he calms down."

Oral was hesitant. "I suppose that could be done."

"Look," said Levent, taking his tone down a notch. "If you don't believe me, go up and talk to Turan yourself. He might not be coherent, and you'll probably have a hell of a time getting through the police vehicles, but see for yourself. There's blood everywhere, even on the roses."

"A young woman."

"Yes."

"Not the one with the long black hair and the—"

"You must know her."

"I saw her once," said Oral, his eyes gone suddenly rheumy. "No wonder Turan's out of his mind. That was some piece."

"She's all pieces now, Oral. I have to go back and help pick them up and put them in plastic bags. Small plastic bags. Can I count on your help to keep this situation from going completely out of control?"

Double O put out his hand. "You can depend on me, Onur."

* * *

The stepfather and mother of Sevim had just paid the bill at the cafe where they had eaten. It was not a Turkish pastani but a French patisserie that boasted a magnificent view of the harbor and the rocky outcrops and islands across the bay. They had crossed the lawn to the broad stone walkway when Levent caught up, cutting in before them as they reached a long bench that faced the sea and the declining sun.

"Sit down, you two," he said. "I've got something to show you."

They did not want to. They did not see why they should, but when Levent sat on the bench they did not move away. They were dressed in casual clothes but not in shorts, in colors that were primary but oddly dull. He was tall, she was short, but Levent could tell they had been up most of the night. They were of an age when the years showed in the skin. It had something to do with circulation. With blood.

"I've just come from Turan Yoruk's house," said Levent as he sat and removed the digital camera from the pouch in his hand. "There was an explosion in his car that should have killed him but failed. I wanted to tell you about it because you're bound to be disappointed."

"Inspector, we have no interest in this matter," said Fernan Verbanian in very correct English. "You're mistaken."

"You will have some interest," said Levent. "Sit down."

Neither husband or wife spoke, but they obeyed and sat on the bench beside him. They watched Levent put the camera into view mode and watched his face as he looked into the LCD monitor. He clicked the button twice, bringing in the first bright image—a shot of the catastrophic damage in the driveway.

"You see the results," said Levent, pushing the camera closer to them. "This was a Mercedes before it was destroyed. The explosives were powerful and well placed."

They gave the camera their attention, not as a team but slightly out of tandem. The stepfather of Sevim looked away first. His hand rose to his cheek as if something had landed there. The mother of Sevim studied the image more than Levent would have expected if he had not known her.

"Inspector, this is grim," she said. "Is that all you have to darken our day?"

Levent clicked the button that advanced the monitor to the next image. It was a close shot of a rose bush. The flower was red as these things usually were. The stem, leaves and thorns were red, too, as if painted.

"That's blood," he said. "Are you interested in whose?"

Neither answered.

"A woman was driving the car when the explosives detonated," said Levent. "If I said she was beautiful, it would mean nothing, but she was as beautiful as any woman I've seen. Before she left the house, I watched her tie up her hair from across the lawn. It was long and she wrapped it tight. I recall thinking that she could look like a man from where I sat. She must have looked like that to your son as he watched her come down the driveway at a greater distance."

Levent clicked the button again to advance to the third photo. It was the finger with the ring still on it.

"This is what Sevim did to the woman," he said. "He accomplished nothing. You should tell him that. He may want to try again."

When Suzanne Vardan spoke, her voice seemed to lose a small part of the control that had been everything Levent knew from her. "I'm sorry for this, Inspector. But you were there at the time? There at the house?"

"I was questioning Turan," said Levent. "That's my job. I'm trying to understand what yours should be at this point, Mrs. Vardan. Your son won't succeed in what he's doing. Turan has taken him seriously and won't allow another attempt on his life. What your son did will only ensure that he won't be taken alive. Believe me, the Jandarma will see to that."

"Turkish justice," she said scornfully.

"In this case, yes."

She raised her hand to her eyes as if to shield them from the image in the camera, though she did not look away. Common humanity demanded it, but Suzanne Vardan had passed from that stage. Levent had the feeling she might return to it when she spoke to her husband.

"Could you leave us, Fernan? Just for a bit."

"You shouldn't talk to him," said her husband. "Think of all the things we shouldn't have done and add this to it."

When she did not respond, he rose and walked away as if he was glad to have respite. The stone walk took the loose stride of his sandals in rhythmic clops like any other. Levent supposed it was easy for the rich to find a surrogate husband and father. They must have shuffled through the foreign service lists to find a quiet compliant one. He had been abroad at his job for much of Sevim's life, leaving the mother to raise the child. So the imprinting had been thorough. Total.

Levent waited until the husband who was so vital to his wife's plan had gone too far to hear. He clicked another small button and the lens of the camera closed with a smooth electronic purr.

"I asked my husband to leave because I want to tell you something," she said in a way that was informative but less than confidential. "It's something about my family that Fernan shouldn't have to hear. He knows about it. He accepts it. But he's French. He thinks like a Frenchman. That's not quite true of me."

"You were born in this country?"

"I was an Istanbullu." She smiled in the wistful way that almost everyone did when they claimed that place. "My family had a business in one of the back streets just off the Covered Bazaar. They sold very fine, very expensive jewelry. It was better to have an appointment when you came into their shop. They knew all their customers and never advertised for more in the papers. Word-of-mouth was all they needed to survive. It was all very civilized. Istanbul is the most civilized place on earth because of the past that never ends."

"Yes."

"Then there's the savagery," she said as if she had completed the cycle. "My family survived the genocide in the east because they were never really a part of it. They were merchants and members of a very conservative community. So they stayed on in place. The empire fell and the republic rose. They prospered. They were like American Indians living on a reservation called Istanbul. There were gaps in their genealogy—massacres—but they had prayers for those who had fallen. Armenians have prayers for everything. Hopes, let's say. Then one day the savages came out again and much closer. There was a tremendous riot in the Old Town along Istiklal Caddesi. Every shop with a Greek or Armenian owner was turned to trash in an afternoon."

Levent said nothing. What she said was true. The way she said it was not false.

"My family took that day as a warning," she said, turning her voice like a planet far from the sun. "Their shop had not been caught up in the violence, but what happened told them that nothing was safe in Turkey. They made plans to leave the country. They did it rationally, betting there was time to do it. And they won. I was growing up as they made their plans to move, never knowing I would be leaving the only home I had ever known.

The day I found out was the saddest day of my life. I loved Istanbul. Even now, after all these years, I'm not really a Parisian in my heart."

"I wouldn't have known," said Levent. "You seem like one."

"I'm telling you this so you can understand the present," she said with the same unhurried way that she said nearly everything. "I always felt out of place in France. I was a Parisian who grew up in a tumultuous time and an Armenian who had no thought for victim-hood. What happened was a long time ago. I was modern and there were greater problems closer to home. Probably, I was rebellious. When I found out these crazy Turks had a party boat moored in the Seine, I went to see them out of curiosity. I may have been looking for the past that was stolen by the past, though I never said that to myself. When I met Sevim, I heard all that in his voice and saw it in his beauty. He was a White Turk with blue eyes and brown hair that he wore almost down to his shoulders. He had a sense of humor—a sense of life—no one could forget. I knew we never could have found each other in Istanbul. Not being who we were. Not with all the history. But finding him in Paris was like finding all the things that should have been."

She put her arm around the back of the bench and looked off toward the husband who was a single dot two hundred meters away on the walkway. He saw her and began to walk back as if by signal. She was done. Suzanne Vardan had said what she wanted. She would not revisit her past again, but seemed to await a reaction from Levent.

"From what I heard, Sevim was a remarkable man," he said.

"I don't doubt it. But there's one thing I'd like you to explain."

"If I can," she said, leaving doubt that she would.

"He died long ago," said Levent. "What made you decide to take your revenge after all these years?"

She smiled again in the same way she had when she called herself an Istanbullu. "I received a letter in the mail one day about a year ago," she said. "It was forwarded from an attorney in Istanbul. I put the letter away for several months, because I wasn't sure how I should react to the information in it. It offered an explanation for the terrible things that happened long ago. It brought the past I had put away into the present in an extraordinary way. A sudden way. It filled me with grief—the same grief—but it also offered a channel for my emotions. A way. It changed everything."

"Who wrote the letter?"

"An old woman who made it one of her last acts."

Levent did not understand until he remembered that Sevim, the Libyan Pirate, had left a mother in Istanbul who died about a year ago. She had been responsible for Turan's exclusion from Bodrum and must have known she had a grandson living in Paris. Levent did not believe Suzanne Vardan debated long in showing the letter to her son. He was sure she had only taken the time to calculate every possibility for revenge. She was more of an Istanbullu than she knew or would admit to herself.

So the vendetta had been handed down by the women of two tribes. If this was tragedy, it was not only of Bodrum, but as old as Halicarnassus and the ancient dramatists who passed legacies of bad blood from generation to generation.

"Did you show the letter to your son?"

"Yes," she said as if she might finally regret that. "He knew that Fernan wasn't his biological father, and you were right that he had never accepted it and many other things. He'd been a stranger in our house all his life. Nothing I could tell him made a difference. Worse, he was a stranger to his own feelings. His instincts. They were always more violent and consuming than any of the expensive things around him. But after I showed him the letter, everything seemed to fall in place. Everything, including his drive to right the past."

"That was true for both of you."

"Yes."

"I'm sure you were predisposed to believe the letter," said Levent. "You knew Turan in Paris, didn't you?"

"Oh, yes," she said in a lighter way that was more deadly for being so. "He always tagged at Sevim's side in those days. He was so close that I thought he might have a physical relationship with the man I loved. But the feeling lasted only as long as it took to know him. It was nothing as natural as love with Turan. Never. He was a vampire—a bloodsucker. His lips weren't so red, but they might have been. He fed on Sevim's incredible energy until he felt strong enough to move away. What I know about him is that when he decided to move on the man he envied, he did it with no feeling. No love. Really, he's not capable of love."

"I'd differ with that," said Levent. "Turan loves money and all it brings."

"Then you do know him," she said. "And you know what he did to have those things."

"I'm convinced of his guilt," said Levent. "Having the rest of the world agree isn't possible, I'm afraid."

She looked toward her husband, who was coming up the walk. He was so near that he had nearly regained all his height, as if she had willed him to her as she had willed the past into the future.

"I suppose that brings us to now," she said.

"Yes, it does, exactly. You should get in touch with your son, Mrs. Vardan. Tell him what happened at Turan's."

She said nothing.

"Your son's only hope is to let me handle this," said Levent. "If Sevim comes to me, we may find a way out for him."

"And I'm to believe you're different than all the rest?"

"Wasn't his father?"

CHAPTER 23

Levent left the marina with as much as he had hoped for. Suzanne Vardan said she would contact her son. She must have sensed that Levent was skeptical. As if to seal a bargain, she showed him the new cell phone she had bought at the shop.

She had done one more thing that demonstrated her trust to the man who was presumed to be different than the rest. She flipped to a photograph embedded in her new phone that showed a picture of Sevim, saying that it would be useful for the inspector to know what he looked like. Levent was grateful to have an image of the man who he had chased for days. He had no objection when she took a picture of him with her phone camera, so recognition could pass both ways.

She wanted to make her son human in the eyes of the law, and in that she had success. The young man who appeared on the display might have been the mirror of his father as she described him. Sevim had dark hair that favored his mother, but crystalline blue eyes and a flared nose that spoke of the father. He wore his hair long, but less than his father's shoulder length. He seemed as tall as Yilmaz had said, his limbs long, his body lean and whip-strong. The energy was there too, but it was overdone, feverish, as if the genetic transfer was skewed. This was a young man who had marked out his limits and found them wanting.

Unstable? Yes.

Crazed?

That was a matter of definition that Sevim had defined. No outsider ever got more than a portion of the past, but the image of the young man put flesh to every corner of it. Levent had almost doubted that such virulent hatred could have been passed from mother to son. Now that was a fact.

Sevim's clothing was like any nautical tourist—shorts of more than normal length and a bosun's striped shirt—but Levent saw two things worth noting. Sevim wore boots. They were serious boots, ankle high in dark brown leather.

The second thing he culled from the photograph was nearly a shadow. The background behind Sevim was blurred, but a strange object seemed to jut from his left ear. It looked like a green candelabra. A plant? Yes. Levent could not place it, though it seemed oddly familiar.

Levent thought nothing more of the two anomalies until after he left the Vardans. Then he asked himself how the photo of Sevim had gotten to the camera. The phone was new. Either Suzanne had taken a picture of her son, which was nearly impossible with surveillance, or Sevim had sent it to his mother.

Levent spent a moment doubting both scenarios. He decided on the second when he remembered that some models had timer delays that would allow the photographer to take his self portrait. He could have set the camera in advance and moved into position before the shot was taken.

So Sevim had sent it. He had taken the picture outdoors, where a flare of green vegetation showed. He was dressed in clothes that were unremarkable except for his hiking boots. And even those were unremarkable to anyone but Levent.

The young man planned to use those heavy-duty boots. He was going off-trail and Levent had an idea of where.

* * *

The commandant waited when Levent came to the parking lot. He did not see the other two men working surveillance, which was a distinct improvement.

"Tell me about the mountain behind Turan's house," said Levent. "I need to know if it's possible to climb to the summit from the opposite side."

Metin did not follow Levent's thinking immediately. "You'd have to be a first-class climber," he said. "It's rough as hell on that side—heavy in the sort of brush and trees we have here."

"If you were determined," said Levent, "how would you do it?"

"An asphalt road that runs along the base of the mountain, but it won't take you a quarter of the way up," he said. "A fire road runs another quarter of the way to the top. All you'd need for that is determination. But the rest is bad business. There's no trail I know of. Alexander the Great looked at that mountain and said, fuck it, if they're up there, they're sure to starve if they don't bust their asses in a fall."

"Let's say you had experience climbing and some basic equipment," said Levent. "Is it possible to get to the top?"

"We're talking of a specific lunatic," said Metin, who saw everything now. "So I'd say yes for him. He'll be beaten up and bloody by the time he reaches the top—and I don't know how he plans to get back down before nightfall."

"Let's say he has cheese and crackers to take him through the night," said Levent. "Where would he go in for the climb?"

"He'd head off somewhere near the end of the fire road," said Metin slowly. "Not all the way to the end because it butts hard against a sheer slope. You'd need a harness, pick, pitons, all of it, to scale that part of the mountain."

"So he'd go off short of the hard slope."

"That's my guess," said Metin, who had clearly never made the climb. "I don't know where, but it would be somewhere east of the road."

"I'd like you to take one of your men off surveillance," said Levent. "I don't think much will happen with the parents. They might move to join the boy if he finishes what he started. Until then, we should be clear."

"I'll take your word."

"Send your man up the mountain," said Levent. "Tell him to look for a way in and some sign that it was done. Any houses there?"

"Two small ones," said Metin. "Both sit near the end of the asphalt road. One is nearer the fire road than the other. A goatherd."

"Tell your man to check everything, including the houses. I'd like to know if our man went up that mountain, and even better, when."

"I'll go myself to look around," said Metin. "We'll see what we can find."

* * *

With the commandant's binoculars, Levent scanned the rugged face of the long scabby mountain. From his angle standing on the road halfway between Turan's compound and the opposite side of the mountain, he saw nothing that looked like movement and little variation in color. The predominant gray rock of the mountain carried through most of the slope, and the dark green vegetation did not end even at the top, as it often did on the peninsula.

The cover was thicker farther down where trees and brush hid the sway of the mountain. Some scattered flowers peaked out from the forest, pink oleander that had seeded itself where competition was scarce, and here and there some cactus.

It was pale green cactus with broad leaves and glints of red fruit that appeared in season. Levent focused harder, but could not bring the cactus close enough for detail. Only slowly did he become sure of what he could not quite see. The cactus was common in the wild and often in the gardens in Bodrum. They were Indian figs, and their fruit was called prickly pear.

Sevim was up there somewhere. He had taken the photo with the candelabra of cactus sprouts that were about to bloom behind him.

But as closely as Levent looked, he could not dial in a view of the direction that Sevim must have taken. The bulge of the mountain and several ravines blocked too much of his line-of-sight. The only way he could have seen the eastern spur that the commandant thought was the likely route to the top would have been to back off into the flatland to the north. And that was too far for the glasses to pick out a man.

Levent did not think he was wrong about Sevim, but making that climb with a pack and rifle made for slow going. It would grow much worse with a misstep. Even a sprained ankle could turn into a serious problem.

A miscalculation? His second miscalculation? Would Sevim abandon his target if he learned he had failed on his first attempt? His mother was certainly in touch with him, and she would tell him the attempt on Turan's life had gone wrong. What Levent did not know was if that would keep the demented young man from going on.

Common sense said no.

Hatred said yes.

Levent brought the glasses down to rest his eyes before putting them on the mountain again. It was tedious work with the late afternoon light slanting in, but he could not let go of the feeling that Sevim was close in everything but elevation. He was almost a presence riding on the horizontal light.

Levent put the glasses back on the mountain, working from the declivity that he had left to a rock face he had not covered. It was the same slow nothing again. He did not even get sprigs of random color and no movement.

He did not know when he became aware of a car approaching on the road, but since it was only the second that had passed, he brought the glasses down again. A bright red BMW. The car slowed as it neared him.

He was surprised when the BMW veered onto the shoulder of the road, crunching pebbles and raising dust. It continued to come fast, braking to a stop with less than twenty centimeters between the front bumper and the rear of Levent's Honda. And it slid a bit closer than that.

Turan. He did not shut down the motor of Sultan's rented car as he moved from behind the wheel, slinging himself onto the dirt at the side of the road. He walked the five paces to Levent as aggressively as he had rammed the car to a halt. He stopped at the same distance of twenty centimeters.

"Inspector, I've been waiting for your call."

"I would have called if there was something you should know," said Levent. "I can't say there is."

"One of my men saw you here on the road," said Turan. "He was surprised to see a man studying the mountain and thought it might be you. What I know about Inspector Levent is that he doesn't do anything without a reason."

Levent did not want to talk to Turan for any reason. He was no longer within the shock of the bombing, and his anger was invisible, but that was the gauge of his control. Levent had never seen anyone's skin change color with less than a day in the southern sun. Turan's had done that. It was as if rage had settled permanently below the surface, putting a charred reddish-purple on his clean shaven features.

"I don't have a good reason to be here," said Levent. "Call it a hunch."

"I'll settle for that," said Turan like a threat. "It's never quite that with an experienced man, is it?"

"I spoke to Suzanne Vardan this afternoon," said Levent, returning Turan's tone. "It might be a good idea if you did, too. I can't guarantee your safety, however."

"We keep coming back to that one," he said, touching her name like a thorn. "Do you know what she was in Paris? We called her Boat Bitch. You couldn't get rid of her. She'd be in the toilet powdering her nose every time you wanted to puke or piss."

"There was no toilet on that boat," said Levent. "Not after a while."

"You're missing the point," said Turan, gliding over fact like a fairy. "That woman couldn't know who the father of her child was. It was lottery and she picked the ticket she wanted in the gene pool."

"So the boy could be anyone's," said Levent. "Even yours."

Turan did not like the logic in his argument now. "No," he said. "Never mine. We're not talking about a man murdering his father—and you can't make him into Jevat Shakir. No one's going to exile this mindless prick to Bodrum so that he can find himself. We're dealing with a criminal who murdered a woman in my driveway. That's all. It's your job to find him and mine to make it worth your while. What do you want?" Turan flung his hand back down the road. "My house? You can have it if you bring this filth to me."

For the smallest part of a moment, the idea of having the finest dwelling on the Aegean coast sang through Levent's mind. He saw himself sitting at the pool. He heard his voice calling to one of the servants he would never have.

But that was not the sound that Levent heard. It was more familiar—Benny and the Jets. "Yes."

"Onur," said the commandant. "I'd say we got lucky again, but every time that happens we get kicked in the ass harder. This time may be the hardest yet."

Levent walked away from Turan toward the side of the road that took him closest to Metin. To his surprise, Turan did not follow.

"What do you have?"

"I've got a man who lives at the base of the mountain short of where I said this boy should go in. He has a pickup truck and says he gave our suspect a ride. I don't know what that does to the theory about a small black car, but the hitchhiker answers the general description. He had a large pack and a long case when he jumped in back of the truck this morning. Very early in the morning."

That meant Sevim had hiked up the mountain to get his view of Turan's compound for the bombing, and it confirmed that his distance from the target had led him wrong. It also supplied a reason why Levent had seen nothing through the glasses as he scanned the slope. Sevim had already found his mark. He was not moving. He was waiting and watching, if he was still there.

"What can you do from your end, Metin?"

"Not much right now," he said. "I've called for every man I have, but we'd be lucky to get up that mountain before nightfall, and we can't make headway after that. So we're basically stuck in place until tomorrow. We'll flush him out then."

"What about a helicopter?"

"None available," he said. "There's a fire at Ichmeler that drew all the choppers that way. They won't be back in time to ferry us in. So it looks like morning for them as well."

Levent turned and walked back to Turan. He stopped short of the mandatory twenty centimeters. "Do you know of a way up the mountain from here?"

Turan brushed his hand toward the mountain in the same way as he had offered his kingdom to Levent. "There is one," he said. "I can show you."

"How long to the summit?"

"An hour," said Turan. "Perhaps a little more."

Levent walked away from Turan again, speaking quickly to Metin and hoping his voice did not carry. "I'm going to try to get up the mountain from this position," he said. "It's a faster way to the top, and I should be there before nightfall. I'll keep in touch, so leave your phone open."

"I don't like that, Onur. Not alone at this time of day."

"I won't take chances," said Levent.

The commandant protested twice more until Levent surrendered the connection gently. It would have been a bad idea to irritate the man on whom your life depended, and Levent knew that every minute was precious now. The sun was almost behind the mountain at his back. The light that everything depended on would not last more than two hours.

"Now tell me how to get up the mountain."

"I said I'd show you," said Turan. "The trail starts less than five hundred meters from here, but it won't do any good to tell you how to lose yourself. You have to know where you're going and what to avoid."

"You can't come along," said Levent. "It may be dangerous for me, but it could be deadly for you."

Turan smiled. It was an odd smile that did not seem to begin but wane as it came and put out all the light that touched his face. The smell of carbon dioxide from the car that still muttered gave off the same kind of pollution.

"He's up there, isn't he?"

"I don't know."

"But you're willing to risk your life to find out."

"I control my risk," said Levent. "I know how. Having you along with me is not the way to a pension."

"It's the way to more," said Turan. "Much more."

"Stop that," said Levent with more anger that he intended. "You're making a mistake—the mistake of your life—but I can't stand here and talk the light to death. Shut off that damned car. We'll go together."

CHAPTER 24

They were not far along the climb before Levent realized that his shoes were the things he had not taken into account. The trail, so-called, was not sudden in the lower part, but it was erratic and rocky. His shoes, comfortable for the street, were not made to cushion the shock of so many variable surfaces. The tread gave little purchase on smooth stone and almost none when it changed to pebble and scree.

The only thing that saved Levent from going down hard several times was the fact that there was no moisture on the mountainside. The summer had been very dry, which was normal but surprising as they climbed higher. The bushes that Levent used as levers to pull himself along almost snapped off in his hand several times until he learned to go for the biggest ones. The one creek bed they crossed was so dry that it was impossible to imagine it in spring or winter spate.

But they had made time up the mountain. Turan kept up a good pace without good shoes, as if he had made the climb more than once. His compound could not be seen behind the turning drift of the mountain, but would be visible near the top. He had not spoken except when they came to a difficult traverse from flat rock to a sloping boulder. He offered his hand and said, "You're doing well for a lowlander."

Levent was not doing well. After the first three hundred meters, the bottoms of his feet were so raw that he winced with every step. His breath came hard and then harder, and the increasing elevation had little to do with it. When Turan stopped for a short break halfway up the trail, Levent sat back heavily against a small tree.

"We'll take the final half in one burst," said Turan. "The light should be less tricky near the top, but we want to make sure we have vision."

"Is there any chance we'll be seen from above?"

"Not until we're almost there," said Turan. "We'll want to move fast then. The last twenty meters are very steep with nothing tramped down to mark the entrance. We won't be exposed until we're at that point. Even then we might not be seen from above. That depends on where this killer has staked himself out."

"I think he'll set up close to the edge so he can overlook your compound."

"An observation post," said Turan.

Levent did not want to tell Turan more, but thought better of it. "It could be a sniper's post. We've reason to believe he's armed with a rifle. And he probably knows that his first attempt on your life failed."

"When were you going to tell me this?" asked Turan with a sharp edge. "After his first shot took one of us down?"

"You know now," said Levent. "I told you not to expose yourself at the house. You shouldn't be here either."

Turan said nothing. He reached for his jacket. Both he and Levent were carrying them up the mountain. From the side pocket he took out a semi-automatic pistol. A Zigana T. Turkish made, military issue, with a fifteen round magazine. This one had a laser sight.

"Then we'll have to get close," he said. "Are you ready?"

"You'll follow my lead when we get to the top," said Levent. "If you do anything out of line, I'll shoot you first."

"Understood, Inspector."

"You'd do better to believe it," said Levent.

* * *

Turan was right about the trail being invisible from above. It was nearly so from any angle, growing more rugged and vertical as they climbed the last half of the trail. Several times they worked in tandem as they spanned open rock face, Turan lending his hand after he had made his way forward on hands and knees. Darkness was coming but not steadily, crowding in when they worked the crevices and coming lighter again when they reached more open ground.

Their best help was the vegetation. It gave cover for their movements and was useful for handholds. Levent expected it to play out, but like the opposite side of the mountain, the brush and small trees continued almost all the way to the top. Only on the side facing Turan's compound was the face bare rock.

The wind grew to be a factor. It had been barely felt before the break, but became stronger with elevation. By the time they reached the last hundred meters to the top, the wind was constant, gusting higher and dropping the temperature enough to make Levent go to his jacket. He checked his pistol then, the CZ 85 Metin had lent him. It held sixteen rounds, one more than Turan's Zigana. That was good, because Levent had no extra magazine.

The last twenty meters up the trail were as steep as Turan had promised. Levent moved to the lead then, grappling the bare rock with both hands and trying to keep his forward momentum as those damned shoes tried to take him backward. He could see that he was exposed from above and that made him scramble hard, jamming his shoes into the sheer surface and using them ski-like, chattering so loud he thought he might be heard. He did not think he could have made it if not for the threat of a man with a rifle, but when his hand found the end of the rock, he pulled with all his strength onto the top.

What he saw was a surprise. The vegetation did not disappear as he looked over the high ridge humped like knuckles in a tight fist. There were no tall trees, but plenty of bushes and low brush. All were shrunken, wind-beaten, but still impeded clear sight, so what helped on the climb was a hindrance here.

Levent moved slowly off the top of the near-vertical rock to give Turan his way forward. When bare ground came to his hand, he inched ahead, crawling on his belly until he found the cover of a stunted yew. He went to Metin's glasses then, concentrating on the lip of the ridge overlooking the compound.

And saw nothing. He swept the area twice, knowing there were crevices in the ridge that he could not penetrate. Before he moved to an angle with a better view, he backed the glasses off the lip of the ridge for a hundred meter scan.

And got something almost right away, forty meters from the edge of the cliff. He did not know what it was at first glance, but the way the brush clumped was different than the low-to-the-ground vegetation on the rest of the ridge. He focused tight on it and saw several protruding white edges. It took a moment to decide that they were raw wood showing through. The brush had been gathered and some of it cut or broken. It was a shelter, very crude, but definite.

"What do you have?" asked Turan, who had crawled to Levent's side.

"Not a man," said Levent. "If you look a hundred and fifty meters off and forty from the cliff, you'll see something that seems to be a windbreak. I'm not sure how recent it is. It may have been set up before. There's a goatherd who works this mountain."

"I'm sure he's stupid enough to be a goatherd but not nearly so stupid as to bring his animals that close to the edge of the ridge," said Turan. "I'd say we have something there right now."

"I can't see any movement or color," said Levent. "That's the problem."

"So we move closer."

"I move closer," said Levent. "You stay here in case something goes wrong."

"At your orders, Inspector."

Levent did not like quick agreement from this man, but it was better than an argument that might carry. "If anything goes wrong, contact the Jandarma on your phone. They may have a helicopter free from fire duty by now."

"We can hope."

Levent looked at Turan to fix him in place, knowing that was useless if he took it in mind to ignore good sense. What he saw was a face that had returned to its normal expression and banished anger. Good? Bad? Turan had not found his way ahead by being easy to read.

Levent moved from behind the yew slowly, crawling on hands and knees. Any sign of motion on the still ridge was the thing that would betray him. The thick bushes moved not at all, toughened and bent to rigid angles by the wind. It was blowing steadily from the east, wailing in Levent's ears. That made it almost impossible to hear any noise below the threshold.

But the rush of the wind worked both ways. If Sevim had dug in behind the shelter, he would hear nothing until it was too late. Levent decided to circle north to the shelter—upwind. That made a longer passage, but Sevim would not be able to get a scent of an intruder on the breeze. He had one reliable sense— sight—and that, too, should be obscured by the shelter on the back blind side.

The crawl was slow across the rocky ground and made slower because Levent stopped every fifteen meters to check the area to each side. He had to raise his head to be sure, but he did not want to be surprised from any direction. He did not see movement from the shelter, and he did not think to look back toward Turan until he was a third of the way to the shelter.

What he saw to the rear was nothing.

The bastard had moved from his position behind the yew. Levent waited, scanning the ground for fifty meters around, but still saw nothing. Turan's green shirt would not show up well in the brush, and he would be careful to stay low. With dusk sifting in like a door closing very slowly, Turan would be even less visible. Nothing could be done about that now.

Levent began to move again toward the shelter that was still eighty meters away. This was the most exposed part of the crawl with no brush for the better part of twenty meters. He should have skirted the area that had been stripped clear by the wind and sub-surface extrusions. He should have moved toward the cliff even if it was downwind. He should have done all that if only because Turan was on the loose.

He tried to move as quickly as he could without flagging his position, his back low and tight, elbows digging into the rocky ground. He had only gone ten meters when the shot sounded.

It came out of the wind like a quick hand clap. Levent could not tell if it was a rifle or pistol shot, but the bullet arrived within the sound, making a hole in the air in front of his face.

He went down flat on the ground and did not move. He worked his pistol into his hand, knowing it was useless for a long shot but feeling better for the weight.

Nothing followed. Levent did not know which direction the shot had come from, but he turned his face toward the shelter and the cliff. He shouted.

"Hold your fire!" he said. "This is Inspector Levent of the police!"

Levent listened hard over the wind, but nothing came. No voice. No shots.

"Sevim, answer me!"

He did not. Levent heard nothing from ahead and nothing from behind where Turan should have been. Only the wind returned its steady drilling.

"This is Inspector Levent!" he said again. "You know me! Your mother sent you my picture so you would!"

For a ten-second count—a very long time—Levent heard nothing. He had no idea if Suzanne Vardan had sent the photograph, or if Sevim's phone battery had survived on this mountain.

Then he heard a strong voice heaved over the wind. "Stand up so I can see you!"

That was the worst good news anyone could bring. If Levent stood, he would be in the clear for a rifle. If he stayed down, he had a dialogue.

"Put your weapon aside!" he shouted. "I'll do the same!"

Levent slowly held his pistol above his head. He might pull it back missing fingers, but less was more right now.

No shot came. Slowly, Levent tossed the pistol in front of him. He had snapped the safety off and kept it off in case he had to reclaim the pistol quickly. There was a small chance the weapon might misfire as it struck the ground, but that did not happen.

"I'm unarmed now!" said Levent when he had no answer. "We can talk! Show your weapon and we'll talk! You can trust me!"

For several seconds, Sevim's voice did not return. Levent had been slowly inching forward, and now he pushed harder. He did not want to be where Sevim thought he was, and he still wanted to be able to move fast for the pistol.

"My weapon's down!" said the strong voice out of the wind again. "That's all you'll get! Now it's your turn! Stand!"

In all his years at Homicide, Levent had never been shot. He had been fired at several times, always by other men with pistols. Trusting a lunatic not to cut him down with a rifle made him as crazy as that man. But he made the decision to stand, and he stood, not fast or slow. He turned sideways to the shelter to make a smaller target, but he stood, amazed at his behavior. He was not trembling. He was not himself exactly.

For five seconds, nothing happened from the shelter. As Levent ticked the time off in his mind, he felt fear taking over, telling him how it would be to die. *Take your time,* Sevim was saying. *Mark your spot. Squeeze slowly.*

But Sevim stood up, rising from the brush like a tall dark animal. He was not at the shelter, but twenty-five meters to the rear at an oblique angle. Levent realized that Sevim had taken a position near the head of the V that was visible from Turan's compound. Near but not at the ridge. He had chosen a good position to turn one of those flat trajectory cartridges down the hill.

But it was also easy for him to turn and fire on a man who did not present the thinner target that he had thought. Sevim was facing him on a good angle. His rifle was down, folded in his arms, but ready. He looked enough like the photo in the cell phone to be its distant twin. His long fair hair was mangled by the wind, and he was taller than Levent imagined.

More than that could not be seen until he began to move slowly toward his target. He walked with the angle of his head steady, never taking his eyes completely from Levent, scanning the area and relying on peripheral vision for the rest. He did not stop until he was ten meters off. That would be just beyond the effective range of a pistol if Levent had another. He did not.

"I don't talk much," said Sevim, speaking in slow but not stilted English. "What do you have to say?"

"I want you to come back with me," said Levent. "I told your mother I'd guarantee your safety—and I will."

Levent could not see Sevim's face closely, but he was sure the lunatic smiled. "That means I've done something wrong."

"Wrong's not the word in this case," said Levent, still boosting his voice. "We're talking about your survival. The Jandarma are coming up this hill. There are enough of them to make sure they do the job. You're their job and they won't take you prisoner."

"But I'll be able to walk out with you," he said with an edge of disbelief. "Is that the way it is?"

"Yes," said Levent. "You'll walk out alive."

He seemed to consider the avenue Levent offered until he turned his head and looked toward the long side of the mountain. He looked closely, measuring the thing he had seen against the future. He shook his head slowly.

"I don't think so," he said so quietly that his voice almost did not carry. "I don't think we'll leave this place. Not you. Not me."

Levent took Sevim's words as a lunatic's curse until he looked in that direction, too. He did not understand that what he saw was a pale glow of red light. It was like the quick glimmer of light—the flash of explosion—that he had seen in the video tape of the parking lot of the convenience store. He was sure he would not have known this light had color except for the smell that arrived at the same time. Something was burning. Something stunk and burned, hoisted on the wind.

Fire. The mountain was burning. The last of the light hurried away like an audible thing and darkness began to close fast. The red light that boiled from behind the slope of the mountain began to move faster, fanned by the wind. Levent did not think about the origin of the flames; he did not hesitate; he brought his hand to his jacket pocket and called out.

"Cell phone!"

Sevim did not bring his rifle up to counter. He was too surprised for that. Levent hit the number that brought up the commandant. He was very glad when Metin came on the line immediately.

"We have a fire up here!" said Levent. "We're at the summit and there's fire coming from your direction!"

"I can see it," said the commandant. "I've already called the helicopters in. They should be there soon. What's your situation?"

Levent knew his situation but not the speed that the helicopters would make across the peninsula to the mountain. They had to scoop the water from the sea three kilometers away and carry it in the buckets under their bellies. Minutes were not the question. Seconds mattered.

"We'll get down the mountain the same way we came up," said Levent. "Keep the choppers coming. This whole mountain will burn!"

"We?" said the commandant.

"All of us," said Levent as he hung off. "We're coming down if we can!"

Levent held the cell phone toward Sevim. "We can get off this mountain by the trail we came up," he said. "Follow me!"

The answer to how much Sevim wanted to die by fire came quickly. He moved toward Levent with speed, carrying the rifle in both hands. The threat of that weapon disappeared as he came closer. The monster was really a man. He was a young man with wide shoulders, a flared nose and light eyes. The glow of fear made them his own now, and his voice was not hostile when it came.

"Where's the trail?" he said.

"South," said Levent. "That way."

Levent took a long step to the place where he had thrown his pistol. He said, "Weapon," as he reached down and picked up the CZ85 by two fingers. Carefully, he jacked the magazine from the butt and caught it in his left hand.

"Empty," he said, putting the magazine in one pocket and the pistol in the other.

Sevim had brought the rifle onto Levent when he retrieved the pistol from the ground. He did not take it off target, but nodded.

Levent began to move away toward the side of the mountain. He did not turn his back on Sevim. He waited until the man with the rifle came abreast at a slightly greater pace before he matched it.

At close range, Sevim's eyes were more feverish than they looked in the picture. Levent thought of the amphetamines Achille mentioned as an explanation. The drug had taken Sevim through last night—perhaps the last several nights—and would take him through the ones to come—if there were any.

But two men were going off this mountain together. Partners, yes. Lunatics, probably. They would be able to head off the flames and slide down the rock face onto the trail. The brush on the south side of the mountain might take the flames, it might burn like dry torches, the smoke would be as dangerous as the flames, but if they kept to the rock faces and went low into the crevices, Levent was sure they could survive.

Levent held that thought like a talisman as they crossed the bald and came into thick brush again. He believed it until he saw the tiny red light emerge out of the red glow that was the reflection of the fire at their back. But the light came from directly ahead. It was a specific red dot that moved erratically, jumping from Levent's left arm to the shoulder of Sevim and onto his chest.

A laser.

Turan's weapon.

"Get down!"

Levent pushed Sevim hard to the right as he hurled himself to the left. He heard the near but not loud snap of a weapon. He knew it was a pistol shot from the Zigana and did not think it was meant for him. As he hit the ground, taking the dull edge of a hard rock on his hip, Levent thought he saw Sevim spin down, ripped down, probably from the force of a bullet.

"Are you hit?"

Levent barely recognized the sound he heard. It was a whine, a shrill, clotted sound escaping from an animal.

"Can you move?"

The sound came again, this time with an ending that said it was done. "What was that?" said Sevim, coughing. "Who?"

Levent knew as he spoke that if he had his words back he would give a different answer. "It's your enemy," he said. "The man you want to kill. Turan Yoruk."

"*Vache!*" he hissed. "*Batard!*"

Turan was a bastard and a pig, but Sevim had not limited his curse to the man he could not see. Levent rolled over the rock on which he had landed, coming down hard on another just as the rifle went off.

Not a hit. Levent felt no pain, heard no ricochet, or the air being parted by a high velocity shell. But a response came immediately. Two pistol shots snapped from ahead where Turan had posted himself.

It was impossible to get off this mountain without going through him. Levent took his magazine and pistol from his pockets. He could have shouted to Sevim to keep Turan busy, but that was already happening. The rifle sounded once, nearer than Levent had put it, the muzzle jetting fire toward the trail. The Zigana answered quickly, telling Sevim he had missed.

Missed again. As Levent crawled to the east, rounding back toward the fire, he understood that he had put himself between two killers who wanted more than anything in life to finish the other. He had confidence in that happening if nature let them have their will, but that was in doubt. Fire suddenly sprang over the crest of the ridge, flashing like an explosion with hands.

Levent traced the wind by the rapid patterns that the fire created. Bushes were bursting into flame, leaping from one to the next with tremendous speed. Dry, Bodrum was so damned dry. Where were the fire choppers? Where was the good sea-water in those buckets?

Levent speeded his crawl until he decided that a crawl was not fast enough. He rose, bent at the waist, moving as fast as he could to round toward the trail.

No shots answered from the right angle. Darkness was closing as fast as the fire closed to the edge of the ridge. The flames moved within the wind as if they were the wind, howling, crashing. They took their color from the oncoming night, red and black and fiercest at the core.

Levent could feel the heat at his back as he moved within pistol range of the last place where he had heard Turan's Zigana. He did not think, nor would he ever think, that the fire had begun spontaneously. Turan had set it. He had worked his way east to find the best place to start the fire before working his way back along the same route to block the entrance to the trail.

Everyone was supposed to die up here. Everyone but one.

All but the devil.

It was hard to see him in the night. The constantly flashing fire at Levent's back gave some visibility, but put the ridge deeper in shadow. He looked to the left toward Sevim and saw nothing. If he did not move, the flames would reach him soon. They were within several meters.

Then Levent saw Turan. He crouched behind the same yew that Levent had used to spot the ridge. There was no way to get a good angle on him without rounding to the left. Levent moved two steps closer to be sure of his shot, wanting to be as sure as that laser, when Turan suddenly looked up.

He did not look at Levent. He looked at the sky.

The fire choppers.

Levent barely heard their engines over the noise of the advancing flames, but he saw the two shapes taking the glow of the fire along the cables that reached from their bellies to their heavy cargo below. They were high, two hundred meters, but moving closer to the earth, their Bambi buckets come to rescue the animals of the forest. There were three on the mountain.

And one of them moved. Turan took two crouching steps toward Sevim's position, his weapon held in both hands, the laser invisible. He wanted the kill. He would not have his prey taken from him.

Levent put both hands on his CZ and went to a crouch, too. He put Turan in his sights. "Right there!" he shouted. "Don't move."

Turan stopped his momentum. He turned toward Levent without seeming to move. "Inspector, I wondered about you."

"I said don't move!"

It was hard to tell in the darkness, but Levent thought Turan smiled. The glow of the flames lit the planes of his face, leaving deep hollows of dark matter that seemed to come from within.

"This man belongs to me or the fire," said Turan, wagging the Zigana in his hand. With an invisible flick, the laser snapped on. "You won't get in the way."

Levent could not sort out what happened next, but he must have sensed something from above. It was more than fire—more than the weightless raging of gas and debris. It was the enormous weight of the water coming down.

The placement was bad in the bad light, and the buckets should have dumped toward the center of the ridge. The booming spew of water never should have landed near the edge of the ridge where two men stood.

Levent went to the ground in a reflex, still holding the CZ toward Turan and watching as the laser sought out its target. That technology might have done its work. Levent could have been hit as he squeezed in return. The red dot within the fire would have been the last thing he saw if the crush of sea-water had not hit the best diver in the Aegean so hard.

The last thing he saw of Turan was the gigantic blast of water driving him to the ground, turning him around in a strange twist. The water seemed to break him backward before it took him the rest of the way down.

Levent did not see more. He was hit at almost the same time by the trailing backlash of the water. He felt his pistol dropping from his hand as the flames suddenly roared higher at his back. Fire began to burst from the rear, igniting the bushes on every side and throwing long plumes of sparks on the wind. Levent was engulfed by the smell of burnt evergreen and something like spice.

Rosemary? Thyme?

It was as if the water from the buckets had done nothing to turn back the flames. Levent got to his feet. He was wet, his clothing was so wet it dragged him down, and he could smell the hair of his arms and head being singed by the cascading sparks. When he felt them on his face, he lurched forward, closing his jacket over his head, trying to walk his way through the fire and the mud that the water had made.

CHAPTER 25

Fire Rescue found Levent several hours later. He must have made his way the few feet to the beginning of the trail, though he had no memory of it. He must have slid down the rock surface head first with nothing to break his fall until he struck the ground at the end of the steep incline. He was lucky there was little brush to take the fire at that place.

Perhaps Levent never would have been found if not for the commandant, who flew in with the first rescue teams. He insisted that he had a man on the mountain and that everything possible should be done to bring him in. After they located Levent near the top of the trail, he was flown to the hospital suffering from smoke inhalation and a concussion. Yes, the water had saved him.

In spite of the relief efforts, the mountain had continued to burn throughout the night. The massive buckets of water dropped by the helicopters in relays from the sea were not enough to douse the flames, and the rescue workers were unable to bring serious equipment quickly up the mountain. The fire only stopped at the edge of the ridge and did not make its way over the shoulder of the mountain below where Turan's compound lay. His possessions, as usual with the rich, were saved.

The fire had consumed everything that was alive or combustible on the ridge, including Turan and Sevim. Their bodies were recovered in bad condition, so thoroughly burnt that they were unrecognizable even to their loved ones. Turan had none of those save the corporate, but the French claimed their own, shipping a closed casket back to Paris.

Levent had not seen them. He spent a day in the hospital attended by Emine, who did not mention the fact that he had turned their holiday into a holocaust. She said that she had been out to see the mountain, which was blackened from the point where the fire started until the top. The fire had jumped from ridge to ridge onto the next mountain, burning the eastern part of it almost as badly.

"It's so dry here," she said. "So hot. We might want to try Kash next year."

But they spent the last day of their vacation at Bitez. The beach was never better. The women were never more beautiful or their bikinis briefer. The sun was so high and bright and the sky so seared by its heat that it seemed impossible for the water to be so intensely blue. Aegean Blue. Bodrum Blue.

Levent had just finished his second beer of the afternoon—domestic—when the cell phone he kept in Emine's beach bag rang. He answered it, knowing the caller without looking at the tattle on the small screen.

"Yes, Chief."

"Inspector, I understand I'm to give praise," he said in his best feint at camaraderie. "They tell me you burnt down half the peninsula but managed to bring the case to a satisfactory close."

"It was something like that, yes, sir."

"There's nothing like fire, Onur. Nothing so basic. It's the thing our ancestors feared above all others. Why do you imagine they lived in caves?"

"I'm sure there's another side to it, sir. I'm not sure I recall at the moment."

"Understandable," he said. "You're been through hell and come out the other side. The others weren't so lucky."

"Luck was all of it, sir. Our ancestors probably called it fate."

"I'd like to leave it at that," he said with the pause that presaged great things or disaster. "Certainly, we're sorry to lose such a fine citizen as Turan Yoruk, but his timing may have been better than his considerable achievements."

"Something happened, sir?"

"Something *will* happen," said the Chief like a soothsayer. "They're bringing in new indictments nearly every day in the Ergenekon investigation."

"Yes, sir. I read the papers here."

"There's no telling where all this will end," he said. "We have so many retired military officers under arrest that it's hard to find a reliable assassin these days. Apparently, Turan was more in that business than the Chamber of Commerce would like to think. If he'd survived, he might have wished that he hadn't. Toast may be toast, but this would have been like a spit turning slowly over a fire."

"I'm surprised to hear that, sir."

"You are?" he said. "You're sure?"

What the Chief wanted Levent to say was that he had not found any of Turan's connections to the Deep State. That shadowy entity was always half fiction and always half real. What was fiction was often as useful as the real to instill fear. And that was being done again, gently.

"Nothing in my investigation discovered a connection between Turan Yoruk and any governmental or extra-governmental institutions. You can rest easy, sir."

The Chief's momentary silence said he was satisfied to hear what he wanted to hear. Now he could go back to the people in the shadows and report that their asses remained black and invisible.

"It's too bad we can't rest as easy on everything," he said. "But we have to worry about our own people. We don't know what names were caught on these wiretaps. We don't know what peripheral evidence or hearsay can be brought into court. We have to realize that the indictments will continue."

Reading between the Chief's lines was not always easy, but Levent knew when the man said "we" he meant himself. Something in that sprawling investigation must have grazed the hide of the slipperiest governmental official Levent knew. The Chief was apparently having trouble keeping his balance between the Islamic government and the things he had done in his time to further the Deep State.

"My advise, sir, is to go on holiday. You might want to think about an overseas destination."

"I may do that," he said. "Suggestions?"

"The water, sir. Try the water."

"Yes, so forgiving—that's what saves us, isn't it?" The Chief seemed to consider that vast watery promise. "I may well take your advice, Inspector. My best, as always, to Emine."

Did you enjoy this book?
Visit ForemostPress.com to share
your comments or a review.

LaVergne, TN USA
29 October 2010
202734LV00004B/150/P